CHOSEN KING

BOOK 1

DREAM
OF
EMPTY CROWNS

Cover design by Fiona Jayde Media ~ fionajaydemedia.com

Edited by Emily Glisson

Map by Angelina La Pointe

SEWALL

Sewall Publishing
P.O. Box 246
Lompoc, California 93438

To contact the author, please visit:
MJSewall.com

ISBN - 13: 978-0692478646
ISBN - 10: 0692478647

Chosen King Book One: Dream Of Empty Crowns

First Edition - July 2015

CHOSEN KING
BOOK 1

DREAM
OF
EMPTY CROWNS

BY
M J SEWALL

SEWALL

New Kingdom
Thure
Old Kingdom
Port
of
Thure
Port of Dralinn
Mount
Ansthia
Kingdom
of the
Thirteen
Gordon's
Village
Palace
City
Oil Fields
King's Port

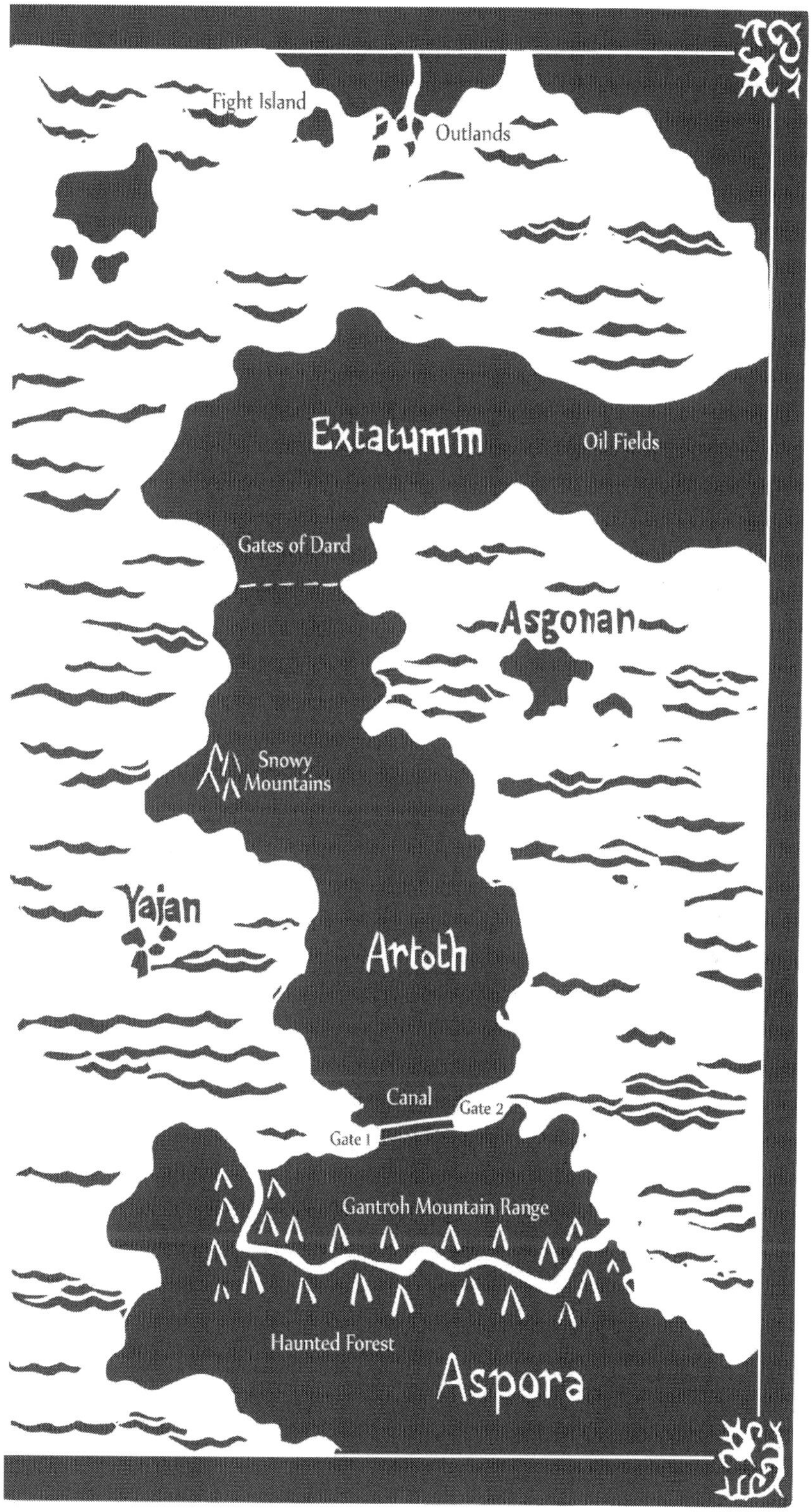
Fight Island
Outlands
Extatumm
Oil Fields
Gates of Dard
Asgonan
Snowy
Mountains
Yajan
Artoth
Canal
Gate 2
Gate 1
Gantroh Mountain Range
Haunted Forest
Aspora

This book is dedicated to my son Preston
Steps no longer apply

Now I write of two kings born from the same story
I will set down the tale of fire and blood
And those that would lead kingdoms
No false history, no fantasies of flawless heroes
I will tell of those who changed our world
And the tragedies that befell them

~ Llawes the younger

CHAPTER 1
THE TOWER

Gordon was falling from the airship, again.

He was on deck watching his kingdom's soldiers fighting the man with the patch and the fierce warrior girl, her long blond hair swinging as she leapt onto a soldier. The clanging of longknives rang in his ears and he could actually smell the sweat and the metallic tinge of blood in the air. Almost glimpsing her face this time, something heavy hit him and Gordon was over the railing and falling. His body turned and he was now facing the vast armies below.

Gordon's eyes darted wildly over the massive sea of men crashing against each other. Fire was everywhere, surrounding them, washing over buildings and forests. Gordon flinched as the massive, strange airships exploded out of the sky around him. As the ground rushed toward him, Gordon looked away from the armies and saw the shadow, which appeared as big as the world, blotting out the sun, making everything else seem gray. It was almost like a man, with dark eyes.

It was laughing.

Gordon jerked awake, hoping he had not screamed like last time. He didn't want to worry his uncle Loren in the next room.

Gordon concentrated on slowing his breathing and wiped the cold sweat from his brow. He decided against getting up and lighting the gas lamp on the wall. Instead, he lay in his dark bedroom with eyes wide open; trying to forget his dream and forcing his thoughts back to the beginning of the exciting day.

Asa, Gordon and Skyler had decided years before to put their names in the tower together. They were all ten then. Now, they were thirteen and it was King Stathen's last trial. Gordon and Asa were certain Skyler would be chosen; Skyler won at everything, he always seemed to know more about any subject, and everyone looked up to him in school.

Gordon's uncle Loren told them to put their names in long before today, but they made a pact to do it together, and Asa always did everything late. The law said every thirteen year old had to put their name in, as long as it was before the choosing ceremony. On the road to the palace, Asa, thirteen and small for his age, swung his name board at his side. As usual, he was bare footed. Gordon scratched his thick brown hair and thought, *my uncle's right. I do need a haircut*. Not wanting to drop his board, Gordon held it tight in his right hand. Skyler had carelessly slid his into a back pocket. Gordon smiled as he realized they looked like steps, Skyler half a foot taller than he was, and shorter Asa walking next to him, all in order of height.

"So Asa, is the paint still wet?" asked Skyler.

Asa glanced quickly at his name and let it hang by his leg so the other boys couldn't see. "Shut up, Sky. When did you paint yours?"

"About two moons ago, like I was supposed to," replied Skyler, "How about you, Gord? When did you paint your name board?"

Gordon didn't answer as he popped a sweet into his mouth.

"Gord?" Asa asked, concerned, "you okay?"

Gordon chewed for a moment. "I'm good. It's just a little longer to get to the tower than I thought. I think I brought enough sweets and sour cakes, though. And I finished my name board a while ago."

The road to the palace was alive with activity. The closer they got to the tower courtyard, the more crowds of people they saw. The roads had become markets. All along the road, there were pots of stews, and sweets, and traders selling three pointed banners. Gordon got out a coin and thought of buying more food, just in case. He decided against it, but smiled as he rubbed his finger over the triangle on one side. He flipped it over to see the profile of the famous firstcouncilor Trunculin on the other.

As the boys continued toward the tower, Gordon began flipping the coin carelessly. Asa made a grab for it and missed, just as a girl from school came up to them.

"Want to see my name?" Enricca had broken off from her group of friends to come over to the boys. She held up her name board to Skyler. Enricca had painted it with at least five different colors, with tiny triangles all around her name.

Truly impressed, Asa asked, "How long did that take you?"

"Probably forever," offered Skyler, "That looks dumb… no one's going to see it anyway."

"Shut up, shoe boy. When I'm queen, I'm going to… throw you in a deep hole to rot. I'll ban the name Skyler forever," replied Enricca.

"Sure. Except there hasn't been a queen chosen since before Salenn the Peacemaker, like a hundred years ago. Asa has a better chance than you," replied Skyler.

Asa said, "Hey!"

Gordon jumped in, "Come on, you know any thirteen year old can be chosen, even Asa."

"Hey!" protested Asa again.

"Your name board looks nice, Enricca," offered Gordon.

Enricca smiled, "Thank you Gordon," as she sneered at Skyler.

"Oooh, Gordon, why don't you just kiss queen Enricca, then?" mocked Skyler, pushing him toward Enricca.

"Stupid boys..." Enricca walked back to her pack of girls across the road, with a wry smile.

Gordon shook his head, confused, "Sky? I thought you liked Enricca."

"Shut up," was all he said, looking straight ahead. Gordon realized it was Enricca calling him 'shoe-boy' that had made him mad. Pointing out that Skyler's father was a shoe maker always seemed to embarrass him. Gordon also knew that Skyler *did* like Enricca.

They could just see the top of the tower. There were lots of people everywhere they looked. It was loud, but with happy, friendly sounds, thought Gordon. Everyone seemed to feel they were a part of the same excitement, old and young alike. Gordon recognized many of the boys and girls his own age from his village. He spotted at least four boys and girls from his school, name boards in hand. As the three boys made their way closer to the tower, they saw the long line of thirteen year olds, all ready to climb the steps.

"Ugg. This is going to take forever," moaned Skyler. "Why did you have to wait so long, Asa?"

Gordon jumped in before Asa had a chance to say anything, "Uncle Loren says the lines have been this long every day for a while. He says it's the biggest choosing he's ever seen."

They all looked at the line in front of them.

Skyler shook his head, "How are there this many thirteen year olds in the kingdom?"

Gordon just smiled. The only thing that Skyler wasn't good at was being patient.

They could feel the nervous energy and knew everyone was thinking the same thing. "What if one of us does get chosen? It could happen you know: King Skyler of the airships…" offered Gordon.

Skyler replied, "King Asa the awesome…and late for everything..."

Asa ignored Skyler's jab and finished their ritual, "…King Gordon the Great."

"Yeah, right, like a kid like us will ever be chosen king? I've heard it's not really fair anyway," said Skyler, "I've heard the rich councilors pay to have their kid's name put in lots of times."

"It has to be fair. Everyone puts their name in, in front of everyone. You can't cheat. There are palace guards watching the tower, even at night," offered Asa.

Gordon agreed, "That's right. Besides, it's happened before. King Rolenn and King Giber were village rats like us. They didn't come from rich families."

"Yeah, over a hundred years ago. Look at that tower. There must be fifty of us in line now, and kids from all over the kingdom have been putting their names in for two or three moons. There are probably thousands of names in there. Even if it is fair, the odds are pretty bad."

Asa looked at his name board and shrugged, "Well, someone has to be chosen, right?"

They were through the entrance, and in the large palace courtyard. They were close enough to see a boy who had just rounded the last turn and was standing on the platform around the mouth of the tower, just standing there, leaning over the large tower opening.

"What's he waiting for?" asked Asa, extending his neck to see over the crowds.

"I don't know. Just toss it in already!" yelled Skyler impatiently, startling the person in front of them.

Gordon said, "He's probably thinking how his life will change if he's chosen. I mean, what if it actually happened?"

The boy finally tossed in his name board and began the walk down the stone tower steps. Gordon popped another sweet.

"You sure you're okay Gord?" asked Skyler.

Gordon shot Skyler a warning glance, "I'm fine, Sky."

"Has anyone with sweetblood illness ever been king?" asked Asa innocently.

Skyler said, "Shut up Asa, he doesn't like to talk…"

Gordon said, "No. Sky, it's okay. No Asa, a lot of people with the sweetblood don't live very long. I've just been lucky."

"That, and your uncle Loren was the firsthealer for the palace," offered Skyler.

"Yeah, my uncle has saved my life a few times. But there is still no cure for… what I have," changing the subject, Gordon asked, "Asa, what's the first thing you would do if you were chosen king?"

Asa thought for a second, "I would take the fleet of airships and drop fire on Extatumm."

Skyler slapped his own name board across Asa's shoulder.

"Oww!" shouted Asa.

"And start a war with the only other kingdom with airships? You dolt! The two councils have to approve a war anyway. Dumb…" said Skyler.

"No one has airships but us." Asa tried to hit Skyler with his name plate, but he knocked it out of Asa's hand instead. "Hey, don't. The paint will smear," said Asa.

"Ha! You did just paint it this morning!" Skyler laughed.

"Shut up, Sky." Asa said.

"Alright, Sky. What would you do as king?' asked Gordon.

The three boys laid out their fantastical kingdoms as each thirteen-year-old climbed the tower and threw in their name. It took over an hour until they reached the tower. Asa and Skyler went first. They both came down, exclaiming how big the hole was and how many names they saw. Then it was Gordon's turn.

As Gordon climbed, he passed the small doors that were built into the sides of the tower. Each one had a number and a lock on it, to be chosen at random on the day of the choosing. Each step brought a new thought. He didn't know how to tell his friends that he was glad he would never be king. He couldn't imagine how anyone his age could make those hard decisions. What does it feel like to be looked up to by millions of people? The whole idea was overwhelming.

Gordon pushed his thought aside as he reached the landing at the edge of the hole. As he stood over the massive opening, it reminded him of a large lake, this one filled with names instead of water. He smiled as he threw in his name. After seeing all of the thousands of name boards, Gordon knew he had nothing to worry about. His name board dropped into the lake of names.

The line of thirteen-year-olds looked even longer now as Gordon came down and rejoined his friends. At the bottom step, a girl brushed past him. She was clearly older than Gordon. *Maybe she's here with a younger brother or sister,* he thought. She looked into his eyes for just a second. Her eyes were deep blue and a wisp of blond hair fell across her forehead. It only lasted for that brief moment, but he thought of it frequently on the way home. He didn't know why, and he didn't tell Asa or Skyler about it.

The boys made their way home in high spirits, talking of everything that would happen at the choosing ceremony in a few days. Gordon was thirsty and made his way home. It was getting dark, but he was within sight of his house. He saw the lamp lighter at the gas lamps along his street. He saw movement to his right as the shadows fled from the light of the lamps. A man was standing by the wall. The man's hood was up, so Gordon couldn't see his face. The man didn't speak to him, and Gordon looked away, hurrying to his house.

The streets in his village were safe, but better not to get too close to mysterious strangers at night. He wasn't sure if the man was looking at him or not. Strangely, he thought of the girl again. Her blue eyes. Gordon thought, *I wonder why people are staring at me today* as he went through the front door of his Uncle Loren's house.

CHAPTER 2
FALLING

"Gordon?" called Uncle Loren.

"It's me; it took a lot longer than I thought," answered Gordon.

"I'll say. I was going to send out a hunting dog to fetch you," Uncle Loren came around the corner from the kitchen, "I told you the tower would be overrun by other thirteen year olds. Hungry?"

Gordon said, "Thirsty mostly. I took enough food, sweets and sour cakes just in case, but not enough water."

Loren looked over Gordon, with the concern Gordon had grown up with. "Let me look at you." Loren took Gordon's face in his hands, looked in his eyes, and then took his hand, "Hands numb at all? Any tingling?"

"No, they're fine." He often got annoyed with how much his uncle checked him over every day, but he loved that he cared so much.

"Here, you know what to do," Loren said, handing him a small metal pot.

Gordon sighed, "Now? Can't it wait?"

"You know I have to test it. Either that or I take some blood," insisted Loren.

"It's okay, I need to go anyway," Gordon said as he went into the next room and relieved himself into the pot and brought it back to Loren.

"I can smell a little sweet from here, I'll go test it. Food's almost ready."

"Food smells good," Gordon offered as his stomach began to rumble.

"I got some good stag meat and circle bread," Uncle Loren left for his work room and Gordon went to the kitchen pump. He pumped the handle at the metal lined sink, and held his cup under the spout until he had finished two cups of water.

"It's too sweet, nearly two hundred parts. Here's some sour cake. Better let that work until you have any more food," Loren handed Gordon a small, round purple cake, which Gordon finished with another cup of water.

Later, they ate the delicious stew and had the fresh bread. Gordon told him of the day's events and how much his friends wanted to be king, "…I'm just glad I won't ever be chosen. Maybe I'll be the king's healer one day like you were."

Loren said, "You'd make a fine king, Gordon. You are brave and kind. You never let anything take your good spirits, not even the sweetblood. But I wouldn't wish the kingship on anyone. Working at the palace is not the fun it seems."

Gordon said, "If you say so… well, I'd better finish that book you gave me. Only two days to go, and you said it had to be done by the choosing."

"That's right, study your history carefully, otherwise you will be doomed to relive it," said Loren, taking the dishes.

"But I'm thirteen, I don't have any history yet," Gordon said with a smile.

Loren smiled back, "Ha, ha, you know what I mean. Get to your book. We can discuss it tomorrow when we visit the sick."

Gordon thought about his own history from time to time. He loved his uncle. All he could remember was living with him since his parents had died. His father died in a terrible accident aboard ship, before he was born. His mother had drowned in a river the same year he was born. It always made Loren sad when Gordon asked about them, so he tried not to. Gordon had a lot of questions. As he got older it was harder not to ask.

Gordon made his way to his bed and finished reading *The Kings And Queens, Great and Small.* Gordon realized why Uncle Loren wanted him to finish it before the choosing. The last two kings in the book both had memorable choosing ceremonies. Bartomm the Bold was chosen king during the second revolt. There had been actual fighting at the ceremony; more than fifty people died in the very same courtyard where he had been earlier in the day. Bartomm had to continue the war at age thirteen while learning to be king. The other king, Jamesson, had tripped and accidentally fallen off the choosing tower and broken both legs. He began his kinghood in a wheeled chair.

Loren often found ways to teach Gordon about things using something that happened in history. When Gordon was helping Uncle Loren with the sick, he was constantly explaining what he was doing so Gordon would understand. Some of his favorite memories were of the talks they had as they traveled from house to house, helping the sick. Gordon also read many books from Uncle Loren's private library. None of Loren's books were taught in school. Whenever Gordon asked why, his uncle always shook his head and said, "I have my theories. But they should be taught."

Gordon put out the gas lamp and fell asleep quickly. He didn't dream that night. At least, nothing he could remember. The day before the choosing came too quickly. It was a regular day of chores and going around the village as Loren's helper. He carried the bags of healing herbs and mixtures that his Uncle used. There were only five people to visit that day. Most everyone seemed to be in good health, awaiting the excitement of the choosing ceremony. The streets seemed more alive somehow; people carrying bundles home excitedly, all the wagons and carts full of food for sale lined along nearly every road, and everyone talking of nothing but the ceremony.

The day passed quickly and ended with the dream again. Gordon was falling from the airship. He could feel the cold wind rushing past his face. He passed through a cloud and he saw his kingdom, and many more beyond. Large armies from every kingdom were smashing into each other like great waves on the sea. Everywhere there was fire, great plumes of smoke rising to the sky he was falling from. This time the sky was surrounded by the shadow, its eyes burning. There was no mouth to the shadow, but the laughter got louder anyway, coming from nowhere and everywhere. As the ground rushed towards Gordon, he could smell the smoke and feel the flames begin to burn his skin.

Gordon woke up, breathless.

"Gordon?" called his Uncle. Gordon realized he must have screamed again.

Gordon called back, "I'm okay, Uncle Loren."

Loren rushed into the room. Gordon threw his blankets off. He still felt like he was burning. He was sticky with sweat. Loren came to him, "Are you alright?" putting his hand to Gordon's head, "You're burning up."

Gordon concentrated on slowing his breathing, "I'm fine. It was just the dream again."

Loren asked, "The same dream? This has been happening since spring."

Gordon nodded, "I know. It was the same dream, but it's changing. I was falling again. There was fire everywhere. And the shadow is getting bigger, closer. I just wish I knew what it meant."

"A terrible dream. I've consulted my books. Falling dreams means you feel out of control. Is that how you feel, Gordon?" Loren asked.

"I don't know. Sometimes I feel like I have no control. I mean, I trip over my feet, I'm not very good at games, and the stupid sweetblood..." he said, trying to smile.

Loren continued, "I understand. Fire in a dream can mean lots of things: transformation in your life, something about to change, needing to change. Seems like many elements of your dream are about things out of control… but this shadow figure is the strangest part."

"It sure is, and the scariest. I don't know why it scares me, not exactly. And why is it laughing during all the fire?"

Loren offered, "Anything I can give you to sleep would complicate the sweetblood. But I suppose I can give you something just for tonight…"

"No... Thanks anyway," Gordon said, "I think I can sleep again. I've never had the dream twice in one night."

"Alright," Loren said, kissing his own hand and putting it on Gordon's forehead, "Love you, Gordon. About the control issues: we all have to be thirteen once. We all feel out of control sometimes, even at my age. Hopefully that was the last time you'll have the dream. And don't forget we leave early tomorrow for the choosing…. Oh, did Asa finish his name board?" Loren asked.

Gordon smiled, "Yes, finally. Sky thinks he painted it that morning."

Loren smiled, "Asa's a funny boy. Goodnight then, the choosing doesn't wait for sleepy boys," said Loren.

Loren went to his own bedroom. The dream scared Gordon, and he didn't know if he should tell his uncle, but in some ways, it also excited him. It almost felt like flying. It had to mean something, dreaming it so often. Gordon always wondered why his dream ended before he hit ground, or why he woke before he puzzled out what it meant. He had heard that if you died in a dream, you died in real life. He wondered how anyone could know that, since the person dreaming would have died. How could anyone tell what they had been dreaming if they were dead?

Uncle Loren was right, though, he did want to be rested for the choosing. He had been only eight for the last choosing ceremony, and didn't remember much. Gordon tried not to be, but he *was* getting excited about the choosing after all.

CHAPTER 3
THE CHOOSING

Loren and Gordon were up at first light. Nearly the whole village was on the road to the choosing with them. Gordon knew how lucky they were to be so close. Some villagers had to make journeys of days and weeks to make it to the choosing on time.

Since everyone was going the same direction, it was strange to see one man leaning against a wall, not moving at all. He was just standing there. Gordon thought the man was staring at Asa's family up ahead, but he couldn't be sure, since there were so many people. He wondered if it was the same hooded man he had seen before, "Loren, do you see that man? Why do you think he's just standing there?"

Loren glanced at the man with little interest, "Attendance isn't required by law. Not everyone is excited about the choosing ceremony. The law requires all thirteen years old put their name in, but the whole world will know who the king is by tomorrow, whether they attend the choosing or not."

Gordon still thought there was something strange about the man, but he soon forgot. Gordon waved to other friends as he saw their families along the road. Asa's family was way ahead of them now, and Sky's was behind. There were too many people in between to walk together. Besides, Gordon was still eager to discuss the history book he'd finished with his uncle. They discussed many kings and queens on the trip. It didn't seem that long before they were at the courtyard awaiting the ceremony to begin.

Gordon had never seen so many people in one place. There was a kind of excitement from every direction; people were laughing, eating, drinking, and having a good time while they waited. The courtyard still looked huge, even filled with all the people. Gordon looked at the statues of the three sisters standing over the courtyard. The three figures made of white stone all stood for something different. He looked on, trying to remember what each detail of the statue meant. The statue that stood for Freedom was a young woman with flowing hair. She was clearly running someplace, the movement carved into the beautiful stone. She held a small book in her hand. Gordon always wondered what it was, but even Uncle Loren wasn't sure. The Justice statue was a woman standing still, holding a longknife high in one hand. The other hand held a thick judge's staff. The last statue was an old woman, standing in the center of the two, and stood for Humanity. She had her arms wide and there was a boy and a girl carved on each side of her.

Gordon looked all around at the balconies overlooking the courtyard. There were people seated on both sides of the courtyard, he assumed they were from the two councils. The choosing tower was at the center of the courtyard, the palace entrance behind it. Three loud gongs rose from the third terrace of the palace and bounced around the great courtyard. The crowd began to quiet.

A wooden walkway had been constructed from the first balcony of the palace to the top of the tower. The enormous hole at the top of the tower had been topped by a round wooden stage. Gordon wondered how they had built all of that so fast, since he had just been here a few days before.

There was a rumbling in the crowd that turned into cheers as Firstcouncilor Trunculin emerged from the first balcony. He walked slowly towards the stage, his long robe hiding his feet. Gordon saw men with longknives and arrowmen behind the firstcouncilor. The firstman of the kingdom, Brenddel, stood by Trunculin's side. He knew it was the firstman because of the one inked stripe across each cheek.

At first, Gordon thought it was strange that no guards came out ahead of Trunculin. He excused the thought quickly when Trunculin reached the stage and smiled brightly. The crowds cheered loudly as he raised his arms. *No one would hurt Trunculin,* he thought, *he's the most popular man in the kingdom.* Gordon had to stretch his neck to see, as many in the crowd raised their arms in response.

Trunculin, the firstcouncilor to so many kings, gently motioned for the crowd to quiet down. He smiled his famous wide smile, and a large glass jar was set next to Trunculin. It reached to the height of his waist.

The ceremony had begun.

Trunculin announced to the crowd, "Friends, neighbors, subjects of the kingdom of the thirteen, welcome to the solemn choosing of a new king... or, maybe... a queen?" he smiled widely to the crowd. There was a smattering of laughter.

"From the days of our first great kings, through the dark days of war in other lands, older kingdoms have fallen away. But our kingdom stands proudly, stronger than ever! The first thirteen kings came and put this great system in place so long ago. Knowing the darkness of their own hearts as men, they formed the amazing idea: After their rule, let the wickedness of men fall away. Let the innocent child lead us. Let the child shape the future that is theirs to command!" said Trunculin.

A great cheer rose from the crowd. Gordon couldn't believe the sound of the crowd cheering as one.

Trunculin continued, "As the great kings said: Let the child that has grown up in innocence, in this great kingdom, put their name in this tower. Since that child has not yet been corrupted by the evil ways of men, let one be chosen king. Only through innocence can we find strength!"

The sound of the cheering crowd got louder. Then there was another sound, a kind of humming sound.

Gordon got close to Loren's ear so that he could ask, "Loren, what is that sound?"

Loren did not answer, but pointed his finger toward the edge of the courtyard, up to the sky. Gordon was one of the first to see the large shape coming over the wall of the courtyard. Only a moment later, the rest of the crowd started to see, and the cheers got even louder.

Trunculin continued, "...and let that child who leads us, lead the greatest kingdom ever seen! The only kingdom with the power to fly!"

The large shape overshadowed the courtyard. The airship seemed enormous, probably because it was so close to the crowds. Gordon could see the tips of the large arrow guns all around the square deck. The flat deck hung from ropes, suspended from the giant gas-filled ship above. It didn't stop to hover, but kept floating over them until it passed out of sight. It had made its intended impression. Gordon wondered if he might be witnessing the greatest choosing of his lifetime.

Trunculin called for calm again only with his gestures, "Let us begin," Trunculin reached into the great glass jar next to him. The jar contained strips of paper with names on it.

"As you all know," Trunculin began, "the eight year olds of our great kingdom have their own type of choosing, putting their names here to have a chance to choose the new king. "

He put his arm deep into the scraps of paper and pulled out a name, "Sanjee, would you come join me for the choosing?"

Though the crowd was enormous, later everyone would claim that they heard the gasp from the little girl Sanjee. Gordon could see movement far into the crowd to his left. Soon, the eight year old girl Sanjee slowly made her way up the tower steps. She was shaking and shyly came up to Trunculin. He bent down and she whispered something in his ear. Trunculin smiled broadly and said to the crowd, "Sanjee asks if I could pick someone else!"

The crowd roared with laughter and cheers. Trunculin put his arm around the girl's shoulders and said, "Sanjee, I think that question makes you more than worthy for this task." The crowd roared again. Sanjee offered a small smile.

"Since the beginning, a boy or girl of eight is asked to choose the door and pick out the name board of our new king. After the new king's fifth trial, this girl will be thirteen and will place her own name in the tower. Sanjee will now choose the door number from this bowl, thus revealing our new king."

A small glass bowl with thirteen bits of paper was given to Trunculin by a guard. Trunculin bent over, and offered the bowl to Sanjee, "Let's find out who our new king or queen shall we, hey little one?"

The crowd roared their approval like a beast alive. Gordon leaned over to Loren, "The firstcouncilor sure knows his audience, doesn't he?"

Loren issued a low chuckle and stared ahead, "Yes, Gordon, he certainly does."

The girl reached into the bowl and pulled out a small paper number. Sanjee whispered in Trunculin's ear, and he smiled again, "She wants me to read the number!"

Trunculin had to calm the crowd down again before he spoke, "Very well, Sanjee, we go to the last door, number thirteen! A very fateful number." The girl, Trunculin and the firstman Brenddel proceeded down a few steps to door number thirteen.

The firstman gave the large key ring to Trunculin with the thirteenth key first. Trunculin turned the lock and a jumbled pile of wooden name boards could be seen through the opening. The girl put her hand in the door and pull out a name board.

She showed it to Trunculin. The girl said something else, but Trunculin shook his head. They both stood facing the crowd. Apparently the girl would read the name herself.

Trunculin scanned over the crowd, but he was not smiling as widely as he had been. Gordon began to wonder what the expression on Trunculin's face meant, but the crowd had erupted with shouts.

"Gordon!" a man shouted from near him. Gordon looked at his uncle. Loren's face had gone pale, and his mouth was open. He stared at Gordon when another man shouted, "Gordon!?"

Then everyone seemed to be shouting his name. *The girl must have said the name wrong,* he thought. Gordon started to feel light headed. He worried that it was a sweetblood reaction. *Do I need something to eat?* He thought. He turned back to his uncle.

Before he could form another thought, hands were grabbing him in all directions. He felt lighter than air. The crowd was lifting him up and passing him to the tower, like he was a boat on a sea of people. *My people now?* He thought briefly. *No, this is a mistake.* But they had not stopped shouting his name.

He got to the tower and the firstman Brenddel took his arm and lifted Gordon up to the steps by door number thirteen. The man was incredibly strong, and Gordon nearly flew up to the steps, like he weighed nothing at all. He hoped he would not fall and look foolish as he stood there on wobbling legs. He thought of the king that had fallen from this very stage, and swallowed hard.

Trunculin took Gordon's hand and bent at the waist. He said, "Congratulations, my king."

Gordon didn't know what to say. He was about to speak when Trunculin stood upright, raised Gordon's hand in the air and announced to the crowd, "Your... New... king... Gordon!" Gordon noticed that the old familiar smile was back on Trunculin's face.

The cheering from the crowds seemed to go on forever. Gordon kept looking over the crowd, trying to find a familiar face. He scanned where his uncle Loren should have been, but he couldn't find him.

He also looked for his friends, but the crowd was too big. He was sure he heard Skyler shout his name, but Gordon couldn't see him anywhere.

Sanjee whispered something else to Trunculin, "She wants to know if she can kiss the new king's cheek!"

Gordon looked to the girl and smiled. He bent down and the girl kissed him quickly on the cheek. She blushed and Gordon was sure he was blushing too. Just then, the crowd started to go quiet and uneasy. Gordon was sure he had done something wrong.

He looked at the crowd, who were all looking behind Gordon. Along the newly erected walkway, guards were marching in. He wondered briefly if the temporary wooden walkway was going to collapse as it shook with their marching.

The soldiers came right up to Gordon. They were not smiling. They stopped and made a kind of shout, "Knives up!" At the signal, they all stepped back and faced each other, raising their longknives. It formed a corridor through which appeared the current ruler. King Stathen was a young, handsome twenty-two and the only king Gordon could remember.

Stathen was not smiling either.

He walked through the guard's archway of longknives and came to within a foot of Gordon's face. King Stathen glared down at Gordon, who hoped he didn't look as terrified as he felt. The king said nothing at first, but slowly shook his head and then turned to the crowds, "Was I this short when I was chosen?"

The crowd exploded with laughter. A wide smile came across King Stathen's face.

As the crowd cheered, King Stathen turned back to Gordon, serious again. He winked at Gordon and whispered, "Time for the serious part." The king motioned for quiet, "Gordon, do you accept this honor and responsibility fate has chosen for you? Or do you put aside the crown for another to be chosen?"

Trunculin said quickly, "You may put it aside at this point only. It is your legal right to do so," just loud enough for Gordon to hear him. King Stathen shot an annoyed glance to Trunculin.

Stathen continued, "...What is your free choice, Gordon?"

Gordon looked at the king, then uneasily looked at the crowd, "I...I..."

"If you accept, say I accept." King Stathen whispered.

"I... accept," said Gordon as loud as he could. He hoped it hadn't sounded like a question.

The king smiled down at Gordon. With both hands, he took the crown off of his head and put it on Gordon's. To Gordon's great surprise, it nearly fit his head, "Now, face your people, our new king.... Gordon!"

The crowd went on cheering for what seemed like days. King Stathen motioned for Gordon to go through the corridor of guards, "You are king now, Gordon. You should go first."

Gordon glanced back to where Loren had been standing, but still couldn't see him. He reluctantly made his way through the guards and their longknives. He tried not to look at their faces. He didn't want to see disappointment on them. He was relieved to see that they all stared straight ahead. King Stathen followed him, then Trunculin and the firstman after. Another guard led Sanjee back down the stone steps of the tower.

They made their way into the palace until Gordon could no longer hear the crowds. The ceremony was over.

CHAPTER 4
OUR NEW KING

As soon as they were all inside, two guards produced a large wooden box trimmed with gold. The crown was quickly removed from Gordon's head to the box, and the crown and the guards were gone before the new could ask anything. Brenddel made a quick, courteous bow and left as well.

"The crown will be stored until the crowning ceremony, when everything will be official," said Trunculin, anticipating Gordon's question.

"You only have to wear it for special occasions anyway," offered King Stathen, "thing's heavy, isn't it?"

Before Gordon could reply, Trunculin interrupted.

"Yes, now, my king ... Gordon. This is my assistant Rolem, who is now also your assistant. He has the list of events and will show you around the palace. If you need anything at all, consider Rolem the man to get it done," said Trunculin as he left them with a bow.

King Stathen added, "The first order of business is the king's meal. It will happen in a few hours. It's where we try to eat together, but everyone will be stopping by to interrupt every bite. My advice, eat something before you get there."

Gordon said, "I think I do need to eat something. How do I… where…?"

"Rolem here will get you what you need. Just don't treat him too badly, you don't want Rolem to poison you or anything," Stathen said smiling.

Gordon looked with alarm at Rolem, who glanced at Stathen uncomfortably.

Stathen laughs, "I'm just jesting with you. Rolem's a good man. He's been working here a long time. Knows everything that is going on."

Gordon gave Rolem a weak smile, unconvinced.

"I must be off, a lot to do before I stop being king," Stathen put a hand on Gordon's shoulder, "You'll do great. There are a lot of councilors to help you. Most of them have been here a long time too. We'll talk more at dinner… I hope," Stathen said as he left Gordon.

Gordon turned to Rolem, "Can I get something to eat, please... um...? Ro…"

"Rolem, my king," the assistant offered back professionally, "There is a lot to learn, I know. Let me show you around the palace. The kitchens are this way."

"Here is the upper council chamber…" Rolem was casually naming each chamber as they passed. Gordon wanted to stop at each room. The main hallway that connected the rooms were massive. He figured at least five of his uncle's entire house could be stacked in the hallway with room to spare.

His uncle! He had almost forgotten him. It seemed like uncle Loren must have left the ceremony when he was named king. It was strange that he would do that, more likely he was just swallowed up by the crowds. It all happened so fast. Gordon remembered Loren's expression of horror when he had been chosen, but maybe he was just worried. Loren worried too much. Still, he wished his uncle was here to share in all the excitement.

"Hey, um, Rolem… Can I ask for my uncle to come visit?"

Rolem offered a courteous smile as they walked down the great hall, "Well… my king, you can ask for anything you wish. You are king now, almost officially. Anything that the laws allow, of course. I will talk to the firstcouncilor about it."

"Of course. I know I can't just do anything I want. I mean, I know I can't just make a law up on my own or anything. That duty is for the upper and lower councils. I just have to agree and sign them, right?" inquired Gordon.

Rolem laughed.

"Oh no, did I say something wrong already?" asked Gordon.

"No, no. I'm very sorry, my king, but that is correct. It's just… it took King Stathen nearly his entire first trial to learn that concept," offered Rolem, "Oh, I probably shouldn't have said that."

"That's okay. I forgot each year of the…my…kingship is called a trial. Why don't they just call it a year? I learned why once… I just can't remember it right now," Gordon asked, embarrassed.

"My king, there is much for you to learn, and quickly. No need to be embarrassed that you don't know everything. No king does, even after each successive trial," Rolem said. "You will be learning how to fight, about the law, dealing with other kings, and much more. It will be a very intense, trying time. Thus each year is called a trial."

Gordon stopped suddenly and had to lean against a wall.

Rolem looked worried, "I'm sorry, my king, I didn't mean to alarm you. Trunculin will council you about…perhaps it wasn't my place…"

"No, no, I just feel a little dizzy. I do need something to eat. My uncle makes me special… wait, I have some here…" Gordon took a small sweet out and started eating it. Rolem looked at it carefully. Gordon noticed this and put it back in his pocket after taking a bite, "Sorry. I'm thirsty too. How far to the kitchens?"

Gordon thought he saw a curious flicker on Rolem's face, but the man quickly smiled. "The kitchens are very close. I can fetch some water sooner if you need it. Are you feeling well?"

"Oh, no, I'm fine," Gordon didn't want to lie, but he wasn't sure how the news of his sweetblood illness would be received.

Rolem looked at Gordon for a moment, smiled and said, "This way then, my king."

Like everywhere he had seen, the kitchens were massive. Everywhere there were long tables piled with food in different states of readiness. There were easily a hundred people working at the fire ovens, stirring impossibly large pots, and hurrying food out through several different passages and hallways. Gordon wondered if he would ever find out where they all led. Rolem had gone to talk to a man with a red hat. Gordon thought it looked more like a long piece of cloth rolled up and laid onto his head in a kind of orderly pile.

The man with the red pile went to the table and came to Gordon with a tray full of food and three cups of different drinks. Every bite was like he was eating food for the first time. Everything he ate and drank was better than the last. He spent a lot of time looking around. Everything was enormous; the fires, the ovens, the ceilings, even many of the cooks were large around the middle. Gordon imagined that the first kings must have been twelve feet tall to build such a large palace. He left the kitchens stuffed and happy.

They went to the seventh and highest level of the palace. Rolem and Gordon came to two giant doors, towering over them as tall as five men end to end. A guard stood at either side with a long weapon, and at the top of each there was a large blade.

Rolem said, "This is Gordon, please open the door for our new king," The two guards did not look at Gordon, but both pushed their doors open to reveal the king's chamber.

Gordon's breath caught in his throat.

Rolem smiled, "It is said quietly that a few kings have fainted when these doors opened," he cleared his throat and led Gordon into the room, "I never actually said that, of course."

The chamber was circular and rose to a round dome. As Gordon looked around, he thought maybe the space was shaped a little more like an egg than a circle. The celling was painted with scenes from the kingdom's history: The first thirteen coming to these lands, the first wars, and the great banner of their kingdom.

It was the best quality banner Gordon had ever seen; much better than the cheap small banners they sold along the roads. It showed the triangle symbol in the middle, surrounded by thirteen longknives radiating out from the triangle. Unlike the cheap versions, the triangle was filled in with the three oak branches that stretched to each corner of the triangle.

In the middle of the room stood the great king's chair. Gordon felt small next to the chair he would be expected to sit in. He felt that as they went higher into the palace that somehow his body had gotten smaller and smaller. He had a strange thought that he might disappear altogether. Gordon looked up at the ceiling and was feeling dizzy again.

"Ah, our young king has found his way to his new home." Trunculin had quietly entered the room. "Apologies, my king," he bowed. "I didn't mean to surprise you. Thank you, Rolem, I will finish the tour."

Rolem nodded at Trunculin and bowed his head to Gordon, leaving the room without another word. "Uh, thank you, Rolem…" Gordon began, but Rolem was already gone. Trunculin took his arm and lead him toward the great chair.

"Now, there is much to discuss. The king's meal is in a few hours. After the crowning ceremony tomorrow you will officially meet your firstman, Brenddel and begin your fight training. After that, I will discuss all the learning: the law you must study, and really just how it all works. Of course, at high sun is the crowning ceremony. All of Stathen's powers will transfer to you. Officially that is. Your speech has been written, and it would be best to study the copy I left in your chamber. Come this way and I will show you."

Trunculin led Gordon behind the king's Chair. If he hadn't been led, he would never have guessed there was a hallway leading in either direction into rooms behind the chair.

They passed guards along the curved hallways as Trunculin led him into a chamber with a large window. The room was the biggest bedroom Gordon had ever seen. The walls were white, with hundreds of books lining one of the large walls. There was also a bed big enough for three people, comfortably, and a writing table and chair. Trunculin demonstrated how the cover rolled up into the desk and disappeared, revealing pen and paper and lined with small square holes that Gordon couldn't wait to explore. Trunculin let Gordon look around the room and found two doors, one leading to a large bathing room, the other a room for clothes, which was empty.

Trunculin smiled, "I hope this will be enough space?"

"Yes…yes, this will be…uh, fine," said Gordon, looking around.

"We are bringing some clothes for dinner now. Starting tomorrow your clothier will start making your garments. Tomorrow you will meet all of the important people that will be a help to you…" Gordon was looking around the room, "Is everything alright, my king?"

"Sorry. It's just… this is a lot to… it's just a lot," Gordon said.

Trunculin smiled again, "Of course, my king. I have counseled many kings before you. Every one of them felt overwhelmed at first. But, you were chosen. And I'm sure you were chosen for a reason."

Trunculin was smiling the warm smile he was famous for, but Gordon still felt uneasy. A thought occurred to him, "Oh, can we find my uncle? I guess he got lost in the crowd. I would sure like to see someone I know right now. Oh, no offense… I just…"

"Of course. No offense taken. We are looking for Loren right now, in fact. He will be brought to the palace as soon as we find him, I promise you that," Trunculin said.

Gordon replied, "Good, thank you. Wait, how did you know Loren was my uncle? Did I tell…?"

Trunculin interrupted "…No, no, my king, as soon as a king is chosen, there is a whole army of people whose job it is find out as much as we can about him. Oh, I almost forgot, in the next few days we will also have the firsthealer look you over…"

Gordon interrupted, "Oh, um, Loren is my healer. He used to work here at the palace. He knows how to…."

"How to what, my king?" Trunculin looked very interested.

"…How to… to take care of me." Gordon didn't know how much to say before he talked to Loren. He never liked talking about his illness with people he didn't know. He wanted to talk to Loren about everything else too, and soon.

Trunculin said smoothly, "Of course, my king. As soon as he is found, all will be well. I must go prepare the king's meal ceremony. If there is anything you need, just tell a guard. They will know what to do."

Okay. Thank you, um… Trunculin. Is that what I should call you?"

"Or firstcouncilor if you'd like. Please don't hesitate to ask for anything. I will see you at the king's meal." Trunculin bowed his head slightly, leaving the room quickly.

Gordon went to the large window and looked out over all the people. There were still large crowds of people that would stay close to the palace for tomorrow's crowning ceremony. Gordon wondered if the people were truly glad he was king. He was all the way up on the seventh level. The people looked very small from here, as did the purple mountains in the distance. Gordon backed away from the window, realizing how far it would be to fall.

CHAPTER 5
WHAT WENT WRONG

Trunculin made his way to the sixth level of the palace. He went past the guards without looking at them, straight to Brenddel's chambers and pushed the door open without knocking, "Where are they?" he demanded angrily.

Brenddel was signing papers and calmly looked up from his work. His thick arms pushed on the edge of the desk while he raised himself from the chair with a soldier's economy of movement. Taking the name board from his desk, he said, "Room three," as he led Trunculin back to the holding rooms, "They all claim they switched the name boards. They tell the same details. No one can explain it."

"They will explain it to me. How could this happen?" Trunculin fumed as they reached the door. Brenddel had the key ready and unlocked it. The moment the door opened Trunculin heard the tail end of a scream.

In the room there were six men. Three knifemen of Brenddel's guard stood around three men in the middle of the room. In the middle, the men were hanging from a bar by their arms. Their feet were not touching the floor. Trunculin walked up to the man hanging closest to him, "What happened?"

"I don't know. I swear it. We switched the name boards like we were supposed to. I swear it!" answered the man.

"You are swearing that between last night and the choosing, someone else snuck into the tower tunnels and placed name boards like these inside the tower near every door?" Trunculin grabbed the name board from Brenddel and held it up to the man's face. Through his pain, the man saw the name Gordon.

Trunculin said, "We found hundreds of these – all say Gordon – just behind every locked door, so that his name alone would be chosen," The firstcouncilor got closer to the man's face, "His name should not have been in the tower at all!"

"It's not possible. We replaced all of the name boards. I swear…" One of the knifemen hit the hanging man across the rib cage with a wooden training weapon. The man screamed.

Trunculin got even closer to the man's terrified face, "Every choosing we find men just like you. Men desperate for coin, men that no one will miss. We hire them quietly, then dispose of them quickly. Not this time. This time it will be slow. Scream all you want; no one can hear you outside this room."

The man began to protest, but Trunculin and Brenddel were already leaving the room. As the door was closed to the sound-proofed holding room, they heard the last, "Pleeeeeasse!" anyone would hear from the men.

Brenddel walked quietly beside Trunculin as he raged, "Never! Never has a name been switched by anyone but us. How could this happen? How many of your men do you think are involved?"

Brenddel glanced briefly at Trunculin, "I put some of my best on guard last night outside the tower. It was a small, loyal three that stood guard inside while those men changed the tiles from the tunnels under the tower. They witnessed those men switch the boards. I am still questioning those guards separately. The top of the tower was covered just like every choosing, so it had to be from the tunnels. I do not know how this happened, but I will find out."

Trunculin said, "I know you will, Brenddel. I apologize for my fire, but it upsets years of planning. Have you found Loren yet? I knew we should have killed him before he became the hero healer of the villages. They must be hiding him in the filthy low lands."

Brenddel replied, "That is the first place we looked. We are still doing a house by house search and nothing yet. He couldn't have gotten far, but with so many new faces here, because of the choosing ceremony, many of the houses are empty. Nearly everyone is here in the palace city. My men were ready for the extra crowd control, but we are spread thin. But we will find him."

"To make this happen, it has to be more than a few. Who is leading them? The conspirers could be many. And I have to go play the kind councilor to our empty-brained King Stathen, and the new boy king from the dirty villages. I'm counting on you," said Trunculin.

Brenddel asked, "What will we do with our new king? He may not be as weak as your first choice. We weren't watching this Gordon boy."

"I can keep most of the plan the same, with a few alterations," said Trunculin, "I'm meeting with the mystic guild now."

"He's already arrived through the tunnels. No one knows he is here but us. He knows you are coming," said Brenddel.

"Of course he does, he's a mystic," replied Trunculin. Brenddel simply looked at the firstcouncilor and walked away as the sun slowly disappeared from the world.

CHAPTER 6
DANGEROUS NOTE

Gordon was looking at the clothes they had brought him. He was trying to work out what the fabric was made from. He felt it between his fingers and loved the way it almost slid off. The outfit was too big, but he was promised that would be fixed tomorrow.

As he was checking his pants, a woman and a girl walked in carrying more clothes. They startled Gordon a little, but he didn't want them to think that they had. "Some more garments for you to choose from, my king. These might fit you a bit better," said the woman as she draped the clothing over the chair. The girl laid her clothes down as well.

"Do I … do I know you?" Gordon said to the girl, trying to remember where he had seen her.

"No, my king, I don't think so," she said as she looked him right in the eyes, "I think you might like this blue one, my king, it has lots of pockets."

"Aline, remember your place, girl. I am sorry, my king, they are all very nice," Gordon barely noticed what the woman said as he stared at the girl named Aline.

"I remember! You were in the courtyard when I put my name in the tower." Gordon said smiling.

Aline looked concerned as she shook her head. "I am just one of the many who serve the king," she said and kept looking directly into his eyes.

"We will leave you now, my king," said the woman turning her back to exit. Aline kept looking at Gordon, and pointed to the pile of clothes. He looked confused as they left. Gordon had no idea what had just happened, but he was sure it was the same girl he had seen that day. Those blue eyes. Gordon went to the pile of clothes and went through them until he found the blue pants. They did have lots of pockets.

He checked to see if any other girls were going to come around the corner from the hallway. Though he was well guarded, Gordon realized that the room had no actual doors, only open hallways. Gordon wondered why everyone thought they could just come in when he was dressing. He would have to figure something out. Then he saw the door. In the bathroom, he tried on the pants. A piece of paper was in one of the pockets. He unfolded it.

Gordon – Great forces are at work. You are not safe. Trust no one but Aline. Be ready for anything. If all goes well, I will see you soon. Be alert. Destroy this note.

Love – L.

It was from his uncle Loren, but he had no idea what it meant. Why should he trust this girl Aline? He didn't know her. How did she know his uncle? Where was Loren? Great forces? Not safe? Gordon suddenly felt very alone. He jumped at a knock on the bathroom door.

"My king, it's time for the king's meal. I am here to show you the way," said Rolem through the door.

Gordon looked at the paper. He looked around quickly, "Um, yes, I'll be out soon."

Seeing the toilet, he put the paper in the bowl and pulled the chain on the wooden box above. The water went from the box through the pipe and down to the bowl, the note swirling down the drain. He washed his hands and splashed cold water on his face. Drying off, he opened the door, "I'm ready."

Rolem smiled, "Yes, my king. Might I make a few suggestions before we go?" he said as he looked at Gordon's outfit. Gordon looked down. His shirt was wet from where he had splashed his face and his pants were inside-out.

"Yes, Rolem. Thanks. I could use some help."

After Rolem had suggested a few ideas on appropriate clothing choices, he led Gordon to the main dining hall. Like many rooms in the palace, Gordon noticed there were no doors here either, just a large high archway through to the hall. As Gordon passed into the room, he stopped and had to remind himself to breathe again.

Rolem smiled as he looked around with Gordon, then back to Gordon's face, "Like it?"

"You could fit an airship in here!" exclaimed Gordon.

The room fell silent. Gordon didn't realize that he had been that loud, and had just noticed how many hundreds of people were in the room. They were all staring at him, then the rumbling started. At first Gordon didn't know what was happening. He then realized that everyone was banging the tables. It sounded like thunder. Trunculin appeared out of nowhere, "Please, welcome your new king… Gordon!"

The banging got even louder. Gordon smiled uneasily again. *This is going to take some getting used to,* he thought. Gordon started to feel a bit light headed and realized he needed something to eat again. He must have eaten too much sour cake in his room to try to balance his blood.

Rolem had drifted away, letting Trunculin guide Gordon through the room. The large triangle tables were scattered on both sides of the large hall. There was a central aisle of purple carpet down the middle, leading to the far side of the room where a long raised table was on a stone platform. To Gordon, it looked almost like the table was set on a stage. The long table was lined with many people. The entire room of people stood as Gordon made his way to the table. Standing behind the table, king Stathen had an ornate purple glass in his hand. He was wearing the crown again. Gordon had a sudden urge to run out of the room, but it was far too late for that.

As they reached the table, Trunculin said, "May I present our new King Gordon to you, my King Stathen, for the first symbolic shifting of power at this peaceful meal?"

"You haven't gotten rid of me yet, Trunc. Not until the crowning ceremony," replied Stathen.

The whole room laughed, and Trunculin joined in, "My king, we will all miss your good humor, especially at my expense."

The king laughed too, "And I'm sure you hope no other king calls you Trunc."

They all laughed. Gordon smiled along.

As the laughter trailed away, Trunculin said, "But jesting aside, my king, you do have to say the words, or this poor boy will not get to eat."

"Fair enough, Trunc. We wouldn't want to starve our new king. Trunculin, firstcouncilor of the kingdom, I agree to lay down my powers beginning tonight, in peace, if the new king will agree to pick up this heavy burden."

Everyone looked at Gordon. Stathen's face was very serious as he looked at Gordon. Trunculin leaned close to Gordon and whispered, "Just say 'I do,' my king."

"I do," was all Gordon had to say as another thunderous round of banging washed through the room.

"Good, I'm starving. Let's eat. Come on around," Stathen gestured to his right. Trunculin led Gordon around the very long table. They must have passed in front of twenty people, then they went up a few stairs and passed behind the same twenty. Everyone turned in their chair to look at Gordon. Most were smiling, some just stared, and some had just the whisper of a smile to offer, as though they weren't sure what to make of this thirteen year old boy who was to be their king.

He didn't know anyone. A few were dressed very strangely, like they were from other lands. *Maybe they're envoys from other kingdoms*, Gordon thought. He would try to ask Trunculin who they all were. They finally reached King Stathen at the middle of the table. There were two empty chairs. Trunculin motioned to Gordon to sit in one chair, while Trunculin sat in the center chair, between the two kings.

As they sat, Trunculin said, "It's one of the old customs. The firstcouncilor sits between the two kings as a symbol of a peaceful continuing of the kingdom."

"That, and old Trunc here likes to be the center of attention," offered king Stathen.

Trunculin replied, "Oh, my king, nothing could be more untrue. I would be attending to all the details for tomorrow if not for old traditions. I prefer to work behind the scenes."

The meal began and Gordon had never seen so much food, not even in the kitchens earlier. He only recognized a few dishes and was glad for the advice Stathen was giving. He was nervous to try some of the dishes, but Gordon knew he had to eat something to keep himself balanced. And he sure didn't want to offend anyone.

He hoped they found Loren soon, so that his blood would stay balanced. Only his uncle Loren made the sour cakes, and Gordon only had a few more left. He knew he shouldn't, but he ate all of the sweet potato on his plate. Sweet potatoes were his favorite, even though his uncle warned him about eating too many. He politely tried many of the other dishes.

"Gordon, stay away from that…" Stathen said as Gordon was spooning a dish he had never tried, "Its orangefish mixed with spice. We also call it brownfish. It will keep you in the bathroom all night."

"Oh, my king, don't listen to him. It's quite a rare dish! Stathen is just jesting again," Trunculin said.

Brenddel, his soon-to-be firstman came up behind Trunculin and whispered something to him. Gordon looked at his spoon and back to Stathen, who shook his head quickly. Gordon put back his spoon full of spicy orangefish.

Trunculin turned to Gordon, "Oh, our new king Gordon, I would normally do this tomorrow after the crowning, but may I introduce Brenddel. He is the firstman of your knife guard."

Gordon had just taken a bite, and swallowed quickly as he stood. He extended his hand. Brenddel was bowing at the king at the same time, and Gordon held his hand out awkwardly. Brenddel looked to the firstcouncilor, then took Gordon's hand. He offered a professional smile, "My king."

Trunculin smiled, sighed and said, "Well, my kings, if you will excuse me. There is another urgent matter to deal with."

"Nothing too serious, I hope?" asked Stathen.

"Oh no, just another boring detail. If you will excuse me," Trunculin didn't wait for a reply, and simply left the table with Brenddel.

Stathen grabbed his glass and moved into Trunculin's seat, next to Gordon. "Good, I thought he'd never leave. How are you feeling?

Feeling? Gordon wasn't sure what to say. Did they know about his sweetblood illness already? Gordon answered, "Umm…very full."

Stathen laughed, "I would wager. You will never go hungry as king. I meant, how are you dealing with all this?"

"Oh. It's…I'm… it's a lot. Everything is happening so fast. I don't even really know what my duties are, exactly," replied Gordon.

Stathen said, "I'm sure. I remember my king's meal. It was king Adinn before me. He had died in that riding accident, so there was no one in that seat for me. No one to talk to except for Trunculin. I was so nervous that I spilled my drink in the first course. I had no idea what I was doing."

"How did you learn it all?"

"I didn't. I still feel like an imposter some days. The people seem to like me, and we've passed some good laws… I think. I'm just lucky that I didn't have any wars to deal with," said king Stathen.

"But you had the battle of the marshes," offered Gordon.

"Ah, you know all about me, do you?"

"No, it's just I like history the best," said Gordon, "Even though it happened when I was young. I read a lot of books."

"Hmmm. Well, the books aren't always right, exactly. It wasn't really our war. We were just helping out a councilor from Aspora. I was only there that one day for a meeting with their leader, Dinmar. It was an enemy agent that I spotted. We protected Dinmar, then we gave chase. The poor enemy's horse was pretty slow, so we caught up to him at the marshes. His friends were there, so there was a brief battle of sorts. But we had twenty men, and there were only five of them. It didn't last long. Hmm, funny if that's the only thing I will be remembered for," Stathen said staring at his glass, like he was trying to remember something, "Gordon, my boy, come take a kingly walk with me. I need some fresh air. Air with less… ears."

They left the table and walked outside under a covered balcony with great pillars all along the walkway. Gordon was amazed at every new place he went in the palace, "Is it okay to be out here?"

Stathen laughed, "Gordon, you are nearly king. You've already taken my room. This will be your home for the next five, or maybe ten years. You can go wherever you wish. And look down there, and there. We're safe anywhere near the palace grounds," Stathen pointed down the covered walkway on either side of them. A guard was posted at regular places.

Stathen suddenly looked serious, "Listen Gordon, we won't be alone again, and there's not much time. I wish I could tell you everything that is really going on. The reason we have kings by choosing is because the men that founded this kingdom believed we are all equal, and therefore anyone can be king. That is the way it is supposed to work," He put his hand on Gordon's shoulder, "If you weren't scared you would make a bad king. A king should be scared, a little. But you will find your strength. You will need it. You are special Gordon. Play along, just don't trust Trunculin. He is..."

"Ah! There are my two kings. I thought you had run off," Trunculin made his way down the long corridor to them, "Gordon my boy, I wanted to go over the ceremony with you tomorrow, so there will be no surprises."

Stathen looked intensely into Gordon's eyes for a moment, then his face changed and broke into a wide, happy smile, "Trunc, we had almost made our escape. That's too bad, Gordon. You will have to be king tomorrow after all."

Trunculin smiled at them, "I never get tired of your jests, king Stathen. Do forgive me, my kings, but we have so little time before the crowning. May I steal him from you, Stathen?"

"He's yours now," Stathen took his hand off of Gordon's shoulder, "Good luck tomorrow, Gordon."

"Thank you, King Stathen. Good luck to you," said Gordon.

"Only for one more day, almost-king Gordon. Trust me, you'll need much more luck than me," Stathen went back into the dining hall.

Trunculin led Gordon back to his bed chamber behind the king's chair, overwhelming him with more information as they walked.

Later that night, alone in his room, he put down the speech Trunculin had told him to memorize. He laid back on his enormous bed and relived the day. Was it really only this morning that he had been chosen? Was it possible? Then he thought of Aline and the note from Loren. He had no idea what it all meant. What was Stathen really trying to tell him about Trunculin?

He thought that he might not be able to sleep at all, or worse, that he was sure to have the dream of falling. He was thinking of Loren's advice; to be ready for anything as he drifted off to sleep. If he dreamed, he did not remember it when he woke the next morning.

CHAPTER 7

TROUBLE AT THE CROWNING

The morning was nonstop activity. They brought Gordon breakfast in his chamber. Most of the morning was getting his clothes just right and memorizing the ceremony speech, so breakfast was almost an interruption. There must have been thirty different people in and out of his room. The ceremony was to be held at high sun, when it would be directly overhead.

Out of the windows, he had seen the airships coming into position around the choosing tower and courtyard. The crowning would be outside in the courtyard for everyone to see. It was also symbolic that it be held on the choosing tower stage.

The morning quickly passed and everything was ready; it was time. Rolem was again in charge of getting Gordon to where he needed to be, "My king, are you ready?"

"No, Rolem," asked Gordon nervously, "Do you think they would miss me if I didn't go?"

Rolem hinted at a smile, "I think Trunculin might notice, my king. Not to mention the thousands that have assembled to watch."

"Thousands?" Gordon asked.

"Thousands, my king."

Gordon took a breath, "Then I guess we should go."

As Gordon left the room, he felt a little dizzy again. That was happening too often, he thought, especially since he had plenty to eat. He knew he hadn't been tested for the sweetblood for a whole day, but he felt mostly alright. Except for the slight headache he felt coming on. *It's just nerves,* he thought.

The walk seemed very long going to the tower. He was sure he would forget all the things he was supposed to say, or get them in the wrong order. He could hear the crowds as they got closer. Gordon saw the walkway down to the tower stage.

The courtyard had been changed again. There were now two walkways leading to the platform stage over the hole in the tower.

Trunculin was there with another man. They were dressed in similar clothes. Gordon guessed that it must be the secondcouncilor, who was in charge of the lower council.

Gordon heard the gong and Rolem stood inside the archway, motioning for Gordon to begin the walk. *Just don't trip and fall,* Gordon kept repeating in his head. His headache had gotten worse, and now there was a kind of buzzing in his ears. Or was it his head? *Just keep it together,* Gordon scolded himself. As Gordon walked into the light, he said, "Thank you, Rolem."

As Gordon started down the platform, he saw Stathen do the same from his opposing walkway. The crowd was so loud, Gordon could no longer hear the buzzing in his ears. He looked around at the crowd, and it seemed like there were more people here now than had been at the choosing. Gordon and Stathen reached the platform at the same time, Stathen wore the crown.

In the center of the platform, was an exact duplicate of the king's chair. He knew it was a copy, because he had just passed the real king's chair on his way down from his chamber. Stathen and Gordon got to each side of the chair, just as Gordon's script had instructed.

Trunculin gestured for the crowd to be quiet. "Good citizens, men and women. You are here to make the final approval. Do you accept the will of fate and your new king Gordon?"

The crowds roared its approval.

"Then let the crown pass to Gordon, along with all of its powers. Then King Stathen will rejoin the people," declared Trunculin.

Gordon's head ached very badly now. But he smiled anyway, knowing it was just nerves and excitement. Trunculin went to Stathen and took the crown from his head. Stathen winked at Trunculin and gave a little smile. Trunculin's own smile wavered a bit, but it was so quick, no one else seemed to notice. Gordon faced the crowd, Trunculin began to place the crown dramatically on Gordon's head. As he did, Gordon's mind exploded.

Gordon no longer saw the crowd. He was falling, staring up at an enormous airship. An arrow flew in front of his face, and he looked to his right to see the firstman Brenddel shooting at someone. A quick glance to the left and there was an enormous man lunging at him with an axe. He had a patch on one eye. Gordon was still falling. It was very cold, and Gordon was having a hard time breathing. Both men were hanging from ropes and fighting and reaching for Gordon at the same time. From nowhere, the girl Aline was attacking with a longknife. Gordon twisted in midair. Now he was staring at the world below, fast approaching. The whole world was on fire. Everywhere he looked there were armies fighting and fire, fire, fire. There were two shadows now. One was right in front of him, this time with Trunculin's face.

Gordon felt as though his head was about to split open. Still on stage, he screamed and collapsed. The crown flew from his head and went clanging on the platform. He screamed again, holding his head. He was back in front of the crowd again and had no idea what was happening. The vision was slowly fading, the faces of the men and the girl flashing in his mind. His head felt like it would rip in two, as he tried to hold it together with his hands.

Trunculin rushed for Gordon, but Stathen got there first. Not knowing what to do, he tried to pry Gordon's hands from his face. He feared he had been shot by an arrow, or poisoned somehow. Gordon's eyes were tightly shut and he was groaning.

"Quickly, get him to the healers!" shouted Trunculin. Stathen began to lift Gordon. "No, Stathen, you are no longer king. Return to the crowds," said Trunculin as the firstman Brenddel rushed to Gordon and lifted him.

Gordon opened his eyes briefly and thought he was back in his vision when he saw Brenddel. He grabbed his head and screamed again. Trunculin was saying something to the crowd, but Gordon couldn't make out what it was. Before he shut his eyes again, he saw Stathen look at him seriously, then walk into the crowd to be swallowed; just another man now.

The last thing he saw was Trunculin's angry face, or was it the shadow? Gordon closed his eyes again and was taken by darkness.

CHAPTER 8
STRANGE VISION

Rolem knew Trunculin was in one of his rages. He didn't want to say anything that would make things worse as he tried to keep pace next to the firstcouncilor.

"Go to the healers. Find out what happened, what is wrong with him. I have to see someone. I will join you there soon," said Trunculin.

Rolem wanted to ask who could be so important to see now, of all times, but working closely with Trunculin had taught him not to ask too many questions. "Yes, firstcouncilor," was all he said.

Rolem went toward the healers and Trunculin headed down another hallway. The firstcouncilor made his way to a small corner of the palace where there were no guards. He unlocked a narrow door.

A very thin man was sitting on a pillow, holding both sides of his head. His eyes were closed. Trunculin towered over the man. The thin man was breathing slowly. He did not open his eyes.

In as calm a voice as possible, Trunculin asked, "What happened?"

The mystic put his hands down, and slowly opened his eyes. "Who is this boy?"

"A poor boy from the villages. We are trying to find his parents. He lives with his uncle, who used to be firsthealer. We cannot find the uncle anywhere. *What happened?"* repeated Trunculin.

The thin man looked calmly at Trunculin and said, "When I tried to install the vision we agreed upon, I had to be very aggressive. The boy's mental walls are very strong; much stronger than they should be for a boy of thirteen. I nearly worked my way over these walls. But before I could install the vision, he has a dream vision of his own."

"How is that possible? Is the boy a mystic?" asked Trunculin.

"No… no, I don't think so. Our guild would have detected him years ago if he had true mystic gifts. I don't know what he is. But I was able to see his dream vision as a passenger in his mind," stated the thin man.

Trunculin sat in a chair facing the man, "Tell me."

"The boy was falling from an airship. But this airship was much bigger than any that exist… at least, any my guild know about," said the mystic.

Trunculin shifted in his chair. The mystic stared at Trunculin, "Don't try to look in my mind, mystic, my walls are stronger than you know. Don't change the agreement now."

"Of course, firstcouncilor," The thin man nodded. "There was a battle between several men on ropes. One man was your firstman Brenddel. He was firing arrows at another man. This man had a patch over one eye." To underline the point, the mystic pointed to the eye the patch was over.

The mystic thought he saw a note of fear on Trunculin's face, but it was just a flash.

"Mantuan?" asked Trunculin.

"Yes. And there was a fierce girl fighting by his side. There were armies from at least four other kingdoms fighting each other. Around all this, there was fire. It was as though the entire world was in a fiery war. There were two shadows overseeing the destruction," finished the mystic.

Trunculin's face hardened, "But this wasn't a true vision?"

The man said, "It couldn't have been. The boy is no mystic, and there is no airship that large. Also, the kingdoms that I saw fighting have been allies for years. And, Mantuan, of course, is dead."

Trunculin was quiet for a moment, "But if Mantuan did survive… somehow…"

"That would be surprising, but it might explain a few things," agreed the mystic, offering nothing else. He blinked and looked at Trunculin expectantly.

Trunculin looked away. The day had started to show on him. "I am tired. I need to go check on the boy."

"How does this change your plans? Is there anything more you would like to share with the guild?" asked the mystic, blinking again.

Trunculin rubbed his upper lip, "The plans stay the same. We made the boy kings powerless. Gordon is king, only not able to serve. A sick king is easy enough to control. I will make up some illness and rule through him."

"But the crown fell. There may be an issue…" said the man.

"No. Stathen did his duty. He went amongst the people. Gordon is rightfully king, even though he wasn't meant to be. It will serve," Trunculin said. He hesitated, "Before I go, I need your skills."

The mystic opened his palms and offered a nod. He said nothing else. The mystic did his duty. When he was done, Trunculin said, "I have to go to Gordon. My absence will be noted."

The mystic nodded again and closed his eyes. Trunculin left the room more disturbed than when he arrived. He made his way to the healers. He walked past the guards and into the healer's chambers. There were no windows, as this was an interior set of rooms in the palace. The soft glow of light came from the walls and ceiling. Trunculin forgot how bright it was in the healing chambers. He squinted, sniffing the air that smelled so unique to these rooms, and remembered how much he hated coming here. Gordon was in the furthest corner of the maze like area, separate from the other sick. The firsthealer was standing over him, making notes in a leather-bound book.

"How is the king?" asked Trunculin without greeting the firsthealer Corinn.

"He is resting. We gave him a something to keep him asleep until we find out what is wrong with him," she said.

"Good, I have been…" Trunculin started.

"What did you do to him?" she interrupted, turning to face Trunculin.

He began again, avoiding her direct stare. "I had a mystic implant a vision. To guide the boy to the right decisions."

"Why did this mystic try to rip his mind open? This is not what I agreed to," replied the firsthealer.

"What you agreed to was the smooth continuation of this kingdom. The boy has to be controlled. Nothing has changed. He will be kept here and I will make some announcement tomorrow. It is too late for you to have doubts," Trunculin said.

The firsthealer said, "I can keep him like this indefinitely. I am using a weak poison that will keep him asleep, but alive. But no more surprises, firstcouncilor. I will not be so willing if there are any more plans kept from me."

She used to say my name, he thought, "Of course. This developed quickly. There was not enough time…"

She turned to Gordon's bed, made another note. She looked at Trunculin quickly, firmly, and left the room without saying another word.

Trunculin looked out the door she had just exited, then went to Gordon. The large bed made the boy look very small. He was lying still, his face looking troubled as he slept, brow furrowed. Trunculin stood over Gordon for another moment, then he left.

A few moments later, a cabinet near Gordon began to slide away from the wall. A head popped out from around it, surveying the room. Aline quietly slid the cabinet further away from the wall and quickly went to Gordon's bed. She removed a small ball of soft bread and placed it in Gordon's mouth. Aline looked around nervously to the entrance to the room. She wished there was a door there instead of just an open archway. She tapped her hand quietly against her leg and waited.

Gordon groggily opened his eyes and started to say something. Aline quickly put her hand over his mouth and a finger to her own lips. Gordon realized something was in his mouth as Aline said, "No words. The zoress bread will absorb what they gave you," she whispered.

She checked the archway again to see a healer's assistant standing there, "Who… who are you? How did you get in here?"

Aline made a quick movement with her left hand. The assistant collapsed quietly to the floor. Gordon saw the small stick Aline had thrown into the man's neck. Gordon had barely seen her hand move.

"Come on," whispered Aline as she helped Gordon out of bed. She put her fingers in Gordon's mouth quickly and removed the bread. What had been a soft white bread was almost black. She dropped it and it crumbled when it hit the floor. Gordon's legs felt wobbly, but she was able to help him to the hidden panel behind the cabinet. Gordon went through first, and Aline pulled a rope attached to the cabinet behind her, pulling the cabinet tight against the wall; the small passageway was sealed again.

The firsthealer began to walk into the room, but saw the assistant puddled on the floor, "What is…" She looked around and saw that Gordon was gone. She realized that she needed to act fast. She examined the assistant, took out the tiny spear from his neck and smelled the tip. *This just got stranger*, she thought as she quickly exited the room. She told another assistant to attend to the man on the floor, explaining nothing else as she ran from the healing rooms.

She got to the guard level a few moments later.

"The boy is gone." She told Brenddel, out of breath.

"What do you mean? Gone where?"

"Gone. Taken somehow. The room was monitored, I don't know how someone got in or how they got out. One of my men was knocked out with this," she handed the small stick-like spear to Brenddel.

He smelled the tip. "Swamp rot. Who are these people?" Brenddel paused, thinking, "No one saw him leave the room, or another person come in the room?"

The firsthealer said, "No. The room was watched. Someone was checking on him every quarter hour."

"Was Gordon in the last room?" asked Brenddel.

"Yes, how did you…"

"They must be in the old passages. Only a few people know about them. It has to be Loren." He slams his fist on the table. "He was in the palace all this time!"

The firsthealer asked, "Loren? Why would…?"

"He's the boy's uncle," replied Brenddel.

"Strange, the firstcouncilor didn't tell me that," said the firsthealer stiffly.

Brenddel and the firsthealer moved quickly through the door. "I know the passages, there is only one place they lead. You tell Trunculin. I will go catch them. Hurry."

CHAPTER 9
HORSES AND RAIN

Gordon kept blinking his eyes. The passage that the girl was taking him through was very dark and narrow, "Who are you exactly? What is going on?"

"No time," responded Aline.

Gordon stopped. "I'm not going anywhere with you unless you tell me..."

Aline yanked him forward. She was very strong, Gordon realized.

"Sorry, my king, but if you don't hurry we will both be dead. I will carry you out if you slow me down. We're meeting Loren."

Gordon said, "You might have just told me that."

"No time!" Aline said as she pulled his arm. This time he followed her. They came to a rusty gate that Aline had to push hard to open. Gordon thought he saw light around the next bend.

As they exited the narrow passage, the light was bright and Gordon had to shield his eyes. They came out at a place in the palace he had not been to. It reeked of rotting food. All along the wall, there were large containers full of waste. Aline got the hooded cloaks that were hidden there. "Put this on. Quickly," she said as she put on her own.

It was much too large for Gordon, but he had no time to complain. Aline was leading him behind the large wheeled bins of waste along the wall. They suddenly heard an angry shout from the other side of the yard. "Loren! Where are you Loren?" Brenddel shouted.

"Oh no. Not yet..." Aline said quietly.

Just then, a hand covered Gordon's mouth. Gordon quickly realized it was his uncle. Loren was hooded as they were and motioned to a large covered building at the end of the row of bins.

"Formation search, find them!" Brenddel instructed his knifemen. They went in different directions to search the courtyard. "Did you think this would work?' he shouted again, "that you could steal a king from us, Loren?"

Aline, Loren and Gordon had walked through the small door of the building, trying not to make a sound. They heard footsteps getting closer. It sounded like a guard was at the front of the building.

"Here! I think I hear something inside the shack." said the guard.

They heard the feet of the other guards running towards the building. They also heard the men unsheathe their longknives. Brenddel was near.

Loren released the rope from inside and the large door fell downward on one very surprised guard. The two horses leaped out with Gordon and Loren on one, and Aline on the other.

Brenddel let out a growl full of rage. He fired a small arrow from his wrist arrow gun. The horses were very fast, and Brenddel couldn't tell if he hit anything. Other guards had hand held arrow guns and fired as well, but the horses and their riders were too far out of range. Brenddel and his men rushed for the other side of the palace grounds.

*

The two horses were side by side. Loren held Gordon tight around the waist as they galloped. "I know you have many questions. I will answer them all. We're still in danger, but will be safe soon." He looked over to Aline who only shook her head. She obviously did not agree.

Loren concentrated on getting to the docks. He knew they would send their fastest riders out, led by an enraged Brenddel. He knew what Brenddel was capable of if he caught them. He had seen too much to underestimate him.

"Loren!" shouted Aline, pointing behind them.

Loren glanced behind him. They were far from the palace on a deserted road. He saw no riders coming after them. Aline must have known that he was hoping they were safe, because she pointed her finger again, and said, "Up!"

Then Loren saw it. An airship was coming in their direction. He scanned around quickly, "Damn. This way…" He jerked his horse to the right. "Through the trees," he said.

"We won't make it. The trees will slow us down," warned Aline.

"Better slow than seen," replied Loren.

"Look, there," Gordon offered. "See that discolored dirt? Looks like an old walking path. Should lead somewhere."

"Good boy… I mean, my king. Aline, there's a path. It will lead to the docks."

The two horses and their fugitives made their way through the trees on the rough path. They had to reduce speed, but the path was in better shape than Loren had imagined. Gordon could smell the sea.

*

Aboard the airship, Brenddel scanned for the riders and the telltale sign of a dust trail. He thought he saw movement next to a large canopy of trees. He was too high up to be sure, "Over there," he told the pilot, "those trees. They must be headed to the docks." Brenddel knew that the riders were far ahead of them. He might lose them. Brenddel told the pilot, "Increase speed. I won't lose them," and went to the front of the airship to the operators of the rain makers.

*

Loren thought they had a chance now. He could barely see the airship through the canopy of the trees. *That means that we can't be seen either*, thought Loren. The airship was surely over them by now. Loren imagined a large shadow coming over the already gloomy forest. Gordon looked up just as he saw a reddish orange flash through the spaces between the leaves.

Aline yelled, "Rain!"

Loren and Aline both looked up with horror and returned to full gallop, despite the danger. Just then the trees to their left exploded with fire. The heat was instant and their horses protested briefly, as they forced them back into a full gallop again.

*

The pilot of the airship shouted to Brenddel, "Are you mad? That's our new king down there!"

Brenddel said nothing, just stared down at the burning forest and the column of fire raining down. He smiled, "I won't lose them."

*

The fire was all around them. To their right, another tree exploded. Aline was making a sound, but the noise of the destruction was too loud for them to hear each other. Loren realized it must be a shout of Aline's anger. Then the trees abruptly ended and they were in open space again. They could see the docks now, as the sun was just about to set.

*

"There!" Brenddel pointed to the two horses emerging from the flaming forest. Get to the ropes!" The soldiers each threw a rope over the side of the deck. Brenddel instructed the pilot, "Take the airship down."

*

The riders reached the barn at the docks. Two men were waiting for them. As they dismounted, Gordon noticed that both men had necklaces of the kingdom's triangle symbol, but they wore them upside down. As Loren got off the horse he made a sound, "Ungg."

Aline said, "Loren! Loren, you're shot." Then Gordon saw the small arrow from Brenddel's wrist gun sticking out of the back of Loren's leg.

Loren said, "I know. Hurry."

Gordon started to protest, but Loren just pushed him forward, taking a cloth from his saddle and began tying it around his leg.

Loren said a few words to the men, and then turned back to Aline and Gordon. "We need to get on the ship quickly. Soldiers will be everywhere soon. I doubt Brenddel will wait for the airship to land before he searches the docks. They will probably rope down."

They all put their hoods back up and boarded their ship. Gordon noticed that several of the men also wore their triangular necklaces upside down. He noticed how much blood had soaked into Uncle Loren's pants.

The airship was getting lower, right over the docks. Loren could see the palace guards on the ropes and said to the pilot, "Now."

The pilot blew a very high-pitched whistle as they cast off. Aline looked as puzzled as Gordon.

*

Above the docks, Brenddel ignored the sun that was almost down, and slowly descended on his rope. He was going over in his mind what he would do first, when he had Loren in his interrogation rooms. Then he heard a strange, high-pitched whistle sound. He looked at the ships. There were very few ships in the wide harbor, and none were coming in. But he saw that seven ships were leaving the docks.

They were leaving at the exact same speed, but leaving in all different directions. It was like a hand slowly spreading wide and shooting off a ship from each finger.

Brenddel gave out a shout, but it did not form any word. Brenddel's rage made forming any real words impossible. The fingers kept spreading, each ship going at exactly the same speed in seven different directions. The sun made its last gasp of light before it sunk into the ocean, the only comment was Brenddel's rage.

CHAPTER 10
MISDIRECTION

Aboard their watership, they went quickly below deck. Loren insisted, so that Brenddel couldn't spot them on deck by chance. Loren also had to see to his wound. It appeared the plan had worked; the airship was not pursuing any of the seven ships. It had headed to a landing field close to the docks instead.

Loren knew that Brenddel would find out the names of each ship and where they were headed soon enough. The plan bought time, but only a little. They were led to the pilot's room on the ship. The room was cramped, but at least they were able to talk. A few moments later the pilot sent some healing supplies.

Gordon wanted to ask a million questions, but he was very concerned about Uncle Loren's leg. "Here, let me help," said Gordon as he made Loren sit on the stool, "Um…Aline, right?

"Yes, my king." Aline said as she looked at him with her deep blue eyes.

"Um, would you mind leaving the room? I have to take Uncle Loren's pants off to help him," said Gordon.

Loren snapped, "No! She stays…" Loren broke off to groan in pain. Gordon could tell he was in more pain that he was letting on. "We need to stay together at all times while aboard."

Gordon said, "Okay, could you... could you turn your back then?"

Aline nodded and turned her back.

"Okay, what do we do?" asked Gordon as he looked at the short arrow. Loren simply ripped his pants around the arrow.

"Stupid..." Loren said with a groan, "I should have gotten you out of there faster, Brenddel was on us too fast. You'll have to let me pull it out Gordon. It didn't go as deep as I first thought. Over there, pour some of that on the wound. That should keep it from getting infected."

"Okay," said Gordon as he poured the liquid around the shaft of the small, thick arrow. Loren sucked air in as the healing liquid stung him.

"Agghh..." Loren said and started pulling. It slid out slowly and Loren kept his yell as quiet as he could. The arrow was free and Gordon had a clean healing cloth ready to wrap the leg. Uncle Loren's eyes were tightly shut. He whispered, "Wrap it tight," Loren said through gritted teeth.

As Gordon finished wrapping the last of the cloth, he tied it off as Loren had shown him, just like when a boy in the village had cut his arm. "Loren, what is going on? Why did they try to kill us? What is happening?"

Loren put his hand on Gordon's shoulder. "Where to begin? Firstly, this is Aline. You can turn around now, Aline. She saved your life... and put it in danger..."

"I told you, Mantuan thought..." Aline started.

"Mantuan thought of the cause before the safety of my nephew," stated Loren firmly, looking hard into Aline's eyes. "But that is something I will discuss with him," he looked back to Gordon. "Aline and I are part of a group that is trying to stop the corruption of our kingdom."

"Is that why they all wear our triangle symbol upside down?" asked Gordon.

"Clever boy," Loren groaned as he tried to straighten his leg. "Yes, we wear it upside down just as a ship in trouble flies their banner upside down. The kingdom of the thirteen is in mortal danger. The choosing has been corrupt for many years. It seems like a random choice, but Trunculin really picks the king. No one knows that but Trunculin and Brenddel, maybe a few others. Those that are loyal to Trunculin have their child's name removed before the choosing, in fear that their child will be controlled by Trunculin."

"For a price, of course" added Aline.

Loren said, "Oh yes. He's grown quite rich playing a game that he has rigged. He collects their fees, but chooses who he wants."

Gordon asked, "But how? The tower is in the courtyard with people around all the time..."

"There are tunnels under the tower," said Aline. "The night before the choosing, it is emptied from below the tower. The name they want chosen is placed in front of all the doors from the inside, and only by the doors. The rest of the tower is empty. Since the stage has been put over the top, no one can see that. When the child reaches in, all the name boards have the same name, the one that Trunculin wants to be picked."

Loren continued, "They choose a boy that is easy to control. They send men out all year to scout for weaker boys. Always boys. We don't know why Trunculin doesn't choose girls."

"Maybe he's afraid of them," Aline offered, "He should be."

Loren's smile turned into a wince of pain instead, "Trunculin is the one that actually runs the kingdom. He controls both the Upper Council and the Lower Council, and the soldiers. He is destroying our great kingdom from the inside."

Gordon felt something change. "I think we stopped."

"Yes, it's time to change ships," said Loren as they gathered their things.

Loren started out for the deck when Aline said, "Loren?"

She was looking at Gordon, who was sweating and looking straight ahead. Aline asked, "Is this... a sweetblood attack?"

Gordon was breathing heavily, and turned to look at his uncle. "She knows a lot, Gordon," Loren said.

"But I've never seen it. Does he need a sweet, or a sour cake?" asked Aline.

"He needs something sweet." Loren pulled two sweets from his bag. "Eat both of these Gordon. I should have given you something to eat sooner."

Gordon began eating the sweets.

Aline got him some water. "So he needs sweet, not sour cake..."

Loren looked into Gordon's eyes, but spoke to Aline. "Right now he doesn't have enough sweet. We don't know a lot about this illness, but it's all about balance. Many things are in your blood that you can't see. In most people, the body balances how much sweet is in the blood naturally. In some, the blood can get too sweet, or not sweet enough. Almost like the body's not making whatever cancels out the sweet. Too sweet and the blood gets too thick, and goes slower through the body. Over time, blood stops getting to the places farthest from the heart, like fingers and toes. Not enough sweet, and he can feel dizzy, hungry, tired. We just have to keep our king in balance. I have been experimenting with a new liquid, an oil from animals. It's complicated, but it balances the sweet like his body is supposed to. I just wish there was a faster way to get it into his body than sour cakes."

"And they taste awful..." Gordon added, trying to smile.

"I know," said his uncle. "No way around it."

Aline asked, "Feeling better?"

Gordon nodded and said, "Yes. Thank you. If I stay balanced, I'm just like everyone else."

Aline smiled a bit. "Except you are the king."

Gordon said, "Yeah... except for that."

Aline asked, "So you've never told me. What happens if the blood gets too sweet or not sweet enough for too long?"

Loren didn't answer, but Gordon looked at Aline and said, "I die."

Loren gave a look to Aline and said, "Gordon will be fine. Now, let's go."

Back on deck it was very dark. Loren managed the steps up with some difficulty. Another, larger ship was next to theirs. Gordon quietly realized this was the first time he'd been so far from home. The only light was a few lanterns that had a cover over the top, so the light only went downward. "So the airships can't spot us," Aline said, guessing why Gordon looked puzzled.

"Why are we changing ships?" asked Gordon.

Loren said, "This ship will go to a port in Aspora, as planned. They may track the ship to there. We are going to Thure, the old kingdom. Farther away, less obvious."

Aboard the new ship, there were more men. They looked harder, meaner somehow to Gordon. They only spoke to Loren, and Gordon noticed several men look at Loren's leg. The blood had soaked through most of the cloth. They were led to a cabin below, where Loren gave a gold coin to the man that showed them to the room. The man grunted and walked away.

The cabin was small, with three rope beds and two old tree stumps for chairs. "Close the door, and lock it," said Loren. Aline did. "This ship will get us to Thure. We need to get supplies from a few people that are friendly to us there. Thure is called the old kingdom, Gordon, as you've read. It's a place where favors and 'who you know' are the best currency."

"Will this 'Manchuan' be there?" Gordon asked.

"Man-tu-an," Aline said, smiling. "He hates his name pronounced wrong."

"He is not shy about what he hates," Loren said. "No, he is on the move now. When the time is right, he will find his way to us."

"When you finally meet him, don't look at the patch. He hates that too," offered Aline.

Gordon asked, "Patch? Is he a big man, really fierce, with a very big axe?"

"Yes, except he lost the axe a long time ago. How did you know that? He has been erased from the histories," asked Loren.

Gordon told them more details about what he saw in his mind at the crowning.

Loren got very serious. He worried, "I don't know what it means, but if you are having visions with Mantuan and Brenddel… the shadow is Trunculin. That part makes sense. But if he is, he has bigger plans that any of us thought."

"The law keeper will know what it means," offered Aline.

"We have enough problems now, we don't need to add searching for a ghost," offered Loren.

Aline said, "Mantuan thinks he's real. He's been searching for years."

"I know, but we have more pressing issues now," said Loren.

"What do you think is happening back in the kingdom right now?" asked Gordon.

Loren groaned, adjusting his leg. He said, "Why don't you tell me, Gordon? Puzzle it out. You have begun your first trial, my king. There will be nothing but trials from now on, wherever we go. What do you think will be happening?"

Gordon thought for a moment and said, "Well, I was crowned, so I am king. They can't hold another choosing while the crowned king lives. They will need to find me, or the kingdom has only the councils to lead it…"

Aline and Loren gave a knowing glance to each other. Gordon didn't notice. "But the crazy firstman Brenddel tried to kill us, even though I am the king. Something… bigger must be going on."

"I knew you would make a good king," said Aline.

Loren glanced at her and back to Gordon. "Brenddel is the toughest man I have ever known, besides Mantuan. He does not give up, ever. I don't think he had orders to kill us. If Trunculin didn't need him so much, he might have been… dealt with a long time ago. He has a fierce anger, even Trunculin can't control him completely."

"I am king. If I went back I could order his trial before the courts. I could find out what was really going on…" said Gordon.

Loren said, "If you went back, Trunculin would have you killed just like king Daymer."

"Daymer? Was he the slaver king? There isn't much about him in the books at school," said Gordon.

"No, there wouldn't be. He died of Brenddel's shortknife on an airship. I know, I was there. I left the palace shortly after. They only let me live because they don't understand how much I really know."

Gordon asked, "Why wasn't it in my history…?"

"Every book you've read is approved by the council and the courts, or written by them. Trunculin controls them all. Through Brenddel, he controls the army too. Kings haven't had any real power for a long time. The history you think you know is false. Mostly, anyway. The books I made you read are the real history. Many of my books are forbidden. Forget what you've learned in school. From now on, our kingdom will hunt us as law breakers."

There was a sharp knock at the door.

CHAPTER 11
THE LAW ROOM

Trunculin paced in front of the king's chair, still wrestling with the best way to move forward. Corinn, the first healer, came into the room, holding a small jar. "This came from Gordon."

"What do I care about Gordon's blood?" asked Trunculin.

She took the seal off. "Smell it."

Trunculin looked confused as he took the jar. Corinn was the only person he could not see through, and he hated games. "It smells…"

"Sweet. The boy has the sweetblood illness. That could be a way to hold another choosing," said Corinn.

"Interesting… maybe. Maybe not. If it comes out, it may build sympathy for the boy. 'A boy who fights a daily struggle with a terrible illness.' The people may love him more and demand he make an appearance. You know how easily the people are swayed by emotion. No one can find out he's left the kingdom," said Trunculin.

"I told you I would help you control the new king," said the firsthealer with the slight accent that Trunculin used to like hearing late at night in the dark. "My ways are a better control than some mystic slithering inside a person's mind."

"That may be so. But I've told you that the control is not tight enough. I've sensed Stathen slipping away these last months. I wanted to be sure with Gordon. I know that made you angry. I know that's why you don't… why we don't…"

Corinn the firsthealer didn't let him finish, "There are many reasons why we don't…" Trunculin shot her an angry glance. "Oh, sorry, still hate to be interrupted?" Corinn smiled sweetly.

Trunculin hated that Corinn still had any power over him. He hated that he missed her. He has stayed away from women for so long, he was angry with himself for playing with fire again. "Yes, well… I need to consult the law room, to find a legal excuse that the people can swallow…"

"What do the mystics say about it?" asked Corinn, walking with him.

Trunculin answered, "They can't see him. They have been acting strange since all this happened."

"If he's in the outlands, he may never be found. Or the outlanders may kill him for you. It's a big world to hide in," said Corinn.

"I doubt they went that far. Brenddel is tracking each ship they may have been on. We have sent waterships to search," said Trunculin.

"Saying what? That we lost our king?" asked the firsthealer.

"Of course not," Trunculin reassured. "We are saying there is an escaped lunatic murderer named Loren, travelling with a girl and a boy… and that there is a reward."

"That should do it. No one likes lunatics with children. What are you going to tell the people? There are even more crowds coming to the kingdom, worried for their new king…," she continued, "He is our king, isn't he?"

"The crown was on his head and Stathen has returned to his village, a local hero no doubt. The law doesn't allow Stathen to return as king. I may be able to convince them Gordon wasn't properly crowned, but I have to consult the law book. If not, I will tell the crowds that he is being cared for by the best healer in our kingdom…" Trunculin said.

Corinn said, "And I would have been doing just that, if he was still here. Loren must be a better healer than I thought. The fact that he's kept his nephew well and secret with the sweetblood shows us that. It is always a death sentence. But I appreciate the complement, Trunc. Still hate being called that?"

"You know I do," Trunculin said curtly through tight lips.

"Good," Corinn said, as she walked away. "You should have chosen a queen this time."

"You can't be serious," Trunculin said. "Have you ever been around a teenaged girl?"

Corinn shook her head as they walked their separate ways.

Trunculin tried not to stare after her as she walked away. The firstcouncilor finally reached the law room. It was the only level that had just one purpose. He passed by guards and the waiting chamber, where dozens of people were waiting in line to see a law keeper.

One wall was three men high with a series of small rectangular wooden holes. There were hundreds of holes and a ladder leaned up against the wall to reach the higher ones. Each rectangle held a different blank form, depending on what law the person was trying to get clarified.

Trunculin walked past the room, holding his breath. He came to the entrance door to the law room. The guards let him pass without a word. He came to a small desk, piled with requests almost as tall as the law keeper who was sitting behind them.

Trunculin let out his breath. "Uhhh, I can still smell them. I don't know how you work so close to the reeking masses."

The man offered no response to Trunculin's query. "How may we help you, firstcouncilor?" said the man with no emotion at all. Trunculin barely registered it as a question.

"I need the grand keeper," said Trunculin.

The little man nodded once, got up and left the room. He came back shortly and resumed his work.

The grand keeper came out. "Firstcouncilor. I thought we might get a visit. How may I help?" said the grand law keeper warmly.

Trunculin didn't bother to hide anything. A law keeper worked all day in a dimly lit level with no windows. He reasoned that they were not even ambitious enough to gossip. The complexities of the law book kept their minds too busy. "I need to know if a king was crowned correctly, if there is any legal way to replace him immediately. Also, if there is any historical precedent for removal, due to illness."

The grand keeper was not surprised. "We will need to consult areas 47, 326, and 2239. Right this way, firstcouncilor."

This level was vast, and there was only one way in. Trunculin was not looking forward to this visit. He needed the information, and he could not trust it to an underling. He needed to see the words himself, in order to know which way he could twist them.

The law book is a collection of pages on a seemingly never-ending long winding set of tables. There are hundreds of tables that support the law book. *It winds through the level just like a snake,* Trunculin thought. It was mounted in such a way that when a new law needed to be added, any section could be opened to receive those pages. Trunculin thought of each section as a chapter of the book, winding around on the tables. Of course, no law was ever removed.

This level was originally sectioned off into small rooms of offices and living chambers. The first law room had held just one small book written by the first thirteen. That was a long time ago, Trunculin knew. Eventually, walls were taken down and the floor was supported from underneath to account for the vast weight of the serpentine book of laws. Since it was like one continuous book, they would have to walk by the entire thing, only stopping at the relevant sections.

Trunculin always felt like he was in a dark tunnel, the rare times he came here. True, Trunculin had written many of the laws himself, but he did not care to look at the consequences. His job was to pass laws, not keep track of them. Until he needed to trap someone in them, of course.

They stopped by each section and Trunculin was annoyed to find the laws concerning how a king was chosen were very clearly written. Most of them were written many years before, even before Trunculin. They had a different philosophy then. The first kings believed that only a few laws would do. Trunculin had always believed that there must be so many laws, often conflicting, that anyone could be called a criminal when it was convenient.

They came to the last relevant section, number 2239. It was a law concerning an obscure king. Trunculin smiled. *That might just work,* he thought to himself. He left the law room relieved to be away from the great snake.

CHAPTER 12
DANGER ON THE WATER

"What is it?" asked Loren, answering the knock.

"It's me. We must speak privately," replied the voice from the other side of the door.

Loren went out, limping on his hurt leg, trying to shield Gordon and Aline from being seen. Through the door, Gordon could hear only whispers. Loren came back a few moments later.

"Who was that, Loren?" asked Aline.

Loren said, "That was the only friend we have on this ship. Plans have changed. Trunculin sent word that there is a man, girl, and boy travelling, and there is a reward. Any of these men would kill us to collect it. He thinks a few suspect who you really are. We have to get off this ship."

"How? This is a direct ship to Thure," asked Aline.

Loren answered, "Almost. They have to stop and do trading at the port of Dralinn."

"Wait... I read about that port. They also call it Murderer's Cove, don't they?" asked Gordon.

"I shouldn't have given you so many books with real history in them," remarked Loren.

"If there's a reward for us, that's the last place we should go," offered Aline.

"It's the most likely place to find a more reliable transport to Thure. Nobody just passes Dralinn. All ships stop there for something."

"It would be a good place to get better disguises than these cloaks. No offense. Plus some fresh healing cloth to wrap your leg," remarked Gordon.

"The boy king here has a point. If we don't get you fresh cloth for your leg, if will get infected" added Aline. "Should I guess at the other reason you want to go there?"

"We have to take turns guarding the door. You want first watch or second, Aline?" asked Loren, ignoring her last question.

"I'll take first watch," she said.

"Okay. I'll sleep for four hours, then you," Loren said. "Gordon, you sleep all eight. We should be at the bay in nine hours or so." He limped to Gordon and hugged him. "I know you have more questions. They will all be answered. But if I don't lie down now, I will fall down."

"I... I understand. Thank you, Uncle Loren, for everything," said Gordon. Loren nodded at Aline, then went to his rope bed. He was asleep the moment he let his head down.

Gordon's rope bed was closer to Aline, who sat facing the door, shortknife on her lap. He climbed onto his bed, closed his eyes and couldn't sleep. He looked at Aline. "Thank you, too, Aline, for all your help. I don't know quite how to ask this, but... who are you exactly?"

"I am Aline from lower Aspora."

"Why is someone from Aspora helping a king from another land? King - I'm still not used to saying that - king," said Gordon.

"You've never been to my land. Even with what your firstcouncilor is doing to the kingdom, your land is still far better than mine. In my land, the king is not chosen. It is called the land of a thousand kings for a reason," said Aline. "The strong rule in my land. They are never the best kind of men, and they are always the cruelest."

"What is the firstcouncilor doing exactly? I don't understand any of this."

Aline said, "Loren should be the one to tell you. It's not my place."

"Well, he's asleep right now. I just want some answers. It's been a long day of people trying to kill me. I think I deserve a few," said Gordon.

"I can tell you this," Aline said. "The beloved Trunculin is capable of horrible things. I have seen some with my own eyes."

"But he has been firstcouncilor since before I was born. He's one of the most popular people in our kingdom. What are these horrible things?" Gordon insisted.

"Like I said, Loren should tell you." Aline didn't say anything after that, and just stared at the door. Gordon gave up, and sleep finally took him.

CHAPTER 13
UNHAPPY CROWDS

There was no turning back now. Trunculin waited inside the archway leading to the balcony, mentally preparing himself for… well, he wasn't sure. This had never been done before, not exactly. Brenddel approached to his right, nodded and said nothing. The firstcouncilor walked onto the balcony and the crowd had a strange reaction.

They had never seen the firstcouncilor come out without smiling. He came out with his head down, looking at the ground. He still was not smiling as he walked down the walkway and onto the stage. He raised his head solemnly to all of the crowds gathered.

"Our young king Gordon," announced Trunculin, "has fled our kingdom."

The shock among the crowds was immediate. There were gasps and shouts, but from most of the crowd there was silence. The firstcouncilor continued, "What you saw yesterday was a boy that was not ready to be King. Gordon, well… his mind broke down. Our firsthealer found nothing wrong with his health or body. His mind simply couldn't take what was thrust upon him. Under a cover of darkness last night, with some traitorous friends, Gordon fled our kingdom in fear and cowardice."

The crowd was stunned. But there was another reaction too, one that the firstcouncilor had not seen before. A few in the crowd started to shout, "I don't believe it," or "he wouldn't do that," were clearly heard among the crowds. Trunculin motioned for the crowd to quiet, and they obeyed.

The firstcouncilor looked shrewdly at the crowds and declared, "But I have consulted the great law book, and I found something that happened long ago that may help us in this strange time. There was a boy named Joreh. He was a small boy and he was chosen king. The poor boy was so scared he soiled himself right on this platform." At this, the crowd let out a few chuckles. "This is not a time for laughter! It must prove to all of you that what happens on this tower is deadly serious," he continued. "We all imagine what it would be like to stand here and be chosen, for the crowds to cheer. What Joreh went through, and what Gordon has done, should remind us all how great a responsibility it is to lead this kingdom."

The crowds did not laugh again. Trunculin knew he had them now. "Like Gordon did, Joreh said the words; he would take this responsibility and be our king. He was not able to continue, and the poor boy went mad within days. It has given us a precedent. After Joreh, a law was passed and there was an immediate second choosing for a new king."

The reaction to this unusual idea was mixed. Trunculin continued, "And that is what is going to happen today. Both councils agreed that it is the only way to get past this uneasy time. The new choosing will be now, in front of all you good people. Please bring the glass barrel."

The crowd seemed unhappy with this idea. Their murmurs and loud whispers were not what the firstcouncilor was hoping for. He couldn't tell what they were saying exactly, but the general tone of the people was not good. *This could still go badly,* Trunculin thought.

The glass barrel was brought out with names of the eight year old child that would choose the new king. This time a boy's name was chosen, and he walked up bravely and chose a number. The number three was chosen this time and the fanfare grew as they unlocked the third door. The boy reached through the door, pulling out the name board of the new king. The firstcouncilor took it from the boy and proudly said "Asa."

Asa was found immediately and hoisted up among the ranks. The firstcouncilor noticed that the mood of the crowd was different this time. It wasn't somber exactly, but it was muted; not at all the excited scene of Gordon's choosing. Trunculin knew there was no turning back now.

Asa looked even more shocked than Gordon had. Trunculin asked if Asa would accept the kingship, and after a long pause Asa said he would. The crowd mostly cheered their new king, and the firstcouncilor made the same speeches that he had made at Gordon's choosing, trying to rush it so that the people would have no choice but to accept the events as they unfolded.

Trunculin added something to his speech. He motioned for the crowd to quiet down and made another announcement. "And to get past this troubled time even faster, the Councils have agreed that the crowning should also be today."

The crowd erupted as one this time, but not with delight. It was as if the firstcouncilor had thrown a switch. Now the crowd was angry. There came shouts of "No!" and, "That's not the law," and one man was clearly heard to say, "You lie!"

The firstcouncilor was never at a loss on what to say or what to do, but this surprised him. He had not expected the ferociousness of this reaction. He couldn't quite move for a moment, but then he motioned for the crowd to quiet down. They did not. He tried a second time, but it just seemed to fuel their anger. Trunculin was angry now too, but he dared not show it.

Not knowing what else to do, he motioned for the king's crown to be brought. The crowd was still very angry, with shouts the firstcouncilor had never heard. Trunculin placed the crown on Asa's head. Asa started to actually look afraid. He shrunk away from the crown, and some people in the crowd noticed.

"He doesn't even want to be king!" said someone from the crowd, while another said, "Don't force him!" and another, "You're scaring him!"

The firstcouncilor mustered his famous smile: The smile that made him so famous among the people. He always smiled the same and thought the same exact thought. Through his smile, he always imagined the entire courtyard being filled with fire from the airships. In his mind, he saw them all burning.

The firstcouncilor continued his widest smile as he nearly crammed the crown on the boy's head. He lowered his own head so only Asa could hear him, and whispered in a sincere tone, "Now, my little king, your first lesson: you will do everything I tell you to do."

The firstcouncilor's hands were on both of Asa's shoulders, gripping him fiercely. The boy simply nodded silently.

"That's a good little king." Trunculin nearly spit the words into Asa's ear.

The new king and the rest made their way into the palace as they had the day before, but instead of cheering crowds for Gordon, all that they could hear were cries of anger.

CHAPTER 14
A FAMILIAR FACE

Back on the ship, the three travelers all managed to get some sleep, somehow. Loren's leg pain made it hard for him to sleep for more than a quarter hour at a time. He shifted in his rope bed, but no position was comfortable. Aline worried about how much blood he had lost. The waters had been rough during the night which must have distracted everyone on board from taking them prisoner to collect any reward.

When it was time to get off the ship, there was a knock on the door, and once again it was their only friend. This time he came into the room with some food and some advice. "I can get you off the ship, but after that, you're on your own. I'm not exactly welcome in this port. There's not enough hours in the day to tell you why."

"Thank you, old friend," said Loren. "I won't forget all you've done for us." They gathered their things and left the ship, Gordon wondering to himself how well he really knew his uncle. How did he know all of these people that Gordon had never heard of?

They got suspicious glances until they were off the ship entirely. Gordon noticed how many people stared at Loren's injured leg as they made their way onto the docks, like they were emboldened by any perceived weakness. As they walked along the long piers, there were smells of salty water and the overpowering odor of fish. There were people selling their catches and other things right out of their boats as they walked toward the port city of Dralinn.

There were shouts of both anger and joy all around them. Gordon knew right away that this was a dangerous place, but he tried not to smile too much. He had never been very far from home, and despite the danger, he was awed by the place that he had only read about. The port of Dralinn, also called murderer's cove, or the bay of death, was famous for all the wrong reasons: Escaped prisoners, murderers, and sea lords all came here to hide or get supplies. Sometimes both. Gordon realized how much danger they were in, especially with Loren hurt, but he had to admit to himself this was exciting. Just like stories he had read about in his books.

As Gordon looked around, it was hard to believe that this was actually a part of the kingdom of the thirteen, his own kingdom. It was only accessible by ship, because mighty mountains separated the bay from the rest of the kingdom. There were some steep trails, but few people dared go through the narrow passes. They were only used by message dogs too fast to be caught by the marauders that sometimes ventures into the steep trails.

The smells sweat, fish and saltwater was a strange mix this early in the morning. It brought Gordon out of his daydreaming to look around at the reality of Dralinn. Gordon hadn't spent much time down by the king's dock back home. Loren had always said it was a dangerous place to be, lots of people that Gordon shouldn't get to know. Compared to this place, the king's dock seemed safer than his village.

There was a large statue where the docks met. It was over five men high and made of some kind of stone that Gordon had never seen before. The man had a giant spear in both hands, and down around this spear were three crowns. The spear was going through all the crowns and into the ground.

Gordon asked Loren, "What does that statute mean?"

Before Loren could answer, Aline said, "It means they don't like kings here."

Gordon looked up from the docks at the houses and buildings. They seemed to almost climb up the hills behind the docks. As they walked closer, he saw that many were built on logs. *They look like houses with legs*, Gordon thought. The logs were sunk into the hills at different lengths so that all the houses were relatively level.

As they walked toward the narrow streets between the buildings, Loren explained, "They are all very close to each other and some are even built on top of the other. Each house is interconnected to the next, all the way up, until the hills turn into Mount Anthsia."

"So that is Mount Anthsia?" Gordon asked, pointing to the top of the mountain towering over the roofs.

Aline added, "Terrible place to build houses. The fools' just better hope Mount Anthsia doesn't spit fire at them…"

"That hasn't happened in hundreds of years…" Loren said.

"I don't know how anyone can live here," finished Aline, walking ahead of them. Gordon thought that Aline seemed mad about something. He was still trying to puzzle out Aline.

They went through a small, narrow alleyway. The sun couldn't penetrate the alley, so it was very dark. Loren slowed down. The steep, inclined alley was hurting his leg. They only stopped for a moment, when a large man with a dirty smile stepped in front of them. Loren stopped and began to say something to him, when another man stepped in behind them, blocking the alley from both sides.

Loren said, "We don't want trouble. We are only here for the day, looking for transport. Maybe you could…"

The man in front of them pulled his shortknife. Gordon could just see the sharp blade in the darkened alley.

Loren started to say, "There's no reason for that…" when Aline acted.

She ran just a few steps and then actually ran up the wall. She bounced off of it and twisted her body, catching the first, larger man by the neck. She used her own body's momentum to flip the man onto the ground. She punched the man just below the throat and he was on his back, gasping for air.

Before Gordon or Loren could register what was happening, she was already flying at the other man. He seemed just as surprised as Gordon and Loren were. He fumbled for his knife. She flung her body around and kicked him in the face. She took the second man's head and smacked it on the cobble stone street. Both men were down and didn't come back up. At least, not by the time they had left the dark alleyway.

"Are you all right, Gordon?" Loren asked Gordon as they made their way through another narrow passageway.

"Am I alright? Is she alright?" Gordon said. "Are those men going to be alright?

"I don't care," said Aline as she led them up a series of narrow passageways. Gordon looked at Aline and she wasn't even breathing fast. It was like nothing had happened at all. Gordon had questions for Aline, but he decided to save them for later.

Gordon had Loren's arm around his neck and was helping him walk. Loren said, "In case you were wondering, you don't want to make her angry."

Gordon replied, "Uh, I'll write that on my list of things not to do."

They found their way into a courtyard where vendors were selling fruits, fish and other things. As they rounded the corner, they saw a large banner on the second level balcony with an upside down triangle. They made their way to the stairs leading to the balcony. Gordon and Aline helped Loren struggle up the stairs. Before they could get to the door, it opened and a woman pointed an arrow gun at them. She was not smiling.

"So that's how you greet your favorite daughter?" asked Aline.

"My only daughter, you mean. Aline, what are you doing here?" The woman did not immediately drop the arrow gun.

"Believe me, you are my least favorite mother. But right now, we need a friend. Loren is hurt and we're all being hunted. What about it Sandrell, feel like being our friend?" asked Aline.

The woman looked at the boy and Loren, then back to her daughter. She saw Loren's leg and lowered the arrow gun. "Come on in. I've got some spice tea and some clean cloth for that leg. I knew this day was going too well."

The woman led them into the house. She put the arrow gun on a nearby table and went to the kitchen without saying anything. They were all in a small room with a round table. Gordon helped Loren to a chair.

"Your… mother?" asked Gordon, "Why…"

"I don't want to talk about it, in case you were wondering," said Aline.

The woman came back with four cups of tea and a bowl of dark brown sweet salt. Gordon took the tea, but politely refused the sweet salt. The woman seemed offended by everything they did, by their very presence. As Gordon looked around at all the weapons hung on the walls, he wondered what Aline's father must be like.

"Come on, Loren," Aline's mother said, "let's see your leg." Sandrell had Loren straighten his leg and unwrapped the cloth that was brown with dried blood. She shook her head and said, "You're a healer, so you know you'll live. I just hope the other man looks worse."

Loren grimaced and said, "I'd rather not talk about the other man. And we have more important things to talk about than my leg."

The woman noticed Gordon looking at the weapons on the walls. "We are a warrior family."

Loren said, "You certainly don't hide your beliefs either, Sandrell. That's quite the statement to have hanging off your balcony."

"Of all the kingdoms, I'm the saddest to see yours go. It was the world's last hope. The least I can do is hang that banner. The real ways I'm helping the cause, I do in secret… so far." said Sandrell.

Loren replied, "It's not over yet. The kingdom may still be saved. There is much to do, and we're always looking for more allies."

Sandrell sat. "I've told Mantuan, and I'll tell you, I'm a woman who plays the odds. I do my part just in case, but I think your kingdom is too far gone to come back. If I'm wrong, and I think there is a chance to win, you will have all the weapons and help you need. I have a few allies of my own. I keep telling Mantuan..."

"Mantuan? You spoke to him? When? Where?" asked Aline.

"Three days ago in this very room. He was traveling with a few men, not disguised in the least. I would love to see Trunculin's face when he is told that Mantuan is still alive. He will probably wet himself," said Sandrell, just finishing wrapping Loren's leg in clean white cloth. "I will admit that seeing him out in the open like that gave me a little hope… but just a little."

"Did he tell you his plans? Where he was going next? I've not heard from him in months," said Loren.

Gordon gave Loren a strange look at hearing this. How did he know Mantuan? How many secrets had Loren kept from him? He was having a hard time waiting to have his questions answered. He felt his anger slowly growing, then looked at Loren's leg and told himself to be patient.

"Didn't say much, but I can tell he's got big things planned. He must be close to putting them in action, to come out in the open. I don't know which way he was headed," she turned to Gordon with a sneer, "so, who are you then?"

Gordon looked to his uncle, not knowing what was okay to say, and what was not.

Before he could say anything, Aline said, "Mother, this is King Gordon."

The woman started to laugh. It wasn't a little laugh, but the laugh of a person who has just heard the funniest jest in her life. "I'm sorry boy, but I've never seen a king from your land who hasn't been through at least three or four trials. I guess that's why the official portrait is done late into their kingship. I have socks older than you, boy."

"We need safe passage to Thure. We'll also need some weapons," said Aline.

"Well I wouldn't say I have any friends exactly, but I know a few people that might help. I know of a ship leaving tomorrow for Thure. I might be able to get you on it. But right now, it seems like you all could use a nice hot bath." She looked at Gordon. "Even kings can stink."

CHAPTER 15
FEAR AND CHOCOLATE

While Rolem was busy showing the new king Asa around the palace, the firstcouncilor went to see Brenddel. He was still uneasy about what had happened with the crowds. In his many years as firstcouncilor, he had never lost the love of the crowd before. He was always able to make them love him, the fools, even in his younger days. He tried to push those thoughts from his mind. Right now, he needed to know what was happening in the search for Gordon and the traitor Loren.

"Anything yet?" asked the firstcouncilor.

Brenddel reported, "We're making progress. We have found out where five of the seven waterships were headed. Three of them had pilots that we suspect are troublemakers. We found several kingdom symbols turned upside down on them. The other two ships were launched by lesser officers, and the pilots were just as unhappy as we were when they found out. Either way, they most likely switched ships in the night. That's what I would've done."

"We must find them. And I need to know if Mantuan is still alive," insisted Trunculin.

"I watched Mantuan fall. He is dead. I want the traitors just as much as you, but the boy's vision cannot be real. And why do we still need the boy anyway? We have a new king now."

"It's not enough," stated Trunculin. "The crowds will eventually accept this king because they have no choice. But if Gordon was to come back, someone might give him shelter and then he could tell his story. He would be an ex-king calling the new king illegitimate, and me a liar. That would start trouble. Or, he finds his way back here with Mantuan and an army and takes his crown back."

"That won't happen. Mantuan is dead. The traitors can't be that stupid, the boy's weak, they are traveling with a servant girl who worked here in the palace. I'm sure I injured Loren when they were escaping, and besides all that, I will find them," Brenddel said.

Trunculin said, "No doubt, Brenddel. It's just that rarely are things this out of my control… but I need you to do something else for me. Since there is no former king for the king's meal, I need you to go in my stead."

"Me? I don't have time to babysit the king. Why can't you do it? Isn't it some ancient custom that you must eat with them? I need to get things ready for the search," said Brenddel.

"A few of the councilors have a problem with the way I handled things. I have to go put my foot on their throats. It might take all evening. Besides, you can leave tomorrow. There have been too many sightings of those shadow fin things for the airships to be travelling at night. It's not safe."

Brenddel hesitated, "Fine. I'll hold the king's hand for a few hours. But then I must prepare. I have to be ready for anything."

Brenddel walked off before the firstcouncilor could say anything. Trunculin didn't mind missing the king's meal. At least that was one unpleasant thing he would not have to do today. He left thinking about how much he did for the kingdom; things that no one will ever know or appreciate.

Brenddel had only stayed through one king's meal. Usually he was too busy with the security for the crowning event. But since Trunculin had changed the order of things. There was no king to transfer power from, so he would be eating alone. The crowds had made Trunculin more nervous than Brenddel had ever seen him.

He saw the boy, Asa, sitting in the middle chair. He wasn't eating. As he approached the table, he noticed that no one was talking to the boy either. Rolem must had finished his tour and left him alone. He normally did not rank high enough to sit at the table with the king. The most he could do was stand behind him. Brenddel looked at the boy and thought that he was the smallest king he had ever seen. The boy had to be thirteen to put his name in, but he looked much younger. And very uneasy. Brenddel thought the firstcouncilor would break the boy's neck getting the crown on his head. He had been scared then, and it looked as though the young king's first day had not gotten much better.

He approached the boy and said, "Hello, my king."

The poor boy jumped in his seat and almost let out a yell. Brenddel noticed, with anger, a few titters and small laughs from surrounding tables.

"S…s…sorry. I didn't see you walk up. Do you know where… that man that was showing me around went?" Asa asked timidly.

Brenddel's said, "I'm sorry, my king, but Rolem does not rank high enough to sit at the table with you. But I do… at least tonight."

The boy gave a small smile, no longer feeling quite as alone. Brenddel said, "I hope it will be okay if I eat with you. I am…"

"The firstman of the kingdom, the great warrior Brenddel," The boy looked down at his plate again. "I know who you are. I have a whole army at home, and I have three of you."

"I'm sorry… what do you mean, my king?"

"Little soldier men." Asa made a motion with his fingers to show how big the soldier toys were. "You are my favorite one… I even painted one with your firstman stripes. The likeness is okay, but the ones I painted came out pretty good."

Brenddel smiled a little, using muscles he hadn't used in a long time. But he couldn't help it. He was always surprised how popular he was in some of the villages. "I had forgotten about those. Someone showed me one of them once; it was a terrible likeness, looked nothing like me. But they did get my arms right." Brenddel made a fist and raised his arm, flexing his muscle. The boy smiled for probably the first time that day. Brenddel realized he was smiling and abruptly stopped, clearing his throat.

Asa didn't know what to say. Finally he managed, "Do you… know what happened to Gordon?" asked the new king, looking down again.

Brenddel said, "The firstcouncilor told you what happened. He told all of the crowds what happened. He ran away. Why do you ask, my king?"

"He's… he was my friend. We're from the same village. I know Gordon never really wanted to be king, but it just doesn't sound like him to run away," said Asa.

Brenddel didn't know what to say, or how to help this boy. He knew that Asa was Trunculin's first choice, until someone put Gordon's name in the tower instead. This little king would never get the truth from Trunculin. But, the distractions might help him, thought Brenddel. The training would start the next day with others, while Brenddel was away. He might be gone from the kingdom a while, and he was afraid of what this timid king might become under Trunculin.

Brenddel lied, "I don't know why he did it. Gordon was not alone, we know his uncle was involved. It's a very brave thing to accept all this responsibility. You know that more than anyone. I guess Gordon just got scared."

Asa just looked at his plate of food again, picking at it once more. Brenddel had never been around children, not even when he was a child. He went into training soon after Mantuan had found him. He remembered how he felt walking into the training yards when he was only nine years old. The world must seem that scary to this new king.

"You know what always makes me feel better when I'm scared?" asked Brenddel.

The boy looked skeptical, "You don't get scared..."

Brenddel leaned over to the boy. "Only fools never get scared."

Asa smiled a little.

"Whenever I've had a hard day, the thing that always makes me feel better is chocolate."

"Chocolate?" asked Asa.

"Yes. Sounds strange, I know. But nothing is more calming than chocolate. I always take a bit of chocolate before a battle." Brenddel raised his hand for a servant girl to come over.

The new king smiled a genuine smile, as the girl brought over the largest chocolate pie he had ever seen. Brenddel smiled at the king and gave him a small nod. Asa's plate of food was cleared and he ate chocolate pie for dinner.

Trunculin was quietly listening to the Secondcouncilor of the lower council and a leading councilor of the upper council bicker back and forth. They railed at Trunculin, and waved their arms wildly while talking about 'tradition' and 'death of the law.'

"Are you just going to sit there? What do you have to say?" asked the secondcouncilor.

Trunculin replied, "Oh, I think you are doing quite well without me saying a word. In fact, if you'd like me to leave so that you can have a discussion about me, I will oblige. I don't really have to be here for you to have this pointless debate."

"Pointless!? You had no right to do it. The choosing and the crowning ceremony have to take place on different days. Even the king's meal was changed. Chaos! It has never been done," said the secondcouncilor.

"…And to tell the crowds that we approved the maneuver. Unforgivable!" said the other councilor.

"Wrong and wrong," said Trunculin. "Section 2239. The great law book is there for any councilor to use. The precedent is there, just as I said. We didn't have time to have them on two different days. It was done once before. And the crowds are restless. They were… not themselves because of what they'd seen the day before, when Gordon collapsed..."

The secondcouncilor interrupted, "Yes, we all noticed the difference. What happened was a rejection of what you were trying to do. The crowds turned on you…"

Without warning, Trunculin rose from his chair and struck the councilor across the face, "You know how I hate to be interrupted." The secondcouncilor was shocked and immediately sat, holding his face.

Trunculin came around the desk and towered over them, "Gordon seemed to immediately steal their hearts, and then he suddenly collapsed in agony on the stage the next day, then he fled the kingdom. Too much trauma on the people will make them unhappy. When the people get too unhappy, they look to the palace. If there is no king in the palace, they get even more nervous. I know you think I've done some terrible thing. But let's be practical, laws need to be passed. The kingdom needs to be run. It's not run by the king, but the people don't know that. They see a day with no king… even one day… and they fear. You want the people in the throes of fear?" Trunculin looked at each of the men very closely, staring at them one at a time. "And let's not, for even one moment, forget who gave you your positions. It wasn't any king, was it?"

They knew well that Trunculin handpicked all of the councilors. The two men looked at each other and refused to meet Trunculin's stare, "You still should've consulted us, then we would not have looked so foolish, not knowing what was going to happen. That puts us in a very bad place with the rest of the council."

Trunculin stared at both men, then quickly grabbed both men by the arm, and said with his famous smile, "Perhaps you are right. I made decisions quickly. In the future, I will try to keep you two more informed. Come now. It's been a rough couple of days. Let's go get something to drink and put it past us." The two men gave a small, weak smile as they all exited the room.

The firstcouncilor knew he had won the day. Losing was never an option.

CHAPTER 16
FIRST TRAINING

Sandrell took Loren to meet her friends for transport the next day. The baths and having clean clothes had helped everyone's mood. They insisted Gordon stay behind as he may be recognized with all the sailors going in and out of the port. Even one person spotting him would put them all in danger. Better to stay put in the house with Aline as his guard.

After they left, Gordon asked, "Did you really grow up here?"

"No. I told you I grew up in Aspora," answered Aline. "I also said I didn't want to talk about my mother. Nice try."

Gordon shrugged and went to one of the weapons on the wall. It was a beautifully carved wooden pole, with a long curved blade at the end. It was easily one and a half times as tall as Gordon.

"Don't touch that," said Aline.

Gordon pulled his hand back, "So, you don't live with your mother..."

"Can't help yourself, can you?" Aline stared at him, but finally said, "I was raised in Aspora. Mantuan was more of a parent to me than my mother was. She was... gone a lot. When your mother is the toughest warrior in the world, there are a lot of enemies."

"It seems like you are sort of mad at her. Do you not get along?" asked Gordon.

Aline answered, "She wasn't there for me much, when I was growing up. Some of that wasn't her fault… it's hard to describe."

"What about your father?" Gordon asked innocently.

"We don't talk about him," Aline said firmly.

"Okay. Sorry…" Gordon asked, still admiring the weapons, "can you use any of these?"

Aline turned her head slowly and stared at Gordon. "I can use all of them." She stared back out the window, bored.

"You know, actually, in a way, you kind of… owe me," Gordon said.

Aline answered, "How is that, exactly? How many times am I supposed to save your life, my king?"

"Well… you rescued me one day before my training was to begin. How do you expect the king to fight for himself, if he can't use any of these? You owe me a lesson," Gordon stood with his arms crossed.

Aline looked at him, got up from her seat, and walked directly to him. Her face was hard to read, but as she got closer he got more nervous, remembering the two men from the alleyway. He uncrossed his arms.

"Okay, little king," she looked him up and down, Gordon noting how much taller she was than him, "lesson one. Don't challenge anyone until you know if you can beat them. Grab that longknife off the wall."

Gordon went to the longknife she pointed to. She grabbed a longknife off the wall close to her, one of roughly equal size. She heard a "thunnk" sound and said, "No my king, you are supposed to *lift* the longknife."

The longknife in Gordon's hand had tipped down, and the end stuck into the floor.

"Sandrell is not going to like what you did to her floor," Aline teased.

"Very funny. I didn't know it was going to be so heavy," Gordon said as he struggled to get the knife tip out of the floor. Aline walked slowly towards him.

"The second lesson is, always be prepared. An enemy does not wait for you to be ready," she raised her longknife into a battle stance, "and there is always an enemy."

Aline swung her longknife down just as Gordon raised his longknife out of the floor. The force nearly drove the longknife from Gordon's hands. But he had practiced with other boys enough to know to try to absorb the impact. Wooden longknives were much lighter than the real thing, he realized.

"The longknife is for slashing. It's for making your reach longer than it is. You must think of it as part of your arm. The most dangerous part," she lunged for Gordon, who barely blocked the blow. "Ah, wooden longknives in the fields, I'm guessing?" she made a stabbing gesture and came within an inch of Gordon skin.

"I thought you said it was for slashing, not stabbing," Gordon said, realizing how close she had come to cutting him.

"Partial truth. Battle is unpredictable. Never believe what your opponent tells you," Aline said as she stabbed again.

Gordon blocked her attempt. Just as he thought he was getting the hang of it, she hooked her foot underneath his leg and he went sprawling backwards. His longknife clattered to the floor.

Aline put the tip of her longknife inches from Gordon's face. "There are no rules in combat. Use whatever you have ... your knife, your hands, even your feet. Above all, use your brain, never use emotion, and always be ready for anything."

Aline put her knife aside and offered Gordon her hand. Gordon got up, a little embarrassed with his performance, but unhurt.

"Not bad for your first time," said Aline.

"Really?" asked Gordon.

"Yes," replied Aline, "You're still alive."

Loren and Sandrell walked through the door, just as the two were putting their longknives back on the wall.

"What happened to my floor?" asked Sandrell.

"I told you," whispered Aline to Gordon. She said to her mother, "I was giving our new king a combat lesson."

"Don't be so sure that he is king," said Sandrell.

Gordon looked confused, he asked Loren, "What does that mean?"

"It means that Trunculin has made a move that I wasn't expecting. He crowned another king on the same day as his choosing. The new king is your friend Asa."

"Asa?" Gordon said, "I guess it does matter when you put your name in the tower."

"No, Gordon, it's not because the name boards were close together in the tower. Asa must have been Trunculin's choice. He just went back to his original plan. Asa is small and will probably be easy for the firstcouncilor to control," said Loren.

Gordon brightened, "This is good news, then. That means they won't be hunting me anymore."

Loren shook his head. "I wish that was true. Now they will be hunting us even harder. They need you dead, so that you can't come back to challenge the firstcouncilor's lies. He needs the kingdom to believe that you are a coward and ran away."

"Oh," said Gordon letting out of long breath. "I just wish this was over."

Loren went to Gordon. "I know Gordon, I know. But there is much more to do. We booked passage to the kingdom of Thure. We leave tomorrow morning."

Sandrell said, “There’s more good news…”

“What’s that?” asked Gordon.

“You survived a training session with Aline,” she said.

CHAPTER 17
BRENDDEL'S GIFT

"Why can't I see my family?" asked Asa, barely able to get the words out. He nervously shuffled his bare feet on the carpet.

Trunculin said, "I'm afraid it's the law, my king. Long ago, it was decided that when a king is chosen, he must totally belong to the kingdom during his trials. Of course, you'll see your family on special occasions. But you will be learning so much, so fast, and eventually there'll be so many decisions to make that you will have no time for friends or family."

Brenddel cleared his throat, entering the room.

"Hello, Brenddel!" Asa said smiling.

Trunculin was surprised by the reaction. "Oh yes, you spent some time together at the kings meal. I'm sorry I couldn't make it, my king. I hope Brenddel was a suitable substitute and didn't bore you with too many battle stories."

"No. It was pretty fun," said Asa.

"Our new king was a fine dinner companion," said Brenddel as he approached the king with something wrapped up in his arms. "I'm just sorry that we can't spend more meals together, my king. I have to go on mission to a far corner of the kingdom."

Asa didn't know if he was supposed to say anything. He didn't know if he had any real authority yet, or if he ever really would.

Brenddel continued, "But I wanted to come by first with a parting gift." He gave the wrapped package to the king.

"What is it? Can I open it?" Asa asked, looking from the firstcouncilor to the Brenddel.

The firstcouncilor said softly, "You are king now, go ahead."

"I feel like it's my birthday!" King Asa opened the package and it was a large soldier that looked just like Brenddel.

Brenddel said, "Long ago, there was an artist here at the palace that made the only likeness of me that I can stand to look at. I thought it might make up for all those toy soldiers that looked nothing like me."

Asa took the large figure, and was amazed that there was an actual longknife in the sheath.

"Be careful with that, it's sharp," warned Brenddel.

"I love it!" Asa said, amazed that the boots came off as well. "Thank you Brenddel."

"If you will pardon me, my king, I do have to be off. I hope your first day of training goes well," said Brenddel.

As Brenddel was leaving, Trunculin said, "And it is getting late for me as well, my king. First trial has begun, and your training awaits. We'll be up early in the morning. I will see you then. Good night."

"You can stay a little longer if you want to, I don't mind," said Asa, looking very small in his large chamber.

Trunculin said smoothly, "I'm sorry, my king, I'm not as young as I used to be. But if you need anything, the guards are just outside. Good night."

"Oh… okay. Goodnight," said Asa as Trunculin and Brenddel left.

Outside in the hallway, Trunculin said, "I thought we agreed you would leave in the morning. There have been sightings of those creatures whenever we get near open waters. You will be flying blind at night."

"I can't delay any longer. I will be over land most of the way. I just got information that they may be in Dralinn. They did switch ships in the middle of the night. I'm guessing that they must have done some trading in the port. They may still be there. If not, someone at the port may be able to point me in the right direction. If I leave tonight, I can make it to the port by morning," Brenddel reasoned.

"If you must. Just be careful," Trunculin's tone changed. "You seem to have grown close to our king very quickly. Considering how much you hated the last few kings, it surprises me."

"The last two kings were fools. I'm not close to the boy, I just feel sorry for him. He seems more lost than the others. I know he will be easy to control, but I… worry for him." said Brenddel.

"Why, Brenddel, I didn't know you were getting sentimental," Trunculin smiled.

Brenddel responded, "There is no room for that in my life, or my duty. We only shared a meal together. I'm sure I will learn to hate this king, just like the others."

"No doubt," said the firstcouncilor as they both made their way down different paths.

CHAPTER 18
A NEW PRIZE

"Your throw, Gordon," said Sandrell.

"A six?" said Aline, "Well, you're beating us all on this battlefield, my king."

"Good that we are only playing for seashells, I would have no more coin for our journey, otherwise," said Loren.

Gordon smiled. "I've been playing card dice with my friends since I was little. It's the first time in days I felt like I could do anything right."

Sandrell handed him six more cards from the triangle stack. "Make your wager."

Gordon pushed ten small seashells into the middle of the table. He picked up his large hand of cards and smiled.

Aline threw the dice, cursing when she rolled a one. Sandrell gave her a triangle shaped card, "Make your wager."

Aline pushed all of her shells in the middle of the table and stood up to make her point.

Gordon tried not to smile. "Very scary. Standing won't make your cards any better."

Aline narrowed her eyes, "If I win you get a long lesson of weapons training,"

"No throw," said Loren.

"No throw," said Sandrell.

Gordon looked Aline right in the eyes, which seemed to be on fire, staring back at him. Apparently, Aline did not like to lose at anything. Aline laid out her cards face up. Gordon did the same.

She looked at Gordon. "I think I hate you," said Aline as she sat down.

Eight of Gordon's cards were kings and two were queens. "Well, I have to be good at something, since you're all good at everything else," said Gordon, as he dragged the large pile of seashells towards him and said, "I think I'll go buy the sea."

They all laughed, even Aline, and cleared the shells, the cards and the dice. Sandrell went to the next room and came back with dessert.

"Mother! You really do love me!" said Aline.

"Just don't tell anyone, child." To Gordon, she said, "Apple cakes are her favorite, especially with hot syrup. Just leave some for the rest of us, Aline," Sandrell said as she placed the dish on the table.

"I think this is the first time I've seen you really smile," said Gordon.

"I would fight Brenddel for apple cakes and syrup," said Aline diving into her dessert.

"And we were having such a nice time. Did you have to bring that monster into my house?" asked Sandrell.

"You know Brenddel?" asked Gordon.

"You might say that," said Loren. "We really don't have to talk about this if you don't want to, Sandrell."

"No, I don't mind. It was a long time ago," Sandrell raised her sleeves up to her shoulder. There was an old scar that wound half way around her arm, "This is a souvenir he left me, the last time we met."

"Now we both have Brenddel scars," said Loren. "You left him with a few scars as well. It took me days to heal him.

Whenever Brenddel was awake during those three days, he was cursing your name."

"Good. I've cursed his name a few times myself," said Sandrell.

"It's hard to believe that you fought side by side once," said Loren.

"I hear they did a lot more than that…" said Aline between bites of her dessert.

Sandrell laughed, "Oh yes, we did. That man was gorgeous way back in the abyss of time. Another lifetime ago. We made a good team until he chose Trunculin over me."

Gordon asked, "I don't understand. Why is Trunculin so bad?"

Loren answered, "Besides murder, putting people in prison for no reason, and forcing every councilor to do what he says, Trunculin has poisoned our kingdom. He's twisting it into a place secretly controlled by only him. I'm guessing they didn't show you the law room?"

"I don't think so. Why?" Gordon replied.

"It used to be a small room, open to the public. But now the 'room' is one secret snake of many inter-connected rooms. It's one very long book of laws, but it has really become a monster that will bite anyone Trunculin tells it to," said Loren.

Sandrell continued, "Trunculin has been in power a long time. He controls the choosing, so that just the right kind of boy will be chosen. Girls put their names in too, but a queen hasn't been chosen for a long time. We don't know why. A boy with good looks and not much in the way of brains is what Trunculin wants. No offense to your friend, Asa. Trunculin needs a boy that will be easy to control, that will do anything the firstcouncilor tells him to do."

Aline added, "And if a king suddenly got smart enough to figure out what was really going on, Brenddel would push him off an airship, or he would die of some mysterious illness."

Gordon said, "But I don't understand. The king and the two councils are all supposed to make laws together. The law has to be signed by all three, right?"

Sandrell continued, "That is the way it's supposed to be, but the reason we wear the symbol of the kingdom upside down is because it hasn't worked that way in a very long time. Everything is upside down. We know Trunculin has subverted the original laws. That he controls both councils, and whichever king he has chosen. He makes it seem as though fate is making these decisions, but it's really him. No one man should have that much power and control. Other kingdoms have had cruel iron-willed kings, which is why the first thirteen walked away from the other kingdoms. It only works if the people have a say and are a part of how their kingdom works."

"But if that's true, how do we convince people what's really going on?" asked Gordon.

Sandrell said, "Some of us believe it's too late."

Aline replied, "That is why we have to get to Mantuan. He has been hunting for the law keeper. He was a councilor that fled the kingdom long ago. Mantuan believes this man has an original copy of the law book; one that shows how the kingdom is supposed to work. He may also have proof of the crimes Trunculin has committed."

"And who exactly is this Mantuan?" asked Gordon.

Loren answered, "Mantuan is the leader of our cause. He has paid the highest price because of it. Brenddel threw him off an airship."

"And he survived? How?" asked Gordon.

Aline smiled, "It's a great story. No one tells it like Mantuan."

Loren continued, "It's vital that we meet up with him soon. He is the only man that Trunculin truly fears. The firstcouncilor has nearly erased him from the histories. If he can't find the law keeper, Mantuan himself knows things that will expose Trunculin."

Sandrell changed subjects. "That's enough for tonight. You need your rest, I made up some beds in the other room. You sleep with me, Aline. I hope you don't snore anymore."

Gordon said, "But I have so many more questions…"

Sandrell said, "I'm sure you do, my young king, but there's much to do. Let's all get some rest."

The next morning came quickly and Gordon did feel better rested. His mind was overrun with questions, but they would have to wait, again. He swallowed his growing anger as best he could. They gathered the gear and weapons that Sandrell had provided. Sandrell agreed to walk them to the docks.

The ship was smaller than the one they had been on before. The pilot met them at the docks himself. "So just you three to Thure? Hmm, they're always raising their fees. It may be a bit more to land there than I thought last night."

"Don't cheat my friends just because I won't be onboard. A price was agreed on. You will honor it," said Sandrell to the pilot.

The pilot nodded his head. "Sandrell is not a woman that I want a fight with. Agreed."

Aline and Sandrell said quiet goodbyes as men from the ship loaded their gear. They were saying something to each other and their foreheads were touching. Gordon couldn't hear what they said, but he wondered what the real story was behind how they acted around each other.

When Sandrell came to say her goodbyes to Gordon and Loren, Gordon asked, "So why aren't you coming with us Sandrell?

Sandrell said, "I have a different mission. Our paths may cross again, young King Gordon. Be careful Loren. Protect them well, Aline."

Gear loaded, the ship left the dock. Sandrell did not wait for them, and started back home. As they were about to go below deck, Loren's eyes got very wide. He stopped.

"Loren, what is it?" asked Gordon.

Aline froze as well. Gordon looked back to shore. He saw Sandrell was now running back towards the direction of her house.

Then Gordon heard the noise. It was very faint. He remembered a similar sound at the choosing. The airship was just coming into view over the buildings, its rotators humming with the unique sound. It was headed in their direction.

"Get below deck!" Loren screamed, but it was too late. Brenddel was at the front of his airship and had already spotted them. He was still far away, but coming fast.

"Damn..." was all that Loren had time to say. They were out of the harbor now, far away from the docks, but Loren knew that the airship was moving much faster than they were, they would have no chance. The airship was headed straight for them. It was floating downward as well, only a few feet from some of the higher rooftops.

From the watership, they saw a figure jump towards the deck of the airship. The figure jumped from a rooftop, seemed to come near the airship, then landed on another rooftop nearby. They watched as one of the four ropes supporting the corners of the deck broke. Sandrell must have cut it with one fluid slice of her blade, thought Gordon. Something fell from the deck of the airship as the rope broke away. It looked like a person. Gordon wondered if anyone on the airship even saw her at all, she moved so fast.

Of the four ropes connected to the corners of the deck, one was now gone, and the back part of the deck drooped dangerously. Brenddel let out a loud yell as two more men fell off the deck, tumbling over the bay. The three other support ropes were still attached, and the other men held onto the rails as the deck hung at a dangerous angle.

The airship was over the harbor now, still coming toward them. Sandrell stood on the roof for another moment, then disappeared into the landscape of houses.

Loren was frantically looking around the deck, trying to figure out what to do. Gordon remembered the fire in the forest, and knew that they could never outrun the airship on the open sea. The airship would float over them and set them on fire. They would burn or be drowned. He could see no hope of escape.

Aline had drawn her short and long knives and was close to the edge of the deck, waiting to attack. Gordon thought this must be instinct, as he couldn't imagine what even Aline could do against an airship. She stood there all the same.

They were out of the harbor and into deep waters now. Gordon could see men standing next to the fire guns on the airship, ready for when they were in position, despite the corner of the deck hanging at the difficult angle.

The airship was very close to them now, and Gordon felt the boat shake. The boat rocked back and forth, the great sails swaying with a motion that seemed to be intensifying. The waves were fairly calm, and there wasn't that much wind. Gordon couldn't figure out why they were rocking so hard.

The pilot shouted, "Hold onto something! Fins up ahead!"

Gordon and Loren went to the side and held onto the rail. Aline just stood there at the back rail, staring up at the airship with her knives ready. She seemed firmly attached to the swaying deck. Gordon looked ahead of the ship, and just off to their left he saw giant fins sticking out of the water. There were two fins, and they were easily taller than Gordon. He had heard of these Shadow fin creatures, sometimes called Jhalgon fish, but he never thought he'd ever see one.

The pilot was trying to control his watership as the airship was almost over them. Gordon felt a strange vibration and looked to the fins again. He saw the beast's wings coming up out of the water. It was enormous. It breached the water just as the airship was almost to them. Its eyes were black and small, compared to its size. It opened its mouth and showed its three rows of giant teeth.

The Jhalgon was longer than their watership as it flew over them, and Gordon saw the belly of the fish. It was unbelievable big. This giant flying beast flapped its wings over their boat, which was still rocking violently as the beast came over the deck. The water from the creature rained down on the deck.

The beast went straight for the airship.

They could hear the men on the airship scream and some of them let go of the rails and fell from the ship where the deck was drooping. Brenddel screamed too, but in rage, and held onto the airship's railing as the massive beast bit into the side of the airship. It ripped right through the ropes holding the floating section that lifted the deck.

More men fell, but not Brenddel, who was hanging onto the side by one hand. The beast was still chewing at the airship, which was starting to fall, losing the gas that kept it in the air. As it sank from the sky, the beast kept biting.

Brenddel had his longknife out, and was slashing and stabbing at the underside of the beast. The beast didn't seem to notice, and chewed at the ropes. It was as though it wanted nothing to be left of the airship.

As the airship went down not far from them, Gordon saw the other large fin break the surface of the water and swim towards the airship. The wake from the beast kept the watership rocking violently. He saw its large wings just under the water, as though it was gliding like a bird in the air. The watership was still moving forward, getting farther away from the crashed airship. The other beast had reached the airship. It was sinking fast, both Jhalgon fish chewing at the ropes as it slowly sank.

Brenddel broke the surface of the water. He climbed onto the back of one of the monsters. Some ropes had gotten tangled around the beasts head, and Brenddel used these to navigate up the beast's back. He sunk his longknife into the back of the Jhalgon, near the fin. The creature finally took noticed. The beast thrashed and tried to throw Brenddel off, but it was caught in the ropes.

The beast and Brenddel went down, rolling with the ropes, still cutting at the creature. Then the airship was just gone. The creatures could no longer be seen under the waves. There were only bubbles and waves where the airship had gone down.

They were far out of the bay when Aline put her knives away. She said, "I guess the gods of the sea are on our side."

*

Sochatt and his little brother Norum were playing in the water. They were taking turns diving just off shore. Their mother told them to stay where they could both touch bottom. They dove after a smooth rock the older brother had found. The younger brother had just come up with it, triumphantly, when he saw the fin. The older boy saw it too, and they both raced out of the water to the rocky beach.

The boys watched as the fin came toward them, then flopped over in the water. There was a rough cut along the fin's edge with some meat still attached. Brenddel climbed up on the shore, breathing heavily. He coughed and sputtered on his hands and knees as the two boys looked on. They both looked back to the deep waters of the bay, then back to the man on the shore.

Brenddel stood up on shaky legs, grabbed the fin, and made his way to the docks. He didn't seem to noticed the boys as they stood there, staring at him. No one bothered him as he walked, staring at the huge fin he was grasping. He dripped all the way to the shops near the docks. He went to the messenger's office, setting his new prized fin on the floor at the counter, and asked, "How much is your fastest messenger dog?"

*

In the palace, Rolem put the bowl of water on the floor for the dog. He unscrewed the lid to the tube attached around the dog's neck. He read it with alarm, and handed it to Trunculin solemnly. As the dog lapped at the water, Trunculin read the note.

His face grew darker as he read. He crumpled the note and regained his composure. "Have another airship equipped immediately. Make sure this time it's armed with the new large arrows guns. I don't know what fate is trying to tell me, but I will not let this boy go, nor his uncle. They have betrayed me, and I will send every airship I have after them, if I must."

"Firstcouncilor, what if they reach a kingdom that will not allow us in to search for them? What if they shield him from us?" asked Rolem.

"We have uneasy alliance with most of the kingdoms. No one would dare give safe passage, let alone protect them. They're either going to Thure, the old kingdom or Artoth, the kingdom of the Gods. Let's hope it is Artoth. If they went to Thure it would be a tangled mess to get them out. The old kingdom loves their old, complicated ways. Also, they haven't been very happy with us since we started building airships," Trunculin said as he carefully wrote the response to Brenddel.

The dog had finished drinking when Rolem put the note in the canister tightly. "I'll send the dog off now. Then I'll attend to the airship."

"Good, do it quickly. We have lost too much time already."

CHAPTER 19
THURE

As their ship approached the great port of Thure, Gordon said, "So this is where we'll find Mantuan?"

Loren replied, "Maybe, but maybe not. But this is the place where he should send word on how to contact him. Thure also offers unique protection. Most of the time you can do pretty much anything you want and no one will care. They also are the largest water ship builder, so they have an uneasy relationship with our kingdom. The airships are not very popular with the king.

"It's a contradictory, lazy, idle kingdom. So complicated that most people are just going about their daily lives, not making trouble, until someone tells them they broke the law. They carefully stay out of wars, choosing trade with other kingdoms instead. They get a fair amount of visitors from other places to see all of the old buildings and artwork. So we will blend in with all the other travelers until we hear word."

"Who are those men?" Gordon asked.

"Those three men approaching the ship? They are the men that will collect the tax for landing. That job could easily be done by one person, everything is inefficient and redundant here," said Loren.

"Three men for every job," Aline agreed.

They had docked, and the crew was unloading the ship. The three men were waiting patiently near where the ship landed. The one who looked like he was in charge wore glasses and had a notebook. He was scribbling feverishly. They paid their fees and the men left.

The ship was unloaded, and they went to some large square buildings painted the pale green and aqua blue colors of Thure. They called it the traveler's gateway. There was an enormous series of waiting rooms with chairs and benches filled with people all writing on stacks of paper.

Loren said, "We're each going to fill out papers. We will wait our turn, and then hand them in over there. Then the papers will be put in a box somewhere deep in a building and forgotten. They will never know our true identities, and we will waste half a day. And if we don't do the forms exactly right, we will have to do them over and over again until they are perfect."

Aline look bored already as she got her stack of forms and started to write, "Why do we have to do this? It just seems like a big waste of time for everyone."

Loren agreed, "It is, and everybody knows it, but it's been that way for so long, that no one knows how to do it any other way. Welcome to the land of paper," said Loren as they all stood at a bench and filled out their forms.

It did take half a day, just as Loren had predicted, and they were finally allowed into the kingdom after the third round of filling out the same forms. As they were walking away from the building through the gates of the kingdom, Gordon noticed men at the back of the building with large boxes of paper.

There were a whole line of them all walking into a different building. When asked, Loren simply said, "As far as I know, they never throw anything away. Those forms are probably from yesterday, or last week, and will be put in some large underground vault somewhere. No one will ever see them again."

Gordon stared at the men and the long building they just come out of, shaking his head. He really didn't see the point.

As they walked through the enormous gate into the kingdom, Gordon looked around. There were people selling things everywhere. It looked like one giant market lining both sides of the streets, but then he looked up to the middle of the market and saw a tall statue of a man with his arms behind his back, lifting his head high to the sky. This was something he had not read about.

"They say its three hundred feet high," said Loren, looking up at the statue.

"Who was he?" asked Gordon.

Aline and Loren looked at each other and smiled. Loren said, "If you ask that woman over there, she will tell you it is Russel the Great, who lived three hundred fifty years ago."

Aline said, "If you ask that man over there, he will probably tell you that it's Jannfarr the Just, who lived a thousand years ago. The truth is… nobody knows."

Gordon asked, "How is that possible?"

Aline said, "The kingdom has so much history, that they seem to have forgotten a lot of it. It is said that their history books are buried deep under the kingdom, but no one can find them. There's so much paper and old books stored in the vaults, that no one can find anything. So they'll hear an old family story, and they will assume it's that person. They seem to have kept such good records about everything, that no one can actually find the truth. My mother describes it like throwing a handful of salt in the ocean and then trying to go find it again."

"Sandrell said we'd find a contact in the new kingdom. We're definitely going to need a map," said Loren. They looked along the vendors and Gordon saw that you could buy almost anything you wanted; there were dishes, weapons, books, clothes, fruits and everything in between. He couldn't stop smiling. He figured it would take a lifetime to make your way through these markets and see everything there was to see.

The three went to a vendor that sold books and purchased a map of both the new kingdom and the old kingdom, they found a quiet corner and unrolled the very large map. Gordon was overwhelmed at the size of Thure.

Loren explained that the oldest part of the kingdom was connected to the new part, and it would be obvious when they would get there, because the buildings were so much different. Both kingdoms were actually connected, with no breaks between. Just one giant kingdom of buildings. Loren and Aline explained that no one could remember when there were forests here, just kingdom. "It just kind of kept growing," is how Loren described it.

"How do you know all of these things, Uncle Loren?" asked Gordon.

"What do you mean?"

"Well," reasoned Gordon, "I've lived with you for thirteen years. You're a healer who only leaves the house to see the sick. You read books. You're kind of…"

"Boring?" Loren laughed, "Gordon, every boy thinks the world began when they were born. Before being your uncle, I traveled all over. I was in my late twenties when you were born. I had a life before you," Loren smiled.

Gordon had never really thought about it that way. Instead of pursuing it further, he asked, "So, how dangerous is the new kingdom?" asked Gordon.

"There won't be any men in alleyways like at Dralinn, if that's what you mean," said Aline.

Loren said, "Actually, both the old and new kingdom are mostly free of crime. They seem to have too much of everything. Everyone is just a little too lazy to cause any trouble."

"It's the most boring kingdom," said Aline.

"Loren, I think I'd better get something to eat soon," said Gordon, slowing down.

"Feeling okay?" asked Aline and Loren almost at the same time.

"Now I have two people to worry about me when I get hungry. I'm fine, I just know I need something to eat," replied Gordon.

They found a small place to eat that sold a dish called kenfren. It was a flaky white fish served in thin, flat bread. Gordon was shown how to hold the bread like a cone in his hand. He chose one of the spicier sauces by accident and sweated the entire meal. He still enjoyed the fried fish mixed with the crunchy cabbage despite his tongue being on fire.

Loren said, "That reminds me, Gordon. I made extra sour cakes and some sweets for you. I want you to carry them with you always, in case you need them. I won't be able to test your blood anytime soon, so you will have to pay close attention to how you are feeling. Okay?"

Gordon took the satchel with the metal box of medicine cakes, "But, we'll be together…"

Loren said, "I know, but it's time you took better care of yourself, without me asking if you feel alright every hour. You are a king now, after all."

Aline added, "He's your uncle, not a king-sitter," she smiled.

Gordon said, "Wait. Was that a jest?"

"Maybe. I make jests sometimes," answered Aline, losing her smile, "don't get used to it." Aline got up from their table.

Gordon was feeling better, so they consulted the map and realized it would be a long day's journey on foot to the old kingdom. They decided to hire a dog team to get them to where they would meet their contact.

The driver took Loren's coin and they all got in their dog coach. Gordon noticed the paper money and coins, all from different kingdoms. Gordon reminded himself later to ask his uncle more questions about his secret life.

They all got in the small seat directly behind the driver. There were two rows of seats. Aline sat alone in the back. There was a looped leather strap in front of each of them and Gordon noticed Aline grabbing hers as soon as they got in. Loren explained that, unlike their own kingdom, the streets were narrow in Thure. It was much harder to accommodate carriages and large teams of horses.

Gordon began to ask what the straps were for, when the driver said "Osh!" and the cart took off like it was fired from an arrow gun.

Gordon grabbed the strap.

"Sorry, I meant to warn you…" Loren said as the cart swept to the other side of the street to avoid another dog cart coming their way. Gordon nearly fell out as the cart went over a bump in the road. He realized that he'd better hold on tight since there were no doors like in a carriage, just open sides.

They rushed through the narrow streets, the man weaving around carts and people. They barely missed a guard on horseback who emerged from across the street. "Slow down!" he warned loudly. The driver used one hand to steer and one hand to wave to the guard as they flew by him.

Aline was standing now, holding the strap in her hands. She was laughing as the wind whipped her hair around her face. Gordon couldn't look backwards long, feeling a need to keep his eyes forward. Loren was casually holding onto his strap, apparently content with the speed they were going.

In the older part of the kingdom, the streets were very narrow. Buildings were stacked high, and had three, five, eight story houses. It was much easier to hire a team of dogs to navigate the narrow streets, even when they got into the new kingdom. *If we even made it there,* thought Gordon, as the cart veered wildly to the left side of the street, missing some very surprised chickens.

Gordon clutched his strap and decided to focus on the dogs. Each one of the six dogs was a different color. They were large and fluffy and seemed to know the streets very well. Gordon focused on watching their tails wag happily.

Loren shouted over the wind in their faces. "Even with this dog team, we won't make it until nightfall."

Aline shouted from the back, still standing. "Who cares, this is fun. I love dog carts." There were a few more close calls, but just after the sun was setting, they finally reached their destination. Gordon was relieved when they stopped. His knuckles had gone white from holding the strap so tight. He opened and closed his hands a few times to get rid of the soreness.

"I'm glad that wasn't during the night. Do they go that fast after the sun sets?' asked Gordon.

"They go even faster when there are fewer people on the streets. Loren asked the driver to go slower for your first time." She smiled at the face Gordon made.

Their contact seemed to live in a very large home with lots of land around it, almost like a small palace itself. Beautiful hand-trimmed bushes and gardens surrounded it, looking almost too perfect. "Who is our contact anyway?" asked Gordon.

They paid the dog driver and made their way to the house. "Someone I've not met," answered Loren. "Aline and Sandrell know him. He's a wealthy merchant that does trading with many other kingdoms."

They had to ring a bell on the large gate. A small man came out. Loren gave the man an envelope with a note that Sandrell had written. The man took the note and returned a few moments later to unlock the gate. He led them into the house that was even larger than Gordon had expected. They walked onto highly polished floors. In fact, everything looked shiny and new. He saw his own face reflected everywhere in polished stone walls. As they were led around a column into a large room, Gordon heard, "Oh, Aline, my favorite little warrior! Come here and give me a great big hug!"

The man was shorter than most, with a large robe and a great sash around his enormous belly. He appeared to be wearing soft slippers and his face was large, round and happy. He wore a wig. Gordon knew this because it looked slightly bluish and sticking out of it was a tiny kitten sitting in a small basket. The kitten was meowing.

"Denny!" Aline ran to the man and hugged him as best she could. Her arms would not make it around the man, and he hugged her with one arm as he steadied the basket on his head with the other. The kitten continued meowing.

"Oh, it has been too long. How is that wild woman out there in Murderer's Bay? I wrote her and told her that she should come here, but she will not have it. And these must be your friends. Welcome! I am Denogg of the family Xoss, but my friends all call me Denny. And I can tell, right now, that we are going to be very good friends."

Gordon couldn't stop staring at the small kitten on top of the man's head. Before anyone could say anything, Denogg said, "Oh, I know, this! It's the newest fashion. Someone on the king's council started doing it at a party, and now we all have to do it; put some small animal in a little basket on our heads. I know someone that put a snake on their head! It's absurd, I know, but you have to keep up with the latest fashion. Still, though, it's so exhausting! I mean, honestly, how silly is it to put a poor little animal on your head?"

Denogg took off the wig and basket carefully. He handed the kitten to Gordon. Gordon didn't know what to say or do, so he accepted the kitten and started to pet it. It began to purr.

Underneath the wig, he had a full head of brown hair, slicked back, "One must keep up appearances, of course, or you are considered a bore. So anyway, you must be King Gordon and the famous Loren that I've just read so much about." He pointed to Sandrell's note.

Denogg came over and gave them each a big hug before they could protest. "You must tell me everything. You must be starving. I have already planned a large feast. Only the most important people will be here tonight."

Loren said, "We are trying to keep our arrival quiet. We don't know how Gordon's presence will be accepted by the king's council. These people that are coming, are they safe?"

"Oh yes, yes. The people that are coming tonight are all from old families. They couldn't care less about politics outside of this kingdom. These people are obsessed with three things: themselves, coin and themselves," Denogg assured them.

"But you are with our cause. Surely some of them might have leanings against us," asked Loren nervously.

"Oh, my dear man," said Denogg, looking at Aline. "They really don't know how it works in Thure, do they? No, in my case, I don't even like politics. I just want to stir things up a little. I see your kingdom, looking more and more like this kingdom. We all used to look at your kingdom as the thing we wanted to be, you gave us hope. Now you're just looking like a newer version of this kingdom. How boring."

"Denny can put up with anything, except boredom," remarked Aline.

"We really appreciate any help you can give us," said Gordon, still holding the kitten, who appeared to be falling asleep.

"Listen to that. I think you are the most well behaved king I've ever met. And I have met dozens of kings. Most of them dumber than a satchel full of rocks. I can see we're going to be best friends. Now let's sit and gossip about our old friend Mantuan," said Denogg, sitting down on a couch.

Loren asked, "He has sent word then?"

"Yes, he did. He sent some close allies. He would have come himself, but there was some other mysterious thing he had to do. Very secretive, that man. Have you already told him not to look at the patch? Anyway, he's convinced the law keeper is in Artoth, or near it. He had to check some things out in Aspora first."

"He's gone home?" asked Aline.

"Not for long I think," replied Denogg.

"What did they come here for, then?" asked Loren.

Denogg said, "Coin and supplies, of course. They got some of both from me, and I've set up a delivery leaving tomorrow from the east side of the kingdom. I'm doing real business while helping Mantuan. I doubt anyone's watching, or even cares. But I keep it quiet, just in case."

"That's why I'm worried about tonight," Loren began. "I don't like the idea of strangers so close to Gordon. Anything could happen."

"My dear man, you're going to put yourself in an early grave worrying like that. I know Thure, better than anyone. Everyone attending tonight is safe!" Denogg leaned in close to them. "I have so much dirt on each one of them that no one would dare try anything. That's the first thing. The second thing is that young Gordon here is going to need to make some connections, friends, and allies. That is what tonight could mean," said Denogg.

"I'm still concerned," said Loren.

"Of course you are. That appears to be your favorite job. Besides, Gordon was robbed of his first day on the job. This will be his debut performance. I think you all should dress the part."

CHAPTER 20
DRESSED TO KILL

Aline was led back to a guest room with three people to dress her. Denogg excitedly led Gordon and Loren back to a separate room, where five people were waiting to help them. Denny made it clear that he wanted to be personally in charge of what Gordon wore, so the five helpers were there to bring whatever clothes Denogg asked for.

Denogg said, "Oh, this is going to be so much fun," as they brought clothes upon clothes for Gordon to try on. Gordon could tell Loren was worried at first, but it was hard to be anything but happy around Denny. He and his helpers all seemed to be very excited about the feast. They all laughed and jested. Gordon could tell that the people worked for Denogg, but they all seemed more like a big family. There were more than a few jests about Denny's weight, with Denny making most of them himself.

Gordon had not seen so many different kinds of clothes, not even at the palace. He didn't know there were this many colors. Gordon wondered if this was what his daily life would have been, back in his kingdom. If things hadn't gone so terribly wrong, of course.

"Oh yes, this is the one. This has got to be it," said Denogg. He had the attendant go and get accessories. When he was done, Gordon was dressed in a purple and black outfit with long boots, a leather breastplate, all richly detailed. Denogg thought of giving him weapons as well, but decided it would be too much.

"I think a crown would be too much, too. Everyone will get the point that you should be taken seriously. You look like a proper king, my boy. No one knows there will even be a mystery guest tonight. I want you to make a grand entrance. Let me tell you all about it…" Denogg explained what he had in mind for tonight's feast. "I don't think the guests will forget tonight for a very long time. When the firstcouncilor of your kingdom hears about it, a vein on his head will probably explode."

Gordon couldn't help laughing, Denny's energy was so contagious. It felt good to laugh. It took just a little longer for them to get everything ready. Loren looks uncomfortable in his new clothes. Gordon had rarely seen Loren dressed up; he always preferred his simple healer's garments. Denogg had left to go attend to his arriving guests. Loren followed him. An attendant would come and get Gordon when it was time.

Gordon didn't know what he was supposed to do until then, so he just looked around the room. It was very large with pictures on the wall of times past. All of the furniture was elaborately decorated. There was a long table under the window, which looked out on the kingdom of Thure. It was dark, so he only saw the outline of rooftops. He imagined families shopping for food, married people strolling along the markets in the softly lit streets.

Gordon thought about how few people he really knew. He only had a few friends back in his kingdom, and that was before he was king. He wondered what they all thought of him, if they worried about him, or if they thought he was a coward that ran away.

As he looked out on the great, old kingdom, he felt relieved to be out of immediate danger. He had never wanted to be king. Neither had Asa, not really. It was just a silly dream that could never happen to them. And now people were actually trying to kill him. He still had so many questions. There just seemed to be no time to have them answered.

An attendant arrived, telling him that it was time to go. He straightened his belt, looked at himself and said, "Thank you. Lead the way."

In the enormous dining room, everyone was seated at a very large, round table. The room was one of the largest dining rooms in any kingdom. The table sat under paintings of great battles and historic figures. Gordon hadn't arrived yet, since Denogg was waiting for just the right moment to have him enter, but he could just make out how massive the room was from the hallway where he waited.

Aline and Loren were already seated. Aline was dressed in a beautiful green gown. Gordon realized his mouth was open and looked away. The table was massive and sat over one hundred guests. That's as high as Gordon could count from where he stood. People were moving around the table, talking to each other. Gordon couldn't make out any conversations, but the atmosphere that floated from the room had a special excitement about it.

Gordon saw Loren, still looking worried as he sat quietly with Aline. Denogg was making his rounds at the table, laughing and talking as he went. An attendant came up to Denogg and hurriedly whispered in his ear. Denogg looked excited as he waved to Aline and Loren.

There was a large group of musicians playing. Denogg hurried over to them and whispered something. The music instantly changed to the familiar march of the kingdom of Thure. As the musicians began, everyone joined in.

From The Mists of Time, the Great kingdom Rose
With The Best Men to Fight, To Vanquish Our Foes
The Most Beautiful Queens, We Never Will Fall
With The Bravest Of Kings, Who Always Stand Tall
With Legends Abound, We Will Always Endure
And Never Will Fall, Our Great kingdom Thure

Towards the end of the song a new group of people were coming into the room, marching three across to the tune. First came soldiers, and then the procession behind it. When the song finished, Denogg rushed over to them. "My king," he said, bowing at the waist.

Everyone stood and gave a dignified bow as the king and queen of Thure entered the chamber along with a large group of people walking in behind them. No one stood up faster than Loren, who could not hide his shock.

The king of Thure said, "Denogg. You know I wouldn't miss one of your feasts for all the wine in my kingdom. And there is a lot of wine in my kingdom." He embraced Denogg.

"My king, my queen, you honor me, and all of us here. Three cheers for the king!" At this, everyone cheered.

"And in honor of your visit, my king, I have a surprise for you," Denogg raised his hand to the band again. The tune of Gordon's kingdom started to play. No one sang the words, just looked confused as to why they were playing the song for the kingdom of the thirteen.

Denogg made a grand gesture and said, "My king, my queen, may I present Gordon, the lawfully chosen ruler of the kingdom of the thirteen."

Gordon walked out of the hallway and down the steps. He was nervous, but he didn't want anyone to know it. The room was nearly silent. Denogg had assured him this would be the best way to stay safe; get everyone's attention in the crowd, and no one dared hurt you. Gordon hoped no one could hear how fast his heart was beating.

Gordon walked straight to the king, who could barely hide his own shock. The queen, who covered her mouth, was not hiding her shock at all. He got within a few feet of the king and got down on one knee, "King Russel the Third, king of all Thure, I offer my fellowship and my friendship if you will have it."

The king said seriously, "Gordon, from the kingdom of the thirteen, you may rise…"

Everyone was quiet. This was an ancient ritual between kings of Thure and other kingdoms. It was a custom whose words had to be spoken exactly, or there would be offense taken. King Russel said, "… As I offer my own hand in friendship and fellowship."

Everyone erupted into cheers. As Gordon got off his knee and pressed his hand into the kings, King Russel smiled. "You know, my fellow king, if you would have spoken one word incorrectly, I would have the legal right to kill you right here. You must be a brave and clever young man."

"Thank you, my… fellow king. I've had to learn very quickly," said Gordon honestly.

The king laughed and slapped Gordon on the back. Gordon tried not to show that the blow almost sent him off his feet. Denogg was still nearby and showed them to their seats. The kings would sit next to each other.

The table was a perfect circle except for a small break, where serving men and women entered and served the guests from the inside of the circle. The guests were all seated around the outside of the circle, chatting happily, but most eyes were on the two kings. The line of people serving food seemed endless, with treats from all over their world.

Denogg had seated himself next to Gordon, and Loren and Aline in the next chairs. Quietly, Loren whispered to Denny, "Why didn't you tell me?"

"Because you would've tried to talk me out of it," replied Denny.

"Yes. It is too dangerous to have him this exposed. Things are moving too fast."

"I told you that I know my kingdom better than you do. There are several ways this could have gone. We could have hidden him away and no one would know he was here. But, if the king found out that he was being hidden, we would all be in danger. What I've done instead is introduced him to a new ally. He'll be much harder to hurt out in the open, even for your wicked firstcouncilor. Look, there, my king's guards are all around him right now, protecting him as a guest of our kingdom. I'm sorry I couldn't tell you. I know he's your nephew, but there's much more at stake, and you know it. Boldness was warranted."

"I trust you because Sandrell and Aline do. But don't keep anything from me again," warned Loren. Denogg nodded and smiled back at Loren.

The two kings were eating together, and Gordon was truly entertained by the king's stories. In Thure, the same family ruled for hundreds of years. The king told him how it was, to grow up in such a famous family, having all those kings before him with the same name. Russel, himself, had already ruled for nearly twenty years, longer than Gordon had been alive.

Gordon instantly liked him.

"You know Gordon, you remind me of myself. I didn't become king until I was twenty three, one year before I met this lovely lady. She is from yet another great family, but I didn't care about that. They left her in my family's care when she was young. They thought we would be like brother and sister. But from the moment I saw her, I was lost," he looked at the queen, who smiled lovingly, "...and found. But I was in the king's house, getting trained by all of my teachers in case one day I would be king. I wasn't supposed to be, you know. Oh no, my older brother was. But he was one for adventure, and he adventured once too many. We all think we're invincible at that age. He was three years older than me. His death was a hard lesson about responsibility. And you are already a king at thirteen."

"Maybe I am. I'm still not exactly sure where things stand with my kingship," said Gordon.

"Yes. It is quite the sticky situation. You know some of your kingdom's first thirteen were originally from Thure. Those men had a very interesting idea: Choose the king from amongst the people to lead them. If they hadn't left Thure and those other lands, that idea would never have started. I believe in the traditional ways, of course. I can trace my family history back fifty generations. That is, If they could find the proof in the vaults."

"Your kingdom seems fond of putting paper in boxes," said Gordon.

The king laughed, nearly spilling his wine. "Many great songs have been written about my kingdom. Many epic poems to describe the great deeds of Thure. And you have put them all to shame by one line that sums up my kingdom. To the kingdom of paper!" the king raised his toast and Gordon took his own glass. They both drank along with the rest of the table.

Denogg leaned over and said to Gordon, "You're doing very well, my boy. Once my king likes somebody, they are a friend for life."

The king was still laughing and telling stories. When he tipped his cup over, there was a servant to instantly refill it for him. In fact, it was hard not to notice how many people were walking by, serving them. The line of people seemed endless. Gordon though, *how much food are we supposed to eat?*

There was food everywhere: Piles of food, and more drink than they could ever finish, much more than in his own king's meal. A servant came by and filled Gordon's cup. He tried to stop him, since he was no longer thirsty, but the servant had already filled it and walked away.

The queen seemed to notice Loren and Aline for the first time. "And who are these fine people, good King Gordon? You are very pretty, young lady. What's your name?"

Aline responded with a bow of her head. "Thank you, my queen. I'm Aline. I think it is Denogg's choice of clothes more than anything."

"Oh, and modest as well. You are a very lucky king to find such a treasure. How did you meet?"

Gordon nearly dropped his drink, "Oh no! I mean… Aline's not… we're not…"

The queen smiled. "Oh, you don't think she's pretty?"

"No! I mean yes, she's… beautiful, but we don't…" managed Gordon.

"Don't what my king?" Aline asked with a smile.

The people around them all laughed, especially the king. "My king Gordon, you are a deep shade of red. We'll stop asking questions… for now. But you could not do better. A toast to the beautiful Aline!"

Aline nodded courteously, but Gordon couldn't look her in the eyes. As Gordon raised his own glass, the king said, "Wait a moment, good king Gordon. Why is your drink a different color than mine?" He took Gordon's cup and took his own and held them up, side by side for comparison.

"Mine is not wine, my king, its berry juice," Gordon explained.

"Berry juice?" The king broke out in laughter again, and this time he spoke to the entire room, "Everyone listen. Our great kingdoms have been friendly for over one hundred years, but always from an uneasy distance. We were born of the same waters, the same dirt. We don't always agree. We have been building great waterships for thousands of years in Thure. Of course, until your airships came along, what we built were just called *ships…*" Everyone laughed.

The king continued, "…We rule our people, and we don't choose kings from among them. But I declare, here today, as long as Gordon is king that our great kingdoms will always be as one. And I also declare that a king visiting my lands can drink whatever he damn well pleases!" he finished, as he put his own cup of wine down in front of Gordon. Gordon looked around to Loren and Denogg for what he should do. Denogg winked at him, and Gordon took the cup of wine and stood himself.

"My fellow king… to… friendship!" Gordon said as he took a drink of the wine and winced at the taste. He swallowed it anyway. The king and queen both laughed at the face Gordon made, as did the rest of the table. The king took Gordon's cup and downed it in one gulp. "Berry juice," the king made a similar face to Gordon's, "Awful! How can you drink this?" The crowd erupted with laughter again.

"Bring me more wine to wash that terrible taste out of my mouth," said the king.

Everyone was laughing as a servant brought more wine for the king. The king smiled broadly and began another toast with his new glass of wine when he started to cough. He laughed at himself for not being able to get out the next toast. He coughed again and stopped smiling. The sound he made after was more like a low growl, when he began to grab at his throat. People stopped laughing as they slowly realized the king was not joking.

Gordon stood up from his chair, not knowing what to do. Everyone was quickly on their feet, with people trying to rush to the king, but the guards were keeping them back. Another guard protected the queen as the king kept clawing at his throat, a thick black liquid now dribbling out of his mouth. His neck was bloody where he'd scratched the skin. His eyes were wild, looking around, blinking, as though he couldn't see. The king flailed as the guards surrounded him.

Loren shouted, "Let me through, I'm a healer!" as he was restrained by the guards. The queen was screaming at the guard to let him through. The king looked at the queen with wild eyes, then just stopped moving. The queen held her husband. She made a sound of grief that Gordon hoped he never heard again.

She let the king's head rock gently back on the chair, shutting his dead eyes. She slowly rose from her husband with tears streaming down her face. She looked at Gordon with naked hatred, "You poisoned him. Guards, kill the boy."

The guards grabbed for Gordon, Aline had no weapons, but pushed the guards back anyway. She picked up a knife from the table to use on a guard when Gordon shouted, "Stop! I didn't poison him. I swear I didn't!"

The guards had drawn their shortknives and were threatening Gordon. Loren said, "My queen, Gordon didn't poison him. He has no reason. It must have been one of the servants."

The queen was cradling her husband again. "Lies!"

Denogg continued the appeal. "My queen. I carefully choose my servants, but Loren must be right. It had to be one of the serving staff. I promise you we will find who did this, but it was not Gordon."

Aline had Gordon to her back, the guards surrounded them with knives drawn.

The queen wiped the tears from her face. "You swear that on your life...?"

"Of course, my queen. I swear that on my life," said Denny.

The queen leaned closer. She stared into Denny's eyes and said, "Do you swear that on your life and your fortune?"

Denogg hesitated for only a moment, then calmly said, "Yes, I swear that on my life and my fortune. Gordon did not do this."

She halted the guards. "If what you say is true, then I will allow you to find whoever you think did this. Take any men you need. But the boy stays at the palace, ready for trial, in case you cannot produce anyone else. Your fortune will be his guarantee," said the queen.

"According to the king's law, my queen?" asked Loren.

"Yes, by the kings law!" said the queen, annoyed.

"My queen, that allows for a volunteer replacement under the law. I volunteer to stand trial in his stead," stated Loren firmly.

"What? No, Loren. You can't!" said Gordon.

"Oh no. The boy comes with me," said the queen. The guards still circled Gordon and Aline.

"But, my queen, by the kings law a substitute is allowed. There are no exceptions," said Denny.

The queen's eyes flared and she took a step towards him. Then she slowly looked around at all of the people. They were all standing, staring. The room was very quiet, "Fine. This man comes with us, but you and the boy are confined to this house."

"What if the murderer has already fled? How are we to find whoever did this if we can't leave the house?" asked Denny.

"Don't test me further, Denny. My husband is dead. The…" the queen paused, tears threatening her ability to speak, "…the king is dead and someone will pay for it, or it will cost you more than your fortune." She looked at Gordon again. "Someone dies for this."

Loren stepped forward to be taken. The guards abandoned Aline and Gordon to do their duty. Gordon said, "Uncle Loren, you can't do this. It's not fair. I didn't do anything wrong; you didn't do anything wrong."

"Don't worry, Gordon, you didn't do this. Denogg will find out who did and why. I have to go now," said Loren, "no arguments."

Guards came up and took Loren roughly. His hands were quickly shackled. Other guards were already putting the king's body on a rug. They draped his cloak over him. The queen started crying again softly, but turned to look one more time at Gordon. She didn't say anything. She just stared, her eyes blazing. The queen gave quiet instructions to her firstman and then they all walked out with the queen, with the king's body and most of the guests. The queen's firstman and some soldiers were the only ones left behind.

Gordon just stared as they took Loren away; another horrible situation he couldn't control. As they led Loren out to be a prisoner for him, Aline and Denogg stood with him, trying to figure out what to do next.

CHAPTER 21
BAD DAY FOR ALL

Brenddel hadn't been this angry in a very long time. The smaller airship had found him in Dralinn to bring him back to the palace. They made sure to stay over land, far away from the coastline as they headed back. Brenddel was now certain the flying creatures were attracted to the rotators that propelled the airships. There had only been a few actual attacks before, nothing like this. They were getting bolder. For a few years there had been sighting of fins, and a few breaches of the water as they attempted to attack the airships. They had never attacked this close to land, and never two at once. The Jhalgon shadow fins were supposed to be just a legend. *The legends just killed seven of my men,* thought Brenddel.

Once back at the palace, Brenddel didn't bother to go see the firstcouncilor. He was too busy making preparations to increase the arms on the other airships. Larger arrow guns meant they could shoot those winged creatures out of the sky, but it also meant more weight. The sun gas that filled their air ships could only lift so much, Brenddel would have to figure out what would have to be removed to balance the new weight of the larger arrow guns.

Brenddel was not used to failing, but he tried not to dwell on the past as he prepared for the mission at hand. He would make sure that the ship would be ready for any threat.

*

The firstcouncilor was at the end of a very long day. The first few days of a new king's first trial were always taxing, but this day was especially grueling. He had heard from the head of every department. Brenddel's secondman in charge was worried that the new king was too frail for combat training. And very distracted, he commented. They had only used wooden longknives, but the boy had barely been able to take even the lightest blow.

The secondcouncilor's assistant was gravely concerned that the king could not learn even the basic concepts of the kingdom or how it worked. He told Trunculin that he was so frustrated three hours into the teaching, that he nearly asked the new king if he had ever read a book.

As the firstcouncilor made his way to see Brenddel, he was approached by his assistant Rolem. He handed Trunculin a message and told him that he might want to go see the king. When he arrived at the king's chamber, he could see the face of the guards looked a little strange, as though they didn't know what to do with this new king.

As he came around the corner of the king's chamber, he could hear King Asa softly crying. Asa was sitting in the chair with his head on the desk, barefoot again. Trunculin could not understand the new king's strange aversion to footwear.

Trunculin was annoyed. The last thing he needed today was a snot-nosed, crying boy king to deal with. He still had to go and make sure Brenddel was informed of the news he had just received. Instead, he had to deal with a weepy king. *Just perfect,* he thought, but Trunculin put on his famous smile and went to the king, putting his arm around the boy's shoulder. The king was startled; not realizing anyone else was in the room. "You scared me. Why doesn't anyone here knock?" asked Asa.

"I am sorry, my king. I simply wanted to say congratulations on getting through your first day. There is no day harder than the first day of the king's first year. That's why we call it a trial," Trunculin tried to sooth.

Asa said, "But I couldn't do anything right. I dropped the wooden shortknife a dozen times in training. The man training me kept making me do the same moves until my shoulder was bruised. I don't understand anything that the councilor was trying to teach me about the law. It just sounded like… like a different language."

"I know, my king, the first day, weeks, even months are very overwhelming. That is why you have me, why you have all of these people working for you to make sure that everything goes smoothly. And I'll tell you a little secret, we do most of the work. We make sure the king is trained in all of these matters just as a precaution. You really don't need to do very much," said Trunculin.

Asa looked more frustrated than ever. "Then why have a king?"

"My king, the people are very simple. They want us to take care of them, make sure they have everything they need; that they don't go hungry, that they have a healer if they need one. Most of all, they need the security of knowing that there is a king to lead them, one of their own leading them. You are the symbol of our kingdom," said Trunculin.

"I just want to go home," Asa said as he broke down in tears again.

Trunculin tried to hide his contempt for the boy by breaking into his famous smile again. He patted him on the shoulder. "Tomorrow will be a little easier," he said as he exited the chamber, quickly going to Brenddel.

Brenddel was busy giving orders and gathering equipment for the airship. He didn't seem to notice Trunculin approach. Brenddel popped a piece of chocolate in his mouth.

The firstcouncilor asked, "Why haven't you been to see me? Since you got back there is much to discuss. We found out the boy is in..."

"In Thure, yes, I know. I've been busy getting the airships armed against those creatures. We can't make our rotators any quieter, so we have to bring more weapons. But that means more weight, so we have to take less men and equipment. It takes time to do all that, so I didn't have time for a chat," Brenddel said, continuing to work.

Trunculin took a step towards Brenddel. "Don't forget who you truly work for, firstman. There is much you don't know. I've just received word that the king is dead."

"Gordon's dead?" asked Brenddel.

"No, Russel, the king of Thure. He was poisoned sitting right next to Gordon. They think Gordon did it," said Trunculin. "They nearly arrested him, but Loren volunteered to stand trial instead. So they're keeping Loren at the king's palace, while Gordon is being kept under house guard with some tradesman."

Brenddel stopped his work for a moment. "This does change things; I'm sure they won't just hand over Loren. Will they give us the boy?"

"I don't know," said Trunculin. "I'm getting information from a few sources, but it's all coming very fast. I don't want to contact Thure in any way until I know what our move is going to be. But I do have an idea that may work."

"Why did you have the king of Thure poisoned? Or was Gordon your target? I didn't know we had those kinds of agents in Thure," asked Brenddel, going back to work.

"What are you talking about? I didn't do it. It wasn't on my orders," said Trunculin impatiently.

"Why would anyone want to kill a king of Thure? They don't have as much coin as they once did, they mostly just have their reputation. The same families will always rule. What possible point could there be?" asked Brenddel aloud.

"Those are all excellent questions. I have answers to none of them. Our relationship with Thure is stable, but not very... friendly. But, one thing is sure, they will have a large funeral for their king. And I think it would be a proper gesture to have our new king be there in his honor. And once we are there, we can negotiate for the release of Gordon and Loren."

Brenddel said, "The custom in Thure is to have the funeral within three days. We would make it, if we left soon. Is king Asa ready for this?"

Trunculin softly chuckled, "No. He's barely able to put on his own pants. But he will have to step up to the occasion. We cannot let this crisis and opportunity in Thure pass us by. Also, you seem to have a connection with the boy. A few days on the airship, you may be able to.... I don't know, find his brains?"

Brenddel didn't much like Trunculin's instant contempt for the boy. *He is small and harmless,* he thought. Brenddel wondered why he felt differently about this king. He pushed the thought aside. "I'll do the best I can. We will leave in two hours," Brenddel turned back around to his duties without saying another word to the firstcouncilor.

The firstcouncilor hated insolence and was about to say something when he noticed a large new addition to Brenddel's wall, just next to Mantuan's axe, "What is that?"

Brenddel said of his prize, "It's a Jhalgon shadow fin."

Trunculin said, "You... you cut that off yourself?"

Brenddel did not look at the firstcouncilor, "Yes."

Trunculin thought better of making Brenddel angry. He rubbed his head as he made his way to tell the king that they were leaving. He stopped by the Mystic's room first, for some special help before he talked to the idiotic boy king again.

CHAPTER 22
ESCAPE

Denogg went over the list of servants again as the midday sun warmed the house. The servants told him how beautiful the red sunrise had been, but it did not lighten his mood. Several servants had fled, probably fearing they would be blamed for poisoning the king. That made it harder to find the real murderers. He hired his servants carefully, always checked out by his most trusted assistants. Something had gone very wrong.

"We have to get Loren out of there," said Gordon.

"That is utmost on my mind, my dear boy, but to do that we must find out who poisoned King Russel. Kings and queens have been poisoned for many hundreds of years... just not lately. Until last night, this was the safest house in Thure. Also, I liked this king. His family has been ruling for hundreds of years, but he was one of the better ones. Russel had a good sense of humor, at least. And he died in my house. Unacceptable." Denogg looked over the list again.

Aline quietly came in the room. "There's a girl outside. You'll want to talk to her, Denny."

A girl of eighteen stood nervously in the hallway. Denogg asked, "My dear Jenae, what is it?"

Aline went to the girl and gently prodded her to come into the room. The girl started crying. "I didn't know they were going to… I can't believe they did this. I'm so sorry."

"Oh, my poor dear. Tell me what you know," said Denogg.

"I know who poisoned the king. It was one of my cousins," said the girl.

Denogg put his arm around the girl's shoulder to calm her. "Were those the two cousins that you asked me to hire last year?" Asked Denogg softly. The girl nodded her head and cried harder.

Denogg asked, "And now you're afraid I will think that you helped them because you asked me to hire them?"

The girl was sobbing. "I had nothing to do with this. I don't even know them that well. They came last year saying that I needed to help them get work. I should have known something was wrong when my younger cousin asked to pour the berry juice."

"Do you know for sure that he did this?" asked Aline.

She opened her hands to show a small jar that was empty. She continued to cry.

Denogg carefully smelled the little jar. "Thorny root," he said wrinkling his nose. "That would do the trick." Denogg hugged the girl, calming her a bit. "Where are they now, my dear?"

"I don't know," she cried. "I went to look for them, and they were both gone, most of their things are gone. They must have fled, but I don't know where they're going."

The guards wouldn't let any of them leave, but they could go anywhere inside the vast home. They immediately went to the servant wing and searched the room assigned to Janae's cousins, looking for anything that might tell them where they'd gone.

There wasn't much left. A basket was in a corner with apple cores in it, and a bit of rope, but nothing to tell them where they had gone. Gordon and Aline searched again, but found nothing else. Gordon looked closer at the little bit of rope that was left. "Denny, this looks like a Gor knot."

"A what?" asked Aline.

Gordon answered, "A Gor knot. I read about them. On old ships, they use them to secure their personal property. They tie elaborate knots around their things. No one can untie the knot and retie the knot exactly the same way. It's like a personalized lock. Old time sailors used them all the time."

"So they might be fleeing the kingdom by ship. Do you have any idea where they would go?" Aline asked the serving girl.

The girl thought for a bit then said, "My family are from the old kingdom of Thure, but my two cousins came from Artoth. They could be going back there."

Denogg said, "Thank you my girl, you may go about your duties. Trust me, no one will punish you, but please tell no one about this."

The girl left, and they closed the door. Denny said, "You need to find those boys. We need to get you both out of here."

"Both of us? Why? I can track them myself and bring them back. Why risk your fortune by having Gordon go with me?" asked Aline.

Gordon asked, "Why exactly would you lose your fortune anyway?"

"I promised my fortune to the crown if you are found guilty, or Loren in your place. We have to get you out of here for several reasons. One, to find those boys. Aline, two searchers are better than one. Gordon, you're smart, let me ask you a question. What do you think will happen if you stay?" asked Denogg.

Gordon thought, then said, "Well, if Aline went and I stayed, I would probably have to go to the funeral of the king, and so would you. Even if Aline found them quickly, she wouldn't get back before the funeral. And funerals attract dignitaries from other kingdoms..."

Denogg nodded, "Clever boy. Go on..."

"If Aline doesn't get them back here, they will k... kill Loren, and they'll give me back to Trunculin as a prisoner to show good faith," said Gordon.

Denogg nodded, "That's right. And I can offer you no protection now. You being far away from here will be the best way for you to be safe. At this point, Aline can guard you much better than I can."

"And your fortune. What about that?" asked Gordon.

Aline answered, "Because he has put his fortune against your innocence; if you are free, you will be safe, but it will look like you are guilty. The queen can seize everything he owns until we can prove your innocence... whether you're here or not."

Gordon shook his head, "I don't want to go if it means that you lose everything. I already feel like Loren is in prison because of me."

Denogg answered, "My dear boy, you don't know how things work around here. The kings and queens of Thure have excellent blood, but most of them have no coin. This kingdom's ship building fortunes dried up long ago. They keep up appearances, but the cupboards are bare. Believe me, my boy. They want my fortune more than they want your head."

"But that's more reason for me to stay. I can't be responsible for you losing..."

"My king, I have been rich for a long time. And when you're rich, no matter how much you give to the poor, or how much you pay your servants, the tax collector always want more. In my long years as a merchant, among other things, I have learned not to keep all of my pebbles in one pocket. I have wealth secured in other lands. Not to mention large pockets in places no one knows about. It will be hard to lose this place," he said, looking around at his enormous house, "but I knew it was gone the moment the queen asked her question. Whatever happens, I will be fine." He rubbed his belly and said, "Besides, I could afford to miss a few meals. Now, let's get you ready, and then we will go off to a little secret of my house I need to show you."

Denogg sent the servant out to do some shopping, or so he told the guards. Denogg quietly told Aline and Gordon, "Okay, I have a ship leaving for Artoth. I sent my servant out for a dog team. Since they only left a few guards, there should be no problem to pull it around the back of the house where my special exit is. Now, let's take a tour of the house."

As they came out of the room, Denogg immediately started talking and pointing to things around the room. "This likeness here was a gift from the third king of Thure. Of course it was not a gift to me, but to his queen, since the third king lived almost two thousand years ago."

Denogg continued as they went down the long hallway lined with art. "Oh, this painting was done by the famous artist Ninian just for me. He owed me a lot of coin. Artists never seem to be able to manage their finances, so he painted this for me as payment." They passed a guard who was not interested in art and paid them little attention.

"Was that the same Ninian that painted the mural of the hundred kings?" asked Gordon, genuinely interested. Aline strolled next to them, decidedly unmoved by the painting.

"Why, very good my boy. He is the very artist that painted that masterpiece that surrounds the king's chair. Are you as interested in art as you are in history?" asked Denogg.

Gordon replied, "Not really. Only when they come together at the same time."

Denogg laughed as they continue down the long hallway, giving quite the performance for the guards. "Ah, I must show you *this* room."

They walked into a large room stacked with rows containing nothing but bottles and large kegs. The room was like a maze and they went through a series of high shelves until they reached the back of the room, well hidden from the entrance.

"The drinks room," declared Denogg, "You see it's in the darkest, coolest part of the house to make sure the wine stays good until I get thirsty," Denogg continued, "and you see the floor. You'll noticed that the floorboards are wider than the rest of the house. Occasionally there are accidents and a bottle drops, or old bottles suddenly pop open on their own. The mess goes down into the sub level." Denogg pushed the only small rug in the room aside with his foot. He grabbed a pole off the wall with a hook at the end, and pulled a section of floor up to reveal a secret door.

"This room has quite a few features. I could go on and on, but I don't want to bore you." As Denogg was saying this, he had quietly opened the trapdoor.

Denogg put a hand on both of their shoulders, just as they heard footsteps entering the room. It wasn't a guard. Instead, it was two servants carrying a basket each, supposedly full of dirty clothes for the laundry, but also full of all of their weapons and gear. They got ready to descend into the hidden room below that led to the exit. Denogg said "Don't worry. The dog team will be waiting for you."

Aline suddenly hugged Denogg very hard.

"What was that for, my dear?" asked Denny.

"For all that you've done, and all that you'll do in the coming days. Thank you Denny," Aline replied.

Gordon started to thank Denogg and put out his hand.

Denogg did not take his hand, "You know, I think that hug is contagious. Come here, my boy, you deserve more than a shake of the hand," he said as he hugged Gordon.

All Gordon could think to say was, "Thank you."

Denny smiled and said nothing else. He simply pointed his finger down to the ladder that led into the secret exit. They both quietly went down, and as soon as they did, Denogg closed the trapdoor above them, putting the false floor back in place, replacing the rug. There was little natural light all along the narrow passageway. But it was clear which way they were supposed to go.

They made their way out of the narrow passageway through a small door. They were careful as they came out, looking around in every direction. The dog team and Denny's trusted servant were there, just as promised.

This was a shielded side of the house that no one could see. There was foliage and large bushes all around, protecting the view. The servant said, "I know the quickest way to the docks. They won't know we're gone until it's too late," said the servant as they left Denogg's house forever.

CHAPTER 23
BAD WEATHER

They were gone for nearly an hour when a guard called through the door. "Denogg, why are these servants guarding the door?"

Denogg said warmly, "Greetings Lantovas. They are not guards. They are waiting to carry the wine for tonight's meal. Let him through, please."

Lantovas, The firstman of the Thurian guards, walked past the servants. Before he could ask another question, Denogg said, "Lantovas, being in charge of the king's guard, you must've gone to a great many events. Can you help me pick out a bottle of wine for tonight's meal?" Denogg picked up a bottle casually and said, "How about this rare Amontillado? It's about time to drink it. It's nearly twenty years old. What do you think?"

The head of the guards looked around, then back to Denogg. He went to the nearest shelf, then cast his eyes to the shelves next to him, scanning them quickly. He picked up a bottle. "I think this one. It was the king's favorite."

"An excellent choice. My family label…"

"Wait, Denny, where are the boy king and the girl?" The guard looked around with concern, "didn't they come in here with you?"

"Oh, they left here a while ago," said Denogg. "Must be on the other side of the house. Probably dressing for tonight's meal. You know young people get bored so easily..."

Lantovas said, "I was just in the other part of the house. My guard said the three of you were in here."

Denogg put the bottle back on the shelf. "I don't keep track of all my guests. That would be rude."

Lantovas stopped listening to Denogg and went around the large room, looking in all directions then went to the back of the room. "Strange that there is only one rug in this room." He spotted the hook on the wall, pushed away the rug, and lifted the false floor. "Damn it," nearly too angry to speak, Lantovas asked, "Where are they? I will only ask you once Denny."

"My name is Denogg of the family Xoss, and I may be a prisoner in my own house at the moment, but you will treat me with the respect I have earned. They have left, with my help. You will not find them, so do with me what you must. But I will not tell you where they have gone."

The guard stared. "Most of your trade is by sea," Lantovas narrowed his eyes. "My guess is to the docks. To one of your ships in the great port?"

Denogg blinked his eyes, but said nothing.

The guard bolted from the room, straight to his second in command. He jerked off his cape, nearly throwing it at the other guard. "I have to get to the docks quickly. Denogg let them go. I don't know how far ahead of me they are."

"Are you sure?" asked the guard.

"It's the only thing that makes sense. He has ships coming and going every day, and he wants to get that boy king out of the kingdom. Gordon has no other friends here as far as we know. We didn't bother to put troops at the docks, since we are only holding a fat man, a girl and a thirteen year old boy."

The second in command motioned for his other guards to get Denogg.

Lantovas continued, "Leave guards here for the servants and take Denogg to the palace prisons. I just hope I'm not too late."

The head of the guard left by the front door at a run, straight to his horse. He figured they were at least a half hour ahead. But he also knew his horse was fast. The streets were narrow and treacherous all the way to the docks. *They must've taken a dog team*, he reasoned. Even in these streets, his horse could out run the dogs.

Lantovas jumped on his horse and raced to the docks. The first raindrop hit his face as he got to full gallop. He knew it would be a long ride, but he had to get there at all costs. He nearly ran over several people along the way. His horse was breathing heavily by the time he finally made it to the docks.

When he reached the docks, it was a hard rain. He scanned the docks for any sign of them. He saw several dogcart teams. He asked a man packing up his fish if he'd seen them. The man didn't say anything, just pointed to the ship. Maybe he would catch them after all.

The ship that was leaving the bay was barely visible in the rain. It was nearly to the open sea. He asked the man again if he was sure they were on that ship. The man nodded wearily and went back to his work.

Lantovas scanned the ships that were docked and saw two with the blue-green royal emblem. One was a large warship that was in the bay mostly for decoration, taken out of service long ago. The other was a small racing boat that had belonged to the king. The king love to participate in small racing challenges twice a year. He went to the ship and said to the man tending it,

"I need to take this ship on king's business, and you're going to pilot for me."

"The king is dead. What business could he have with this boat?" said the man.

"You're going to take me to catch that ship," Lantovas said, pointing to the ship that was almost out of sight.

"In this rain? It's too dangerous," replied the man on the boat.

Lantovas replied, "That ship is carrying the king's murderer away from justice."

The man's face changed. He got serious and went right to work. In just a few moments, they had departed the docks in pursuit of the king's killer.

*

The ship carrying Gordon and Aline away from Thure was a small vessel manned by a crew of six men. They had been very kind to both Gordon and Aline, after Denogg's servant had given the message to the pilot. The pilot now understood that besides the spices, furs and wine, he was now to transport two passengers. The pilot was also told in the note not to ask who they were.

The sun was going down just as they were leaving the bay, and Gordon stared at it. Gordon was tired and worried. He watched the sinking of the sun into the ocean, and he wondered how it would ever have the courage to come back up again. He could just barely see the last sliver of the sun set through the clouds. The clouds came at them quickly and began to spit rain, about to be joined by even darker, wetter clouds blowing towards them.

Aline came up beside him with a cloth to keep the rain off their heads. "None of this is your fault, you know."

"No? So why does it feel like it is? I didn't want to be king. I didn't want any of this. Loren is in prison for me, accused of killing a king I just met and Denny is losing his fortune. And I'm running away… again."

Aline assured, "You are not running away. We have to find the people that poisoned the king. And Denny was right. You're safer being far away. Everyone who is in this struggle knows that they might not see it through. Everyone is willing to sacrifice themselves if it means, at least in one part of this world, that people can be free; to pursue their own fate. What's going on is a lot bigger that you or me, or even Loren or Denny."

Gordon let the idea into his mind and weighed it against everything he'd learned. He had read about other kingdoms and how life was for people who lived there. But he had only known one way of life. "So, why are you in the struggle? What are you looking for?"

Aline looked at the dark clouds and finally said, "In my land of Aspora, we don't have one king. In fact, there's no one in charge. Have you read much about Aspora?"

Gordon answered, "Just that it's big and wild..."

Aline explained, "Not only are there no kings, but there are really no laws. People just do whatever they want."

"No laws and no king? Doesn't that mean everyone's free?" asked Gordon.

Aline laughed softly. "You'd think it would be a great idea wouldn't you? There are no rules, no limits, no one telling you what you can and can't do. Men can get drunk, piss right in the streets, fight and kill each other. Some proclaim they are the king of a street, or a city. Until someone else comes along and kills them. There is always fighting. You have to learn to fight young. No one has the time to write books or invent airships. They are too busy trying to stay alive."

"But at least everyone's free."

Aline stopped smiling. "That's not exactly true. Those little kings proclaim you must do what they say. Maybe people listen to them, maybe they don't. People die all the time in Aspora. Empty, stupid deaths. No rules are as bad as having too many. I remember being scared all of the time, knowing I had to fight or die. I probably would've died, if I hadn't met Mantuan."

"How did you meet...?" asked Gordon, trying to keep his balance as the boat rocked. The waters had grown rough with the wind.

Aline didn't answer, just looked around, like she'd heard something no one else could. The sun was completely down, and the dark clouds had arrived with their wet gifts. The wind gusted harder, and the rain started to sting their eyes. Gordon and Aline almost fell over as a large wave rocked the small vessel.

The crew was running around the deck, tying things down with heavy rope. The pilot was standing at the back of the ship with a long spy glass in his hand, looking backwards instead of forward. Gordon tried to follow his line of sight. Gordon saw a small shape. *Another ship,* he thought. It seemed to be moving very fast, and right toward them.

The Pilot collapsed his spy glass and turned around, yelling orders to his crew. The ship was rocking wildly back and forth. Gordon had a hand on the railing, surprised at how high the waves had gotten. The wind threw seawater in his face.

"Get below deck, now!" demanded the pilot. Just then a flash of lightning lit the sky directly behind them. As Aline and Gordon made their way toward the ladder below, Gordon saw how fast the other ship was approaching. The thunderclap came quickly after the lightning just as the boat was hit by a very large wave. Gordon flew back. He might've gone over, but he caught a rope at the edge of the railing.

Aline, trying to make her way over to secure Gordon, was hit by water coming over the side of the ship. She was thrown down the ladder and below deck. Gordon still had his hand around the rope, but struggled to stay on the boat. There was a lot of water on the deck. Gordon thought they were riding lower in the water, but he couldn't be sure. The waves seemed nearly as high as the boat. Just as Gordon thought the next wave would push him overboard, another wave came the opposite direction and threw him back on the deck right next to the Pilot's feet.

"Get below deck! Damn you, you won't survive out here!" Gordon didn't need to be told again. Gordon got to the stairs and below deck. Aline was at the bottom of the stairs, holding her head. There was blood pouring from a cut on her forehead.

"Are you all right? What happened?" asked Gordon.

Then Gordon realized there was several feet of water on the floor.

"I'm fine, I hit my head on the stairs. We need to find our gear."

"Wait, should I get something for your head?" asked Gordon.

"No, I'll be fine. If the ship goes down we need to hang on to our gear."

Gordon stood there for a moment, frozen. *If the ship went down?* He'd never imagined the ship might actually sink. Aline trudged through the water, grabbing Gordon's arm and forcing him to help her find their gear. Gordon groped for the metal box with his sweets and sour cakes. He breathed a sigh as his fingers found them. He made sure the metal lid was closed tight.

The water was very cold on their legs and it was nearly pitch black below deck. The boat was rocking and they could barely stand, but they found their things. They heard an ominous creaking sound in the ship.

Aline grabbed some rope. "Here. Use this to tie your sack and your gear to you. Make the knot tight."

As Gordon complied, and Aline did the same, he said, "I don't care what the pilot says. We shouldn't be down here."

The deluge was deafening as they climbed the stairs. Another flash of lightning lit the sky. Gordon could see the mouths of the sailors moving, but he couldn't hear anything.

Gordon glanced at the pilot, who had tied himself to the wheel. The other ship was faring no better. It was rocking just as wildly and looked like it was also riding low in the water, probably in trouble too. Gordon could not even see any men on board the dark shape.

Aline grabbed Gordon and pulled him to the mast. She tried desperately to use nearby ropes to tie them both to the mast, but the wind and the rain were too strong. Just as she secured Gordon with the ropes, a large wave came over the ship and she was gone.

Gordon tried feverishly to undo his knot and find her. He couldn't tell which side of the boat she has gone over, or even if she was somewhere still on deck.

Another cold wave came over the railing of the ship, salt water getting in his mouth as he tried to yell Aline's name. The cold water had numbed his hands, but he continued to try and untie the knot. The ship was leaning badly to one side as he heard a loud crack. His ears began to ring and he realized the mast he was tied to just cracked in half. Another wave came straight for him. Gordon felt the boat tip farther as the mast and sails crashed into the water. The broken mast led the boat down towards the cold, dark waters. Gordon didn't even feel the shock of the cold sea as everything went black.

CHAPTER 24
MUCH TO LEARN

The two airships were making good progress. They had stayed away from the coastline, but soon they would be headed out over the open waters. There was no other way to get to Thure. Trunculin had wanted to wait until morning, but Brenddel insisted they leave at night, "Those things wouldn't dare attack me again. We'll fly as high as we can manage. Besides, these two ships are fully armed with large arrows and rain makers. I'm ready this time."

Trunculin wanted to get to the old kingdom as soon as possible, so he agreed. He knew the small contingent of soldiers they brought with them all knew their jobs. The only one he worried about was the new king.

"Firstcouncilor. Look over there, I think that's lightning!" shouted king Asa.

As it turned out, the new king was the least of his worries. It seems the king was fascinated by everything he saw. They had been up in the air for hours already, and the boy wasn't tired of pointing out every little thing that he discovered.

Trunculin heard the faintest roll of thunder. He got up from his chair, and tried to seem interested for the boy's sake. He pulled his blanket around his shoulders. "Yes, my king, I can just see it way over there. It looks like large dark clouds, probably over the water…"

"Oh! Look at that!" The king had already lost interest, and had run to the front of the ship. The firstcouncilor followed dutifully and now the king was pointing at a large trail of lights along the ground. "What is that? Are they fire bugs?"

Trunculin said, "Oh, let's hope not. That many fire bugs in one place could be trouble. No, those little lights down there, looks like some sort of celebration or maybe a farmer's feast."

"You mean, those are people down there? They look as small as bugs," said Asa excitedly.

Brenddel walked up and said, "Yes, my king. Those are people down there. We are the only kingdom that can see people from this high up. The people look like little bugs because they are so far beneath us. Just like if your friend was far away on a hill, he would look very small to you. It's the same thing."

"I thought Extatumm has airships too. That's what my friend Skyler says."

Brenddel stiffened a little. "There have been rumors for years that they have airships. The people that took over the kingdom of Dard, and renamed it Extatumm, are very secretive. They let in no one from outside their lands. But I'm sure they don't have airships. Those are just rumors and lies."

Trunculin took this opportunity to fade back to his chair, leaving the firstman and the king alone.

"Oh! Is this the fire gun? How does it work?" asked Asa.

Brenddel put his hand over Asa's. "Better not touch that, my king. It takes a lot of training to operate one of these. But I will show you the basics. We call it a rainmaker because it rains fire downward. You see this pipe here releases the oil. As it drops, it is caught on fire here," he said, indicating the wick hung near the pipe. "The fire spreads down, and the fireman has a snuffer so that the fire does not travel back up the pipe, you see?"

Asa said, "Wooooah. So, can you aim it at other airships?"

Brenddel replied, "We are working on that. So far, we can only drop fire downward. Why would we want to aim fire at our own airships, anyway?"

King Asa shrugged, "I don't know. I haven't really been taught about the airships yet. So… I still don't get how the ship stays up in the air, or how we go down. A councilor started to tell me but… I got confused. What's in there?" The king asked as he pointed to the massive floating body of the ship above them.

Brenddel smiled and said, "A while back, some men in our kingdom discovered a different kind of air. It comes from deep in the ground, and we have found a way to capture it. It is lighter than the air that we breathe. We call it the sun gas, because it escapes back to the sun if we don't capture it. But, if we capture enough of this light air, like in the skin of an airship, the whole ship floats."

"So, no one else has discovered this light air, except us?" asked Asa.

"No, my king, it was found in our kingdom, and we believe that it only occurs here. It is a jealously guarded secret how we get the sun gas out of the ground, and how we build the airships," Brenddel said secretively. "You will keep this a secret, won't you, my king?

Asa smiled, "Of course. So why is the ship so big, and the deck so much smaller? Wouldn't it be better if we had more weapons and stuff?" asked the king.

Brenddel smiled, "I wish we could. The problem is that the gas can only lift so much. This is not magic. We have to deal with realities. It takes a lot of this special air to lift even one person. We plan everything we load on the ships very carefully. It's a good thing you're so skinny, or we may have left you behind."

Asa smiled. "But, how does it go up and down?"

"I will show you," said Brenddel, leading him to the controls. "It is a little like a watership. This wheel steers the ships side to side. The wheel controls the rudder. When the air passes around the rudder, it turns the ship in either direction. This other wheel does the same thing to give us height or make us go down. If we have to go up very quickly, we can throw sandbags or water overboard. If we have to go down very quickly, we can let some of the gas escape, you see?"

"Wow," said Asa.

"There is a lot more to being a pilot, but those are the basics. Are you excited about seeing the world outside of our kingdom?" asked Brenddel.

"I've never been outside the kingdom before. Is Thure big? I hear it's really old."

Brenddel replied, "Yes. Very big and very old."

"I've never talked to a queen before. I don't know what I'm supposed to say."

"I wouldn't be the one to tell you. I'm just a soldier. That's the firstcouncilor's job. I'm sure he'll tell you all you need to know," replied Brenddel.

Asa shifted uncomfortably as he leaned on the railing. He looked back to see if anyone was listening and said, "I don't... I don't think Trunculin likes me."

Brenddel leaned in close, and with a very serious face he said, "The firstcouncilor doesn't like anyone."

Asa started to smile, too. The two of them stood there, looking down at the line of lights, imagining what was happening so far beneath them. Asa looked up and saw a giant kingdom approaching far in the distance. Even from this height in the dark, he could see how big it was. It made Asa feel even smaller.

CHAPTER 25
LOST

Gordon's eyes shot open to a world of light and pain. He immediately put his arm over his eyes against the bright sunlight. He realized he was, at least, alive. He felt something next to him and realized it was his lumpy sack still tied around his body. He hurriedly searched for his metal can. He found it, and opened it to find only a little water got in. He ate a sweet as he looked around.

There was not a cloud in the sky, almost like there never had been. He was lying on some large leaves, surrounded by sand. *Did I crawl here? I don't remember,* he thought. He could hear the waves break on the beach.

With some effort, and more than a little pain, he managed a standing position as he tried to figure out where he was. The only land he could see was the small bit he was on. Beyond that, it was just blue sea everywhere. The beach was narrow and led to lush green plants and trees three times as tall as he was.

He started to walk along the beach, looking for Aline. He was worried to call her name out until he figured out where he was, and who else was around. He saw bits of wood that had been washed ashore that were clearly pieces of ship.

The sea was gently playing with a large pile of clothes and tangled ropes. It got tugged out a little, then the next wave gently put it back on the sand. He went to it, and pulled back quickly when he saw a face. The eyes were closed and the man was wrapped in a jumble of ropes.

He choked back his fear and got closer again. Gordon could tell that the man was dead. The rope that carried him away from the sinking ship had also wrapped around his neck long before he got to shore. Gordon got up uneasily and walked away, not knowing what else to do.

He had to find Aline.

There was more wood on the beach as he walked, and a few barrels were washed ashore. Some of the things he recognized from the ship, others were just unrecognizable ruins. No Aline. He walked for some time, squinting his eyes in the hot sun, when he spotted someone else lying on the sand. It looked like a person, faced down.

He fought the urge to yell as he ran toward the person. It had to be Aline. *We haven't gone through all this to…* but Gordon couldn't let himself think like that. He slowed down as he approached the shape on the sand.

He was afraid the unmoving shape was dead as well, but he had to make sure. As he got closer, the body appeared to be moving slightly, maybe breathing. He bent down. It was a man and he was alive. Gordon turned him over. Gordon looked at the man's clothes. He was dressed in the bluish green uniform of a Thurian guard. Gordon was just about to bend over to see if he was unhurt when he heard a noise from behind him. "Bhuta?"

Gordon spun around, startled. Standing only two feet away from him was a man like no one he had ever seen. The man said the strange word again, pointing to the man on the ground. The man was carrying a long wooden club, and had ink designs all over his body. To Gordon, they almost look like numbers.

As Gordon tried to figure out what to do next, he couldn't help but stare at what looked like a number eight on the man's neck. He had no idea how the man had gotten so close without Gordon hearing him. The man on the sand moved and let out a groan.

Gordon turned around to see the man was trying to sit up. He was coughing and sputtering as he pushed himself upright. Gordon turned around again to face the man with the number eight, and suddenly there were ten others standing there. He had not heard them approach. They all looked at Gordon and down at the man, saying nothing.

Gordon instinctively tried to protect the men and drew his small knife. He realized instantly how foolish he must look. The one with the eight on his neck smiled. Gordon stood over the man with his knife drawn, not knowing what to do.

The men with ink all over their bodies all smiled and then… dropped their clubs. Gordon was surprised. That was the last thing the expected them to do and Gordon simply looked at them, mouth open. They all began to laugh as their weapons laid silently on the ground. The Thurian guard coughed on the sand and stared at them.

Gordon slowly put his own knife away. He helped the man on the ground get up. The man with the eight on his neck walked up to Gordon quickly, still smiling, and did something entirely unexpected: he hugged Gordon tight. All the men standing behind him began laughing.

CHAPTER 26
OLD WOMAN'S PLAN

"Disaster. How could this happen?" said the queen as she paced back and forth.

"You must stay calm," said the old woman sitting a few feet from her, both hands on her cane.

"I lose the boy king and my best guard all in one day, just after my husband…" the queen began sobbing and sat down in her chair.

"You have to focus now. The firstcouncilor and his new boy king will be here soon with those damned airships of theirs. We don't have much time, and you have things to decide," said the old woman.

The queen stopped crying. "I know. I know, it's just that things are happening so fast. One disaster after another. And that damned Denogg. I am going to have his heart cut out."

The old woman got up with energy and went to the queen. "Good. Anger will focus you. But forget about Denogg right now. You have immediate problems. First, you need to secure your place of power before anything else. You didn't have any children, so that helps you, but…"

"… But my husband has a brother. Yes, I know. I'm surprised he hasn't shown up at my door already, demanding to be crowned."

The old woman reasoned, "He will make his move soon enough. He'll speak at the funeral and if it's a good enough speech, the people may crown him right there and then. We both know the ancient laws of acclamation; if the crowds demand it, he will be king. You need some protection before then."

"Yes. But my main card to bargain with is gone. It's not the young new king I'm worried about upsetting," said the queen. "It's what his firstcouncilor will do when he finds out I've lost Gordon."

"It's also important to decide how honest you're going to be with your new potential ally," said the queen's grandmother. "Trunculin may partner with you now that you have Denogg's fortune behind you. But that will not protect you from the king's brother Darion. He's an idiot, but he has soldiers that are very loyal to him. He's wisely kept them out of Thure and somewhere safe, but they could be here fast enough. And your most loyal guard is probably lost at sea by now, along with Gordon. We would've heard something by now… and that storm was terrible, so I'm told."

"Grandmother, I know how dire my situation is, thank you. But what will the firstcouncilor want in return? He's from the richest kingdom. He doesn't need my new fortune. We can't buy him," said the queen.

"I wager the firstcouncilor is not a man who values coin. I'm guessing he values power. The lines between our kingdoms have been strong in the past, you just need to make it an active, friendly alliance once more. I'm sure he will have some demands. The boy's uncle is one card you still hold, but he's expecting Gordon. What would you tell him?" asked the grandmother.

"I think the truth is best. The boy is presumed lost at sea. With that terrible storm, there's no hope he survived. We sent several ships out to look for them. But there's no word yet if they found anything."

The grandmother reasoned, "Yes, but the firstcouncilor doesn't know that. If you give them any hope that he's alive, they will send that damned floating thing out to look for him. And who knows what they will find? Better to be certain."

The queen said, "I can't produce a body out of thin air. What would you have me do?"

"I have a few ideas," replied the grandmother.

*

The airships landed in a small field just outside the walls of the kingdom of Thure. It was a very tight landing. Trunculin knew it was wise to land as far outside the Thurian gates as possible. Relations had been uneasy between their kingdoms in the years since the airships took flight. Thure's place as the world's shipbuilders had been secure for many hundreds of years. That meant they controlled trade between the kingdoms. When airships were invented, and goods could be moved at twice the speed, Thure had fallen to a distant second in power. Thure had not been very friendly with Trunculin's kingdom ever since.

Since there was very little open land, Brenddel had landed in the only small field left outside of Thure. The second airship stayed in the air, as instructed. King Asa stood along the railing as they floated down to land. Everywhere Asa looked was covered with the great kingdom; one big sprawling Thure.

The Thurian envoys came out to meet them and escorted them into the kingdom. They had been processed through the front gate with no paperwork, having been granted a waiver by the queen. As they made their way through the kingdom gates,

Asa seemed delighted by everything he saw. There was different clothing, strange cooking smells, even the weapons the soldiers held were different.

Asa knew he should act like a king, but he was too excited. Brenddel kept a stony face as they were led through the kingdom on an ornate cart pulled by twelve of the largest dogs Asa had ever seen. He wondered why the dogs weren't distracted by the smell of food everywhere. Asa couldn't even pick out one kind of food he knew as they slowly passed cart after cart of food.

They went slowly, following closely behind the Thurian cart, people parting as they came. Asa seemed too busy looking around to notice the people staring. Brenddel glanced at the young king from time to time, smiling inwardly at each new discovery the king was making. He couldn't remember being a boy. Being the adopted son of the firstman, Brenddel knew nothing but the life of fighting and service.

Brenddel knew that Asa would not have a normal life, either, no matter what happened. He was glad to see the new discoveries through Asa's eyes. He never thought about it before, finding joy in small things. Brenddel wondered briefly why it had never occurred to him.

"What's that, Trunculin?" Asa said as he pointed to a tent selling fresh meat.

Trunculin looked, "That, my king, is snake meat. They say it's quite good."

The young king made a sound of disgust and the firstcouncilor said, "No, no, my king, we don't make sounds like that. We are about to meet a queen from another kingdom, one that lost a husband unexpectedly. We have to be serious and respectful. And whatever they serve, you must eat it."

"Even if it's snake?" the king asked, horrified.

"Snake isn't so bad. A little chewy. Let's just hope they don't feed us spiders fried in batter," said Brenddel.

The king looked even more shocked. He was about to make another horrified sound, but looked at Trunculin and tried to clear any emotion from his face.

"You're not helping things," said the firstcouncilor to Brenddel.

They arrived at the palace to great fanfare. People lined the streets by the palace to see the new boy king. As he had been trained on the airship, he waved politely.

The firstcouncilor noted something strange. The queen and her guard were standing in the forefront waiting to receive them, but off to the side was another smaller group of soldiers dressed similarly. At the head of these men stood a man who could only be Darion, the king's brother. Trunculin loved politics. He thought to himself, *this is going to be fun.*

They arrived and the queen came down to meet them with her guards. Trunculin noticed that Darion made no move to try to interfere. Trunculin got out of the dog cart and stood there, while Asa walked up to the queen, bowed and said, "Queen Eyonna, queen of all Thure, I offer my fellowship and my friendship if you will want it." Asa immediately realized what he'd said wrong, and replied, "I mean... if you will have it… sorry."

The queen smiled and held out her hand. "I think we can forgive the mistake of one word. I won't have your head cut off just yet." Asa kissed her hand, as was the custom of the ruling queen of Thure. "King Asa, newest king of the kingdom of the thirteen, I say rise, as I offer my own hand in friendship and fellowship," she added quietly, "and you did just fine, my king. Welcome King Asa, to the kingdom of Thure."

The crowds cheered as they welcomed Asa and his party into the kingdom. As they were about to enter the palace, Darion's contingent was still off to one side. The queen stopped. "Oh, how forgetful of me. This is Darion, the brother of the king, my late husband."

Darion stepped up and gave the customary greeting and Asa returned it perfectly this time. Darion bowed and everyone proceeded in. Darion said, "And I look forward to seeing you at the funeral meal, firstcouncilor."

"As do I," said the firstcouncilor to Darion. Trunculin immediately looked at the queen for reaction. As she was walking in front of Trunculin, he could not see her face, but he thought he saw her body language change for just a moment. *Oh yes,* Trunculin thought, *this is going to be lots of fun.*

The queen wasted no time in meeting with the new king and Trunculin. They were shown to the formal room where the queen took the king's chair and an old woman took the seat that normally sat the queen.

"I wasn't aware that we would be in the company of the great queen Alonnia of Dard," said the firstcouncilor to the old woman.

The old woman cocked her head and said, "Firstcouncilor, you honor me. And how very tactful you were to use the beautiful name of my old kingdom, and not the name those scum have chosen to call it."

The firstcouncilor nodded and smiled, and the queen added, "And how very bold of the firstcouncilor to speak before the queen does, although I do appreciate you honoring my grandmother. There is much to discuss… and some news that will not be welcome."

"Nothing too serious, I hope?" asked Trunculin.

"King Gordon is dead," the queen said bluntly.

Trunculin tried not to show his shock, but Asa let out a gasp. The firstcouncilor rose quickly to his feet, and king Asa stood as well.

The queen continued, "Some of my guards allowed him to escape and he was drowned at sea during a terrible storm."

Trunculin spoke, "How could this happen? How do you know that he is dead? Did you recover his body? He may have survived somehow."

"There is no doubt about his death." She motioned to her guard, who immediately left the room. "There was a witness that survived."

The guard returned with a man dressed in the colors of Thure. Queen Eyonna said, "Please tell King Asa and his firstcouncilor what happened."

The man said, "We were in pursuit of the escaping ship when a storm came on us suddenly. Both of our ships were damaged. I saw the murderer's ship go down with my own eyes. The two other men in my boat, including Lantovas, the head of the guard, did not survive. There were no survivors from the other boat," the man made his report looking straight ahead, with no emotion. Brenddel said nothing, but was suspicious. The man sounded like he was reciting from a script he had just learned.

"How can you be so sure? You survived. Surely someone else might have," Trunculin reasoned.

The queen said, "We sent out a dozen rescue ships and searched for other survivors. I'm sorry, but Gordon is dead. Thank you, that will be all," said the queen motioning for the man to leave.

The firstcouncilor was gravely concerned as he looked at Brenddel, who was standing just behind King Asa's chair. Trunculin quietly sat back down. Asa was numb. He had never had a friend die.

The queen said, "It is unforgivable that we allowed Gordon to escape, but I can't say that I am saddened by the boy's death. He did murder my husband. But, by law, we still have the guilty party."

"What do you mean?" managed Asa.

"We have his substitute. When Gordon was accused, his uncle said he would stand trial instead. By the laws of my kingdom that makes it the same thing," said the queen.

The new king was confused and looked to Trunculin for guidance. He explained, "My king, in Thure, if a person is accused of a crime and a relative or close friend offers to go on trial for them, they are allowed to do so. They are considered guilty."

"But they're not the one that did it. How is that fair?" asked Asa, quickly turning to the queen and saying, "no offense, my queen, I am new to your kingdom's rules. And... I... I knew Gordon. The Gordon I knew wouldn't have murdered anyone."

The queen said, "No reason to apologize, my king. My land has many laws, some of which are hard to understand. But that is the law, and justice must be served. I was there and saw my husband die. It must have been Gordon."

The grandmother interrupted. "But of course there are other considerations to be made. Let's cut through the horse dung, shall we? We can help each other. I think that is clear."

"My grandmother has always been direct," said the queen, "and she's right. My people demand that my husband's murderer be punished. But there is more at stake here. Since Gordon escaped, he admitted his guilt by his actions. My people might be convinced that the gods of Thure punished Gordon directly for his actions. They might be convinced that his uncle was just protecting the boy and has no part in my husband's murder."

"But... you need protection," said young King Asa.

Everyone in the room was silent. Trunculin's mouth dropped open, and Brenddel barely contained his smile.

The grandmother smiled. "Now that's cutting through the dung. That's exactly what we need. The king's brother Darion wants power. This might be the best time to grab the crown for himself."

Asa said, "And if Darion knew that we were friends…"

"… Then he would be much less likely to make trouble. Exactly," the queen said as she looked at Trunculin, "whatever gods you pray to in your kingdom, they seem to choose smart young kings."

Asa smiled brightly, looking very much like the boy of thirteen that he was. He immediately realized his error and tried to stop smiling. He looked at Trunculin, but couldn't read the firstcouncilor's expression. He looked around the room awkwardly, not knowing what to do next.

Next to Asa, Brenddel gave just the smallest nod to the king. Asa felt like he knew what he was doing for the first time.

Trunculin sat quietly, having decided to himself that it would be the last happy moment he would allow Asa to have.

CHAPTER 27
THE NEW GUESTS

Gordon had no idea what they were saying. The people with inked bodies were leading them somewhere. Gordon hoped it would be somewhere safe, although he was reluctant to leave the beach at all, since he had still not found Aline.

Gordon's vision was a little blurry and he was very thirsty. He had already looked in his sack. The metal can was still sealed. A little salt water had gotten in, but there were still some sour cakes and one sweet. He didn't want to use up too many sour cakes, but he nibbled on one as he walked. Thirst meant his blood was too sweet. He hoped he could get something to drink soon.

His companion was not optimistic about what was happening. "We shouldn't be going with these people. For all we know, they could be cannibals."

"Well, they let me keep my knife. And I don't think cannibals like to hug strangers," said Gordon.

The guard did not look convinced. He kept looking around nervously as though he were going to run off when he got the chance. "Probably just putting us at ease, until they roast us. And speak for yourself; my longknife was lost at sea. I have no choice but the play this out. Whatever happens, boy, when we are rescued you will be put on trial for what you've done."

Gordon replied, "I already told you I didn't do it. We know who did it and we were..."

"Yes, yes, your mysterious servant cousins. That's very convenient. But a man only runs if he's guilty," said the guard.

"I just wanted to save my uncle Loren. If it were up to me, I would have stood trial and proven my innocence. A lot of people have been making decisions for me lately. I'm kind of tired of it," said Gordon.

The guard said, "Well, we'll see about that when we get back to Thure. Because of you, I'm going to miss the funeral of the great king."

Gordon blinked to clear his vision, "He did seem like a great king. I really liked him," said Gordon sincerely.

Just as the guard was about to protest and start another argument, they walked out of the dense foliage and into a large open space. Gordon's eyes were drawn upward as he tried to make sense of what he was seeing.

It looked like a mountain had been carved out. In its place, little houses have been built inside it, as far up as Gordon could see. There were people everywhere. There must have been hundreds of people climbing ladders from one story to the next, cooking meals from small fires right outside of their small houses. After a few moments, Gordon realized that the space must have been formed naturally, and these people had built their houses under the natural formation, well protected under the overhanging rock that formed the huge space inside.

All of the small huts and houses seemed to be interconnected in a complex system. It reminded Gordon of the houses stacked on top of each other in Murderer's Bay, but much more simple. These houses were made of what looked like wood and clay, but just as beautiful in their own way. He thought of

Aline again, her face flashing in his mind. He was worried he would never find her.

Gordon looked down from the hollowed out mountain to the clearing before him. In the center was a large, round structure. At first look, Gordon thought it was a just a mound with grass on top of it, but as they got closer, it was clearly some sort of building. Gordon could see holes that looked like doors and windows all around the building. It looked like it was part of the ground in a way, but at the same time was clearly made by human hands.

From the silence of the Thurian guard, Gordon realized that he must be in awe as well. The people started to look in their direction as they came into the area. Gordon could hear their language bouncing around everywhere.

Some children ran up to them, explaining something excitedly in their language. The children didn't touch them, just looked at them and talked amongst themselves. Gordon noticed that the children didn't have ink on their bodies. *Maybe it's something they do later in life*, he thought.

Gordon wished that he knew how to speak their language, so we could ask questions. He wanted to ask if they'd seen Aline. The men led them into the large, round structure. Gordon was right about the opening being a door. What looked like dirt and grass outside was supported by a beautiful and complicated series of wooden beams on the inside.

They were led through several rooms. All the walls were decorated with objects; things to cook with, exotic musical instruments, baskets and many things he could only guess at. As they entered the series of rooms, Gordon also noticed some weapons and tools hanging on the wall that looked almost as though they'd come from his own kingdom. Maybe they were things they traded for, or that came ashore with other shipwrecks. Gordon couldn't be sure and had no one to ask.

They were led to a third room, this one much larger and round just like the outside of the structure. Gordon assumed they were the middle of the structure, and thought this might be their version of a palace. There was no king's chair or anything like it, so Gordon couldn't be sure. There was also no one that looked more important in any way, but a few of the men went over to an older man sitting in the corner weaving a basket.

The man was wearing eyeglasses that looked completely out of place with his simple clothing. Gordon realized he wasn't much older than the other men. But this man seemed confident, in charge. The man nodded, and his face got very serious. He walked up to Gordon and the guard, and looked both of them over.

The guard stepped forward as though he were protecting Gordon. That surprised Gordon, since just moments before, he was calling him a murderer. The man took off his glasses and looked into the guard's face and then Gordon's. Gordon got a shiver as the man stared into his eyes. Then the man laughed and hugged the guard. Even though he'd seen one of the men hug Gordon on the beach, this was apparently the last thing the guard expected to happen. His body language stiffened, not knowing what to do. His arms were sticking straight to his sides. Apparently the guard had no practice at hugging.

The man also came to Gordon and hugged him. He said something that he couldn't understand. The man motioned with his hand for all to follow. He put his glasses back onto his nose and looked confused for a moment, trying to figure out how to communicate. Then he made a motion with his hand, as though he put something in his mouth and pretended to eat.

That was all the man had to do to make the hungry guard move. Gordon's stomach began to growl too. The sour cake had time to work, but it was always a matter of balance. He may have eaten too much sour cake and now he needed real food. Gordon started to panic, realizing that he had no way to communicate with these people that he needed something sweet to make him feel better.

Gordon also realized that he wouldn't be seeing Loren or another healer for probably a long time. He had no idea what he was going to do after the few sour cakes ran out. He began to feel dizzy. He was feeling very hungry now, like all the food in the world would not be enough.

The man with the eight turned around and looked at Gordon with some concern. The man with the glasses came over to Gordon and looked him over, taking Gordon's face in his hands and looking in his eyes. He put his nose right next to Gordon's mouth and sniffed. He took Gordon by the arm and helped him to some food.

Behind the large, round structure, there was an even larger clearing with many fires, all cooking different foods, all smelling delicious, spicy and strange. Gordon's stomach growled. The man with the glasses led him to an area where they were baking bread. It was flat and thick, but the man went to one, tore it in half, and offered Gordon one half. With the other half, he put his own nose to the bread and smelled it, looking at Gordon. Gordon smelled his own bread and realized it was some sort of sweet bread. He looked to the man, who nodded his head, and Gordon ate some.

It was warm, soft and delicious. He wished he could ask the man how he knew that Gordon needed something sweet, but he would never know. This was another mystery to add to Gordon's growing list.

They all gathered together, and swarms of people came to welcome them. They smiled, laughed and ate together from clay dishes with wooden spoons. People were coming and going all through the meal. Everyone seemed happy.

Nearly all the men and women had ink on their bodies in some way. Some of them had ink all over their body with images of animals or plants. Others had strange symbols that Gordon did not recognize, but only one man had what looked like numbers on his skin. Gordon thought of Brenddel with his firstman stripes on his face. Gordon shuddered and tried to think of something else.

The guard had forgotten his idea of them being cannibals and was filling his belly. There must have been two dozen different dishes. Some of them were meat, some of them were like stews with exotic vegetables, and some dishes were sweet. Everything seemed to have a spice or a flavor that Gordon had never tried before.

The men that had originally found them on the beach were the ones that stayed near them, talking constantly. They knew that Gordon and the guard couldn't understand them, but they kept talking to them anyway. After a while they talked more to themselves, and Gordon and the guard finally began to talk to each other.

"My name is Lantovas," said the guard after they had finished eating.

Gordon put out his hand, which Lantovas took hesitantly. "I guess you already know my name is Gordon."

Lantovas smiled a little. "I guess I do. I haven't thanked you for trying to guard over me from these… um… cannibals," he smiled.

Gordon replied, "I didn't really do anything. There were lots of them. I wouldn't have won that fight."

"That makes the deed more worthy of my respect," replied the guard.

"Do you really think I killed the king?" asked Gordon seriously.

Lantovas replied, "I doubt it. But I am a soldier. I still have to bring you back. It is for the queen to decide what to do with you. I have only to do my duty."

"Or, we could find a way out of here and go to Artoth together to find the real murderers," offered Gordon.

Different men and women offered them sweet desserts to try. Gordon knew he had probably eaten too much already, and wanted to stay in balance. He declined the sweet deserts and drank a delicious tea they offered instead.

Later that night, after it was very dark, the man with the glasses stood up in front of them. There was a clearing with small fire pits all around it, just next to the main eating area. He spoke very loudly to everyone gathered and moved his arms as he was telling a story. Many of the children gathered at his feet, excited.

As he stood in the middle of this clearing, a man and woman came up next to him, walking arm in arm. They were pointing at things and patting each other on the arms, as though they were young lovers.

There must've been hundreds gathered by then, watching the performance. A drum began off to the side. Gordon looked over to see a few musicians that were just on the edge of the fire pits surrounding the primitive stage. A large man slowly walked up to the young couple looking very angry, holding one of their clubs.

The large man grabbed the woman and threatened the man with the club. The young man tried to pull the girl as well, but then the large man pretended to bash the young man in the head. The young man fell. Then, several men and women started to surround the large man. The man made a sound and held up his club, pulling the woman towards him. He said something, which made people quiet. They all got down on the ground and looked like they were praying to him.

Then, one of the women came to him with what looked like a crown made of leaves, and placed it on his head. The rest of them were still on the ground as the large man started to laugh. Next, they brought a chair, which the large man sat on, and held his club up over his head. The woman sat next to the man's chair and was pretending to cry.

People were up on their feet and looked as though they were pretending to build something. The man was standing and waving his club around as though he was giving orders. The man with the glasses was now standing off to the side, narrating the story in their beautiful language.

The people looked like they were working very hard as the large man shouted at them. Then a few of the people entered the stage, coming towards the man with their own clubs. The man got very loud now, and the other men all attacked him. The other people, who had been working, turned to the large man and started to surround him. The large man took the woman that was sitting by the chair and lifted her up over his shoulder. He went around the edge of the stage in a circle.

The other people followed him. He went to the middle of the clearing where there was a large pile of leaves. The man laid the woman down and covered her in the large leaves and headed toward the fire pits. He lit his club on fire, then slowly came back to the middle of the clearing and looked like he was about to set the leaves on fire.

The rest of the people jumped on him, took the club away, and two men cleared the leaves off of the girl. The large man was finally on the ground. A woman took the crown off his head. She walked very slowly to the closest fire pit and threw it into the fire.

The man was still on the ground, and all the people who were on stage and in the audience were cheering. The people all left the stage, except for the large man who was still lying down, pretending to be dead. All the people surrounded the dead man with platters of food. They were smiling and happy. The man with the glasses got louder, and the audience were slapping their legs and cheering.

Gordon and Lantovas looked around, then at each other. "Is it like clapping?" Gordon asked Lantovas. He shrugged and the two decided to join in and slap their legs. Apparently they don't do it quite right, and many people around them begin to laugh.

After a while, they were shown a very comfortable place to sleep. Gordon fell asleep right away. Even Lantovas, who first thought they were cannibals, apparently felt safe enough to sleep among them.

CHAPTER 28
BAD ETIQUETTE

Asa was trying desperately not to make a mistake. He tried to learn so much in the short time leading up to their trip, but there were so many more rules in Thure. He looked at his plate, which was empty at the moment. He knew the food would be coming soon, and he had no idea what they were going to serve. Or how he was supposed to eat it.

There were utensils all around the plate, four at each side and four at the top in two rows. Only two of them looked familiar. One clearly being a spoon, the other maybe a knife. It was like a knife in some ways, but didn't come to a point at the end.

"You know, there are so many ancient rules here, if you use the wrong one, you might start a war between our kingdoms. I'm Darion, by the way. The king was my brother," Darion put out his hand to shake the hand of the new king.

Asa shook the hand and looked nervously at all the utensils, "Any ideas?"

"Actually, like everything else in this kingdom," replied Darion, "it's elaborate, but kind of boring. You start on the outside here, working inward toward your plate. Just go in order for each course. Start at the left and make a kind of half-circle around the plate."

"Wait. There are twelve… they're going to bring twelve things for me to eat?" asked king Asa as quietly as he could.

"Oh yes, we go all the way when there are important people visiting. And don't worry, we've hired a lot of new food tasters just in case. You're going to love how we prepare snake," said Darion, smiling.

"Don't let him scare you, my boy. There is no snake being served as long as I'm alive," said the grandmother, sitting across from them.

The dining hall was large and most of it was filled with long, square tables where people ate together. Where they were seated, it was all round tables. When Asa asked the firstcouncilor why it was different, he explained that the queen or king always sit with dignitaries at a round table so everyone would feel more equal.

Asa noticed that the plain chair he was sitting in was much different than the elaborate chairs the queen and her grandmother were sitting in. Asa also realized that the chair that Darion was seated in was plain like his. Apparently the chairs weren't equal.

"Oh come on now, you must eat all the delicacies, good grandmother. I'm sure you've snuck a bite of snake on your plate here and there," said Darion.

"The kings and queens from my kingdom feel snake is on the same level as rat," said the grandmother, "they are both of the dirt."

Darion teased, "Oh, you mean back in Extatumm? I've heard they eat snake there too …."

"Don't ever say that word to my face again, boy. I've never liked you, and you've never liked me. King Asa should know the real reason why the knives at the tables are not pointed. It's because long ago, royal women like me stabbed insolent little princes like you right at the table."

"I'd like to see you try old woman…" began Darion.

The queen cut him off. "That's enough. You are going to make King Asa believe we are commoners, acting this way."

Asa said, "Oh, it's alright, my queen. I have five brothers. Food and fists get thrown at nearly every meal. I know how family can be," but looked sheepishly as he spoke.

Everyone seemed uncomfortable at Asa's family story, but luckily the first course was just being served.

Brenddel walked up to the table and whispered something into the firstcouncilor's ear. Trunculin said, "Would you excuse me for just a moment, my queen? I have a quick matter to take care of. Pardon me for interrupting."

The queen granted permission for him to leave the table and Brenddel and Trunculin left the room together.

In the hallway, just outside the dining Hall, Brenddel said, "I still think that guard was lying about surviving the shipwreck. Gordon could still be out there. I want to look for him, with your permission."

"I agree that the guard was lying. It would do no good to leave tonight. It's too dark to see anything out on the open waters. You wouldn't see one of those fin beasts come at you until it was too late." Trunculin paused for a moment. "Actually, we might be able to spear two fish with one stick. Let me tell you what I have in mind..."

Back at the dinner table, Asa was on the third course. He was following the utensil directions exactly as Darion had instructed. So far everything was fairly familiar: the two different soups were both good and they hadn't expected him to eat anything too disgusting yet.

Besides, it turned out to be kind of fun. Since Asa had mentioned brothers, Darion had been telling stories of growing up. This was the most anyone had talked to him since he became king.

"…. That's nothing, one time my brother bested me with a wooden knife and the bet was that we had to jump into a frozen pond… naked. I swear it felt like a thousand knives hitting me at once," said Darion.

"One time, all of my brothers had me on the ground, and they were passing wind right in my face…" Asa stopped as he realized how loud he was being. The queen and her grandmother were looking at them. They were not pleased.

Asa was embarrassed and said, "I'm sorry, my queen," and looked down at the latest course on his plate. Darion just kept laughing. Apparently, the king's brother didn't care what the two women thought of him.

Asa whispered to Darion, "You're going to get me into trouble," but Asa was smiling anyway.

CHAPTER 29
TO RULE THE PAPER KINGDOM

The funeral of the king was scheduled when the sun was at its highest point in the sky. The firstcouncilor went over everything Asa was supposed to do that day, which wasn't much. Asa was relieved to find that out.

Asa was informed they were going to make an alliance with the queen. But he wasn't so sure that it was the best idea. He liked Darion. He reminded him of Asa's oldest brother who had a wicked sense of humor. Asa had always looked up to his eldest brother. Asa asked Trunculin, "But isn't Darion supposed to take over when the king dies?"

"My king, this situation is very complicated. The law is not entirely clear. There has been precedent for both the queen of a dead king ruling and of the brother taking over…" Trunculin began.

Asa interrupted, "But Darion was telling me…"

"…. If you would please let me finish. What I was going to say is that, most of the time, the law does favor another male family member becoming king," Trunculin said. "That is true, but there are other considerations other than the law. An alliance with the brother, who is far less connected or respected, would yield us very little. An alliance with the queen, who has very powerful alliances, and a much more respected family name…"

"But what's more important than the law? Aren't I like the protector of the law?" asked Asa innocently.

"If you would… please… stop interrupting me," Trunculin's tone turned harsh, and they both noticed. Trunculin paused and calmly continued. "My king, yes, you are right that the law should be the first thing we think about. But the second thing we must be, is practical. The queen is much more predictable. We already know what she wants and she's already signaled what she will give us. Plus, if we ever need a favor down the road, she knows far more influential and important people to help us. You see?"

"I guess… It just seems like maybe the queen is hiding something from us. I mean, she seems nice and everything. It's just ... I get a weird feeling that she's not telling us the truth, somehow." Asa seemed a little confused again. "But you know best. I'm sorry, I really don't know what I'm doing most of the time. I trust you."

"Thank you, my king, that's all I've ever wanted," Trunculin said.

The firstcouncilor explains that the queen would speak, and then Darion would speak, then the funeral pyre would be lit. Asa had only seen a dead person once, his grandfather. He only saw him for a few moments until his mother made him leave the room. Asa had never seen a body burn before. He was not looking forward to that part. Sitting there waiting, his mind turned to the practical things: *How long will it burn? Will there be a bad smell?*

There were thousands of people assembled for the funeral. Earlier in the day, the people could walk by the king's Pyre. Now, they were all in one area, behind guards. Asa noticed that many of them seemed to be genuinely sad. *He must've been a great king*. At this thought, Asa felt small again. He saw the giant statue peering over the kingdom and that made him feel small too. They would never build a statue of him, Asa realized. *No one will cry at my funeral.*

The queen began her speech. "Good people of Thure. Your king, my beloved husband, is dead. I will not lessen this occasion by speaking of the manner in which he was taken. His place amongst the great kings is secured by his good deeds and his love for you." She paused for a moment. "Those responsible have been repaid by the Gods for what they did. This is a day to remember what a great king he was. And, as his queen, I will fulfill every promise he made to you. His kindness, his combination of gentleness with his people and his strength against anyone who would speak out against our mighty Thure, these will be honored by your queen. We ruled this kingdom together and made alliances to keep the deep and longstanding peace for the love of you, the great people of Thure."

The firstcouncilor was nodding along with what she was saying, and looking around at the crowds. Asa looked at the crowds too and noticed that although many people were cheering for the queen, not everyone was.

"They say blood is thick, which is true. But the bonds of marriage and love are even stronger than blood. Today, I send my husband…" She paused and Asa could tell that she was on the verge of tears. The crowds quieted, waiting for her next word, "…send my husband to the Hall of the great kings. But tomorrow, I will still be your queen and ready to continue the great work that we have begun for all of you!"

With the last sentence everyone was cheering. The firstcouncilor looked very pleased.

It was time for Darion to speak. "Before I begin praising my brother, will you cheer one more time for our beautiful queen?" at which point the crowd cheered even louder. Darion glanced over to the queen and nodded. She smiled back at him courteously. "My brother was a great king and no words I say today can live up to the man that lays behind me. And I'm not here today to talk about myself or my family. But the queen did remind us of the strong bond of blood. I remember not just my brother, but the other kings that have been in my family over the centuries, and how long my family has been here in Thure."

The firstcouncilor glanced at the queen, whose face showed no emotion. She simply looked straight ahead.

Darion continued. "My family was born here. We have been in this kingdom for centuries. My family has seen other kingdoms come and go. But Thure has always been here, strong, like my brother. But what role do *you* have in deciding your own future? I know how smart all of you are, how good all of you are. The king knew it too. He loved you all, and I know that he cares what your future holds. Three cheers for our fallen king!" The crowds cheered very loudly, *but not as loudly as they have been for the queen, maybe,* Asa thought. It was hard to tell with crowds.

"You have power," Darion said. "The power of numbers. And a great people when they are together, united in one cause, can make their own decisions. All you have to do is decide in one voice what your future holds. Use your voice as one and tell your leaders what you will..." The crowds cheered very loudly again.

King Asa wasn't sure what was happening, so he leaned over to the firstcouncilor. Trunculin explained, "If they say in public, as one group, that they want Darion to be king, the queen will have no choice but to accept it, or turn against her own people and rule by force."

Asa looked at Darion, then back at the crowds. The queen's grandmother sat beside the queen and looked very angry. The queen's face didn't change. It still showed no emotion, but Asa thought that he saw her bow her head down just a little.

Darion continued, getting louder now. "So I say to you, how will you, the people of Thure, honor your king? Would you choose to honor the law as he did? To choose from your own people? Or from the people that have lived next to you for centuries? Or would you choose lawlessness and foreign blood?"

The crowd was cheering even louder. But then something strange happened. Half of the crowd quieted down. No one knew what was going on, until the giant airship burst out over a row of tall trees. Most people had never seen an airship before. The crowds were cheering very loud now, but it was for the airship, not Darion.

Before Darion could say another word, the queen took Asa by the hand and led him next to Darion and stood one step above him with Asa by her side. The airship was directly over them. She raised her hands with Asa's, and the crowd cheered so loud it was deafening.

The firstcouncilor stood as well, as did the queen's grandmother. They both looked directly at Darion. The queen and Asa stood with their hands together in partnership and alliance and looked out solemnly as the crowds cheered them on.

Darion bowed his head and started clapping for the queen. He took a step away from her. It was clear he had lost. Darion returned to his seat, as did king Asa.

The crowd got quiet again as the queen bowed her head. The airship had passed over them and was slowly floating away from the crowds, headed toward the sea.

"Let this fire burn in all of our hearts. To Russel, king of Thure." The queen gave the signal, and the fire bearers walked slowly to the king's pyre. The crowds were silent as the queen turned around to quietly gaze at the pyre.

Asa turned around looking for Darion, but couldn't see him anywhere. The queen gave the signal and the fire bearers lit the king's pyre. A new era in in the old kingdom of Thure had begun, as they watched the flames reach for the sky.

CHAPTER 30
MONSTER IN THE TREES

Gordon woke to the midday sun. He had no idea how long he'd slept, but it felt like he had been asleep for a week. He awoke to gentle singing and new cooking smells. Everything smelled delicious. He felt a pang of guilt. He slept soundly while Aline was out there somewhere, or worse…

He went out to see what the day would bring, while trying to figure out how to get Artoth. He knew it would not be easy. He didn't know how to communicate with these people. They had been so kind to him, he almost felt guilty leaving them. But he had to find out what happened to Aline. He would not lose hope that she was alive.

Lantovas still wanted to take him back to Thure without finding the actual murderers. And Gordon had no idea where the murderers were, exactly. All of his problems should have made him feel overwhelmed and hopeless, but somehow he thought there was a way forward. The happiness of these people seem to be infectious.

"Have you found a way to communicate with them?" Gordon said as he approached Lantovas in a group of people. They were all laughing together.

Lantovas was laughing too. "No, but they seem to like to laugh, especially about me trying to talk with them. I have been able to figure out that they're going on a hunt today. I think we have been invited." He turned back to the men and pretended like he was using a club, and then pointed to himself and Gordon. They all started nodding and saying something in their language. It was clear that they were indeed invited along.

Gordon did not know what kind of animals they were hunting. They were each given the club very much like the others had, and they set off on a path into the forest. They hadn't walked very far when they heard something rustling around in the brush ahead. The men got very quiet and started to separate out in a circle to try to surround whatever animal was there.

A wild pig with giant tusks broke out of the brush and ran down the trail, away from them. One of the men tried to jump on the animal and catch it, but he only landed on the ground empty handed. They all raced after the wild pig.

The pig cut back into some underbrush. Lantovas motioned that they should go farther around. Never having been on the hunt, Gordon listened to the guard. Just then, they heard a strange noise. Gordon was sure he had heard that sound before, but it sounded very far away. It was out of place in all this green, and Gordon tried to remember what it might be. It was not coming from the underbrush, and it was not made by any animal. *Rotators.*

Lantovas apparently heard the sound too. Without a word, he started running back towards the beach. Gordon followed him. The other men followed too, confused by the sound.

Lantovas was the first man on the beach and looked to the sky. An airship was floating in sight, but seemed to be flying away from them. It was very high up, Gordon thought, *probably to avoid the shadow fin creatures.*

The guard started to wave his arms wildly and jump around. Gordon panicked and leaped onto the man's back.

Lantovas said, "What… Gordon, what are you doing!?"

"If they find me, they're going to kill me," said Gordon, struggling to stay on the man's back.

Lantovas threw Gordon off easily and said, "Stop it. They are from your kingdom. They are not going to kill you. You're just afraid to face my queen," said Lantovas. "Damn it, boy, they didn't see us."

The guard started to run down the beach, waving his arms wildly and yelling again. Then there was another sound, this time coming from the trees. Apparently, the wild boar was running for the beach. The guard heard the noise and turned back to the trees. Before he could do anything, a giant gray beast came out of the jungle. It was on all four of its thick, muscular legs. The creature was looking at the sky, apparently investigating the strange sound as well.

Then the beast looked down and saw Lantovas.

The creature's feet looked more like giant hands. The creature was nearly twice as tall as Lantovas and grabbed with his two front legs, the ones like hands. The guard looked scared for only a moment, but bravely tried to deflect the animal's attack with his club. The creature was too large and too fast. He grabbed Lantovas around the arm holding the club. Before any of the other men could do anything, the creature had taken the guard back through the trees.

Gordon could barely believe what he had just seen. The men looked at each other, shaking their heads.

"We have to go after him!" pointing in the direction that the creature had gone. The men only shook their heads. "We. Go. Now." Gordon repeated.

The inked men looked at each other with concern. They spoke to each other rapidly in their language. The man with the eight on his neck seemed to be pointing in the direction that Lantovas had been taken.

The other men were shaking their heads. They were getting louder, but it was clear that Number Eight was losing the argument. Gordon tried to motion once more and even took a few steps, showing that he wanted to go after the creature, but it was no use. The men started walking back to their homes.

The airship was completely out of sight. Gordon could no longer hear any hint of the rotators. Gordon was torn. All he had was a shortknife and a club. The creature was huge. He had no chance of saving Lantovas on his own.

Gordon reluctantly followed the men back, not knowing what else to do. He felt completely helpless. It reminded him again how everything was out of his control.

The men quietly argued all the way back. Number Eight repeatedly pointing to the thick jungle forest. They arrived back in the village and went straight into the round building. They went to the man that Gordon thought of as their leader. The other men were clearly seeking his advice.

Gordon thought about the story from the night before. He thought it was about a man who had been their king, but had abused them so much that they rose up against him. Now, he wondered if it was supposed to be about the beast that they had just seen. Maybe it was both, somehow.

The men were talking very fast to their leader, who was listening very carefully and growing more concerned as they spoke. Number Eight started to make his case, and the leader listened to every word and nodded gravely.

The leader stood there for a moment, saying nothing as he put on his glasses. He noticed Gordon for the first time. He looked at his men, and then motioned for Gordon to come over to him.

Gordon went over, not knowing what to expect. He said something to Gordon in his language, realizing Gordon wouldn't understand what he was saying. So he gently took the club from Number Eight and raised it up in his hands and then made a sound. Then he put his hand over the top of the club and gently lowered the stick down and made another sound. Gordon thought he understood. Gordon carefully took his shortknife from its sheath and raised it up in the air.

The man nodded and smiled a sad smile. The leader started speaking very quickly to his men. Forming a plan or giving orders, Gordon wasn't sure, but it had the sense of action. Over the next half hour, the men came and went, and Gordon stayed with the leader and collected weapons.

The leader laid nets for fishing and some clubs together on a long table. He then went to different rooms of the building and came back with more weapons. He laid out spears and even more exotic weapons. He then led Gordon to a room he had not been in before. Along one wall, different things were hanging from a net on the wall.

The leader went to the back of the room and reached behind a broken wooden shield. He brought out a curved longknife. Gordon had never seen one with a curved blade. It had its own sheath, and when the leader slid it out, he could see that someone had taken very good care of it. It looked like it had been made yesterday.

The leader solemnly offered it to Gordon. Gordon looked confused. Was he really giving Gordon a longknife? Gordon took out his shortknife and showed it to the man. The man put his hand over the shortknife and shook his head, offering the longknife to Gordon again. This time, Gordon put away his shortknife and accepted it. It was much lighter than he expected as he hung it around his waist.

The leader nodded and they both left the room. Soon, they were on their way to find the beast.

CHAPTER 31
ROLL OF THE DICE

King Asa didn't like being alone. With Brenddel gone for the day with the airship, Asa had no one to talk to. He always imagined a king would be talking to people all day long: council members, his people, somebody. But it seemed like there was just a lot of sitting around and waiting.

He hoped being a king wasn't always going to be boring.

Asa tried to stay with Trunculin, since it was at least a person he knew. Besides the guards that they brought with them, the firstcouncilor was the only one that talked to him at all.

He had not seen the queen since the funeral. When he asked what they were going to do that night, Trunculin said, "Oh, I am sorry, my king, one of my agents has just arrived and we have much to discuss."

"When are we meeting with him?" asked the king excitedly. He was getting more eager to learn.

"My king, these things would just bore you. It is one of my jobs as firstcouncilor to save you from the boring details. I will meet with my agent and then I will report to you as to what was..."

"But wouldn't it be easier if I just came with you?" interrupted Asa.

".... My king!" Trunculin said, sounding annoyed, "...if I might finish what I was saying. The truth is that these issues are sensitive, and you have just begun your training. I'll be happy to tell you what was said and explain what it all means, later."

"I really want to come with you. I don't know anyone else here," Asa said, trying to sound confident and firm.

Trunculin walked very close to Asa and leaned over, his face right in front of the king's. He put his hand on one of Asa's shoulders and said, "I really think my way," he dug his thumb into Asa's shoulder blade, "would be best."

Asa winced in pain.

Before Asa knew what to do, Trunculin had released him and walked out of the room. Asa rubbed his shoulder. *That really hurt,* Asa thought. He started thinking about his family and how far away they were. *Everyone I've ever known is across the waters,* he thought.

Asa sat there for a while in his chamber, thinking fondly of the fights he had with his brothers. He took his shoes off, straightened himself and thought, *I am king. I am not going to sit in this room all night and do nothing*. So Asa did the only thing he had the power to do, he looked around.

He had only seen a few parts of the Thurian palace. Since there were a few of his guards, and the queen's guards everywhere in the palace, he felt safe enough to walk around by himself. If a guard stopped him, saying that he should wait for the firstcouncilor, he would simply say 'let me pass, I am king.' *Should be easy enough,* he thought.

The fact he was king had not set in completely. *I have some power now,* Asa thought, *I can do what I want.* There was no parent telling him to wash his face or put his shoes on, and no brother hitting him for no reason. He wondered briefly if a guard should walk with him, but strangely enough, the guards didn't pay any attention to him at all. It was almost as if they couldn't see him.

Asa walked around his own level of the palace. He then went down a long, ornate staircase that wound down into the next level. There were people everywhere, but no one seemed to pay him any attention.

In a way, he felt like he was just any other boy that no one noticed. He wasn't sure if he liked that or not. As he wandered, he heard people having fun chatting about things he didn't understand. Then from up ahead, he heard some men shouting and laughing. It sounded like they were having fun, so Asa walked into the narrow corridor and saw a group of men kneeling on the ground.

"Three kings!" one man said, and most of the men cheered, all but a few.

"Three kings and four queens, a full palace. And some very happy kings, I'll wager..." And all the men cheered and laughed as he got closer. He looked closer at what they were doing. Apparently, they were throwing king dice on the floor. He could see piles of coin and realized the men were gambling.

Some of the men finally noticed him and turned around. One man stood up and held his hand out. "No strangers here, boy."

All the men had stopped and were looking at Asa. A voice from behind the man said, "Better be careful now, you don't want to start a war between our kingdoms."

The man looked at Asa uncertainly. The voice continued, "Don't you know who this is? You are talking to a king. Good King Asa, do you want me to cut his throat right here for his insolence? Or should we just send them all to the prisons?" asked Darion, the king's brother. The other men all looked a little nervous.

"No, we can just boil one of his legs in oil," said Asa, playing along.

"Are you sure? You know, back in the old days, they would take four horses and tie one leg and one arm to each horse and have them run in different directions. You think this offense rises to that punishment, my king?" said Darion in a serious tone.

"Or… we could just throw dice," said Asa.

All the men started to laugh. All, except for the man that had almost gotten thrown into prison. He slowly realized it was all a jest.

As they sat down and rolled the dice, Darion gave Asa some coin, since Asa didn't have any with him. He really had no idea who paid for everything. He almost thought about asking the firstcouncilor, but decided he did not want to think about Trunculin right now, or anything else but being around other people.

"So what's a king doing walking around our palace? And barefooted, I see," asked Darion between throws.

"I don't know. Not much. I'm finding you don't have many friends when you're king. I hadn't thought of that before."

Darion agreed. "That is true enough. You have allies, enemies, and subjects. Sometimes they are all three at the same time. But kings have few friends."

"Where did you go after the funeral?"

"Honestly? To get drunk," he said, lifting the cup sitting next to him on the floor. He took a long swallow. "To forget my troubles for a while. No place for the little brother of a dead king, apparently."

Other men were throwing dice and cheering, and others sulked and yelled when they lost.

"I'm sorry. I didn't know any of that was going to happen," said the young king.

"Forget it," said Darion. "None of that had anything to do with you. The story of the families of Thure is long and bitter."

"What will you do now?"

"Travel. I'm off to see the world. You see, I figure if I go off and become famous for some high adventure, I can come back the conquering hero and maybe the people will love me more. Or at least notice me. I'm sure it's hard to be a young king, but it's just as hard to be a king's younger brother," said Darion.

Asa thought about that and realized in many ways they were both powerless, "I only have older brothers. You should have seen the look on their faces in the crowd when my name was called. I'm pretty sure my oldest brother caught a fly. His jaw was wide open!"

Darion had just been taking a sip and nearly spit it out. As he laughed, he managed, "Would have paid to see that."

Asa said, "I think I'd rather go anywhere, than go back to my kingdom and be king. This is one of the first times I've laughed since I was chosen."

"People would certainly talk about you. A young king throws down his crown and runs towards adventure. They might write songs about you."

Asa said, "Probably not. They might have if Skyler had been chosen. He's the leader of my friends. Or my friend Gordon… I still can't believe he's dead. Even Gordon would have been a more famous king than me."

"Your *friend*, Gordon? You actually knew the king that was chosen before you?" Darion put his cup down and seemed to get more serious.

"Oh, yeah. We were close friends. We grew up together. In fact, we put our names in the tower on the same day," answered Asa.

Darion asked, "So two boys that just happen to be childhood friends, out of your entire, vast kingdom, were chosen just days apart?"

"Yes. I hadn't really noticed the… strangeness of that before. How likely is that?" asked Asa.

Darion pointed at the dice. "About as common as me rolling seven kings, 1000 times in a row," said Darion, looking directly in Asa's eyes to make sure he understood how impossible it really was.

Asa didn't say anything for a few moments. Nor did Darion. They just sat there thinking about what it all might mean. Another man threw the dice. They clicked into place as the man rolled seven kings.

CHAPTER 32
ROASTED ALIVE

The longknife hung at his side. It was light, but he felt a new weight of responsibility. He had no idea what was going to happen next, but they were slowly creeping towards a clearing in the trees where they thought the creature might be. Gordon hoped they weren't too late.

As they approached it, they could just see through heavy underbrush. The leader signaled to the men silently, and motioned for them to go in different positions. The leader took Gordon with him. They quietly pushed through the green leaves to get a better look at what was happening in the clearing.

The man that had hunted Gordon over the open ocean was naked and tied to a log. Gordon couldn't tell if he was alive or not. He looks for the beast, but he couldn't see anything. A moment later, the beast walked into the opening on the other side of the clearing. Gordon hadn't heard it coming and wondered how something so big could make so little noise.

It was carrying some sticks. There were other sticks and leaves underneath the guard and the log. The sticks in the creature's hands looked different. The beast was standing on its rear legs now, but it looked nothing like a man. It had thick grey matted fur all over its body, and walked clumsily, like it belonged on all four legs. As the creature came near Lantovas, it took the sticks one by one and twisted them.

Gordon had never heard of another creature using hands like a man. As it took the sticks and twisted them in its hand, they seem to crumble. When they did, they released some sort of milky liquid. It did this with five sticks and then put the sticks on the pile under Lantovas. It went back on all fours and stood a few feet away from the pile under the naked man. Lantovas was still not moving. Gordon could now see some blood and scrapes on Lantovas' face and arms. He hoped that Lantovas was only knocked out.

Gordon started to feel light headed. He suddenly realized that he had not eaten anything. *Not now,* he thought as he began to sweat. He knew they would act soon and was hoping the leader would give some type of signal. Gordon blinked to unblur his eyes, as he willed himself to be okay.

It was starting to get dark, and they saw tiny lights appearing, floating in midair. They seemed to come from all directions out of the forest.

Gordon saw tiny dots of light landed on the pile with the milky liquid. As soon as the little lights had landed there, the creature got up and ran towards them, making loud shrieking sounds and waving his arms wildly. It was almost as though the beast was trying to swat flies away from his meal.

He realized they were fire bugs. The creature was exciting them so they would explode. He saw that there was a plume of fire where the little lights used to be. Quickly, all of the lights turned into little sparks of fire. Gordon looked on, and now the pile of brush underneath the naked man was burning.

The beast's back turned toward them, the leader shouted something, and all the men jumped out of the underbrush and towards the beast. Gordon followed, taking the longknife from its sheath. The beast was startled for a second, but its fear turned into rage. The warriors were trying to circle the beast, but the beast swung its great arms. The first man that rushed the beast got picked up and thrown deep into the brush.

The beast was enormous, as tall as two men, and nearly as wide. Its arm-like-legs were much longer than its body, able to reach out and lash out at anything that got in its way.

All the men were shouting and rushing at the beast. The monster couldn't figure out where to send its rage first. Gordon decided to try to help Lantovas. The man was just waking up and realized there was a fire underneath him. He pulled at the vines he was tied with. Luckily, the beast had not seen Gordon yet.

He started to throw dirt on the fire. The flames were getting higher and the milky substance made a terrible smell, like burning sweet salt. Lantovas was groaning, as the fire was starting to heat up his skin. Gordon couldn't get the fire completely out, so he tried to cut the vines with his longknife. He went around and cut the vines between the man's hands. Lantovas yelled as fire touched his skin. The creature saw Gordon for the first time and let out a terrible sound.

The beast ran and groped for Gordon, who ducked just in time. His knife was stuck under the vines trying to cut them. Gordon pulled the knife toward him, cutting the vines from underneath. Lantovas was free from the log, and they both rolled away from the beast's grip.

The other men were screaming at the beast, driving their spears and weapons into its fur. With one great arm, the beast swatted away their weapons as it kept grabbing for his meal with the other.

Gordon had nearly rolled onto his longknife. Pulling the blade out from underneath him before he got cut, he was safe from his knife, but not from the beast. In one quick movement, the beast grabbed Gordon by the leg and flung him across the clearing. Then he took Lantovas and put him directly on the fire. The guard screamed. Gordon got up, instinctively ran at the beast, slicing at the beast's hand. It hit its target. The beast let go of the man's ankle. Lantovas hurried off the fire and onto the sand.

The other men had closed in on the beast from behind, and the beast howled as several spears were stabbed into its back. The beast wheeled around on the men, knocking them all to the ground. The beast grabbed at its back to try to get the spears. Gordon went to Lantovas to make sure he was okay.

The beast went over to a tree and knocked the spears out of its back, all at once. There were two men standing near, the leader and Number Eight, but they were trying to attend the other fallen men before the creature could attack again. The beast decided against his toasted meal and went for the leader instead.

Number Eight leapt at the monster and swung his heavy club at the beast's face. This hurt the beast, and it staggered backwards. The monster grabbed Number Eight's club and flung both he and his club into the brush. The beast was more enraged and grabbed at another man on the ground nearby. He picked up the man and threw him over the trees.

The leader screamed at the beast and charged it with his own knife. The monster was facing away from Gordon, so Gordon ran at the back of the beast and slashed, using all his strength with his curved longknife. He connected with the beast's leg. It didn't feel like Gordon did much damage, but the great beast had lost its balance and was tumbling.

It tripped backwards and landed right on the fire. The beast let out another wild, inhuman cry as his matted fur immediately caught fire. It scrambled to stand up out of the fire on its back legs, screaming the entire time.

It lost all interest in the men and rushed toward the forest. The leader was standing right in the beast's way. The beast grabbed the leader and hurled him right into Gordon.

Gordon's world went dark.

CHAPTER 33
TRUE NATURE

"How did you know I needed good news today?" said the firstcouncilor as he settled a little deeper into his chair, cup of wine in hand.

"It goes well in Extatumm, it is true," said the small councilor. "They have built them much faster than expected. They seemed to understand the plans immediately and have already made big leaps in design. I just don't know how much longer they can keep such a big thing secret."

Trunculin said, "Extatumm is well secluded from the rest of the kingdoms. As our plans get closer to execution, the secrecy has gotten deeper, as agreed. There have been rumors swirling for years. But there will be a time soon to reveal some of my plans. You have done well Arasta, better than I ever could have asked for."

"Thank you, firstcouncilor, I appreciate you choosing me to conduct this important mission. It is an honor," said Arasta.

"Well, I always knew there was something special about you. So how is it in Extatumm… really?"

"It's a very interesting place. It's almost like a kingdom, one of many contradictions. The transformation from Dard to

Extatumm was based on the idea of equality for all the people, and they still preach that today in public. If you talk to anyone in the markets or on the streets, they talk of the leader TrTorrin like he's a god, not a man. They all call him the father. The people don't seem to notice that they are still looking up to leaders, not equals. There is no real freedom there. It is the best of all worlds," Arasta said.

"But there are choosing's? Or some sort of elections, are there not?" asked Trunculin.

Arasta said, "Oh yes, they have elections of what they call an 'outer counsel.' You can be on this counsel for three years. Then you can be on a lesser counsel for three years and then after the three years, you can be reelected to the outer council again."

Trunculin said, "Let me guess. The same people keep getting elected year after year and just rotate between the councils?"

"Yes, it is a perfect circle. The same leaders are always in control," Arasta confirmed.

"And the people don't seem to notice?" asked the firstcouncilor.

Arasta replied, "Strangely enough, they do not."

Both men laughed at this, as they drink their wine.

"The timeline is still good for the meeting?" asked Trunculin.

"Actually, I was going to ask you the same question. Has the Gordon business changed anything?" asked Arasta.

Trunculin replied, "No, not at all. A mere bump. In fact, I need you to return right away to make sure TrTorrin and the rest know that all is well."

"Yes, firstcouncilor, I expected that. What about…"

The door opened and a boy walked in. Arasta looked over Trunculin's shoulder to the intruder, "We don't require anything, boy. You may leave us."

The boy said, "Excuse me, Trunculin, could I have a few words about..."

The firstcouncilor jumped out of his chair and nearly spilled his wine, "My king, how did you... that is, what can I do for you?"

Arasta was out of his chair quickly. They both went to the king, and Arasta bowed at the waist.

Trunculin said, "My king, Arasta is one of my assistants, and has been traveling."

Arasta finished, "I beg your forgiveness, my king. I was unaware of what you looked like."

"This is one of my assistants Arasta.... as I've said, as he said... what do you need, my king?" Trunculin tried to regain his composure.

Asa looked at the man next to Trunculin and said, "I would prefer to have a moment alone, firstcouncilor," said Asa seriously.

"This is one of my most trusted assistants, my king. Whatever you can say in front of me, you can say in front of him. His loyalty is clad in iron."

Asa looked at the small man again and immediately did not trust him. Arasta looked back at the king in a way that made him uncomfortable, "I really need to speak to you alone," said the young king.

Trunculin stepped towards the king until he was very close, and looked down on Asa. He said in a very serious voice, "And I have told you that Arasta can be trusted," Asa took a step back, remembering how Trunculin had hurt his shoulder earlier. Trunculin continued, "This might be a good time, my little king, to explain how things really work. You are the king for the people. You are trotted out for meals, and you waive and you smile. Besides that, you do exactly as I say every other moment of your day. Perhaps I should have made that clear earlier. Do you understand me now?"

A small smile formed on the other man's face.

Asa didn't know what to do. He did not expect the firstcouncilor to speak in this way and it frightened him, but he didn't want the other man to know he was scared. He was the king, whether Trunculin liked it or not. He looked at the other man. Asa tried very hard not to even blink and said, "I understand that the king is at the top of the triangle and you are far below," he said defiantly.

Asa saw Trunculin's face change completely. He almost looked like a different person. Trunculin raised his hand to hit Asa. The other man was quick to catch the firstcouncilor's hand, and the Trunculin slowly lowered it. Arasta looked down and let go of his hand, not knowing if he had done the right thing.

Trunculin bent lower until he was eye to eye with the king, "My little king. Fate may choose the king, but fate also causes accidents. No one is safe from the winds of fortune. I wonder how sad your parents would be if one or two of your brothers drown in that lake by your house?"

Asa's mouth dropped open.

Trunculin continued, "Do you understand me now? Good night, little king. Don't soil your bed dreaming of your dead brothers."

The other man was openly smiling now, but it was not a smile Asa had ever seen. It was how a snake smiled when it saw a mouse. Asa walked out of the room.

Just outside the room, Darion was waiting for Asa. Darion began, "What did he…?"

Asa stopped and closed his eyes. Darion stopped speaking. Asa knew if he spoke at that very moment, he might let the fear take hold. As they walked away from the room down the corridor, Asa was angry and scared all at the same time. He needed answers, and he knew of no one that would be honest with him. Brenddel had still not returned.

Asa said to Darion, "I need a favor."

Darion said, "What do you need?"

The young king told him, and Darion smiled. They both hurried off.

CHAPTER 34
PATH TO TRUTH

Darion led Asa into the lower levels of the palace. They passed many guards, until they reached the lowest level. They came to a large metal door with a small sliding window in it. Darion knocked on the door, and the smaller window slid open. Darion said to the man behind the door, "Ah, Tobee, I thought you might be on duty tonight. We need to see somebody, open the door."

Tobee replied, "Sorry, not for these prisoners. I have special orders not to let anyone in. Only the queen, that firstman and the councilor fellow from the other kingdom can see them."

"You know, this might get very awkward," said Darion, "You see, this is the king from that very kingdom. He's in charge of the firstman and the firstcouncilor fellow."

Asa said, "Can you please open the door, Tobee?"

The small window slid shut loudly. Darion smiled at Asa. There was a clicking sound and the door opened. As they walked through the door, the guard scowled at them. Darion and Asa nodded their thanks. As they were walking further down the hallway of cells, Darion whispered to Asa, "I'm glad that worked. I thought I was going to have to threaten him with some rumors I've heard about him and his best friend's wife."

They hurried down the hallway and got to the last set of cells. In the cell on the left, they saw a man sleeping on his bed. In the cell on the right, Loren was leaning against the bars. As they approached, he said, "Asa? What are you doing here?"

"Not the best way to talk to your new king," said Darion.

The man in the other cell sat up on his bed.

"King Asa. Of course. I heard you were chosen," said Loren.

Asa went closer to the bars and said, "Hello Loren. I was chosen, and I'm beginning to think there's more going on than I was told. I don't see anyone else I can trust."

Loren replied, "I will answer any question that I can."

Asa asked, "First, how is it that I was chosen right after Gordon? It seems too strange."

Loren said, "It isn't strange. I think the firstcouncilor meant to choose you. It certainly wasn't fate. The choosing has been rigged for years. Trunculin has ways of hiding the truth."

"Well, that would explain that," said Darion.

Asa reasoned, "But if that's true, that means Gordon wasn't chosen by fate either. Do you know Gordon is...?"

Loren bowed his head and said, "Yes, I know. The firstcouncilor came down here and told me personally. He couldn't wait to give me the news."

Asa said, "I still can't believe it."

Loren said, "I can't either."

Asa asked, "So then...who made Gordon king? Why did he run?"

"Asa, there is so much more going on than you realize, that I don't know where to begin," Loren said. "We didn't run by choice. Gordon was going to be killed. He had already been poisoned after he collapsed at the crowning ceremony. For some reason, the firstcouncilor chose you. But someone in our movement decided it should be Gordon instead. I don't know why. I haven't talked to the man who made that decision."

"What movement?" asked Darion.

"Why is Darion of Thure suddenly so interested in the politics of another kingdom?" asked the voice from the other cell.

"Denogg of the great family Xoss. I heard that they had put you down here. I guess that's how you get repaid for hiring the wrong people, Denny," said Darion.

Denogg replied, "Very strange that you say that. Only a very, very few people know what actually happened in my home. What makes you think it was a servant?"

Darion replied, "I can hear the implication in your voice, Denny. I hear all the rumors. No, I did not poison my brother. I loved him. It's a shame about your fortune, now that Gordon is dead. The queen now has your coin to go along with her good name."

Loren said, "Asa, listen to me. You have to be very care. Trunculin is the most dangerous man I know…"

"The second most dangerous," said Brenddel, coming up behind them.

Asa and Darion turned around, startled.

Brenddel said, "Whenever I get back from patrol, the first thing I do is make sure the prisoners are where they're supposed to be," said Brenddel looking straight into Loren's eyes, "We don't need your lies in the king's head, healer."

No one said anything.

Brenddel broke the silence. "I think it would be best if I escorted you to your chambers, my king."

"Yes, I think I'd better go to bed too," said Darion. "There's only so much a man can take in one day. If I may take my leave, my king?"

Asa nodded to Darion. Darion left, nodding to both men in the cells. Brenddel waited for the king to come with him. Asa turned around to look at Loren for a moment, but Loren and Denogg had both faded back into the shadows. Asa and Brenddel left without another word.

They walked toward king Asa's room in silence until Asa finally asked, "Aren't you going to ask me what I was doing down there?"

"It is not the place of the firstman to ask the king why he does what he does. My job is to keep you safe, guarding you personally, when I can. I'm sorry I had to leave you today," replied Brenddel.

"Are you going to tell the firstcouncilor where I was?"

Brenddel replied, "I am your firstman; therefore, my duty is to you first. Although, I am required to answer any questions asked by the firstcouncilor. So, if he ever asks me if you were in the prisons talking to Gordon's uncle, while in the presence of the dead king's brother, I would have to say... yes."

"Do you think he'll ask you?" said Asa.

Brenddel replied, "Well, my king, if you were him, would you ask that question exactly like that?"

Asa smiled and said, "Probably not."

"Probably not," Brenddel said as they continued on to the king's chamber.

CHAPTER 35
DANCE FOR THE DEAD

Floating in the ocean. The water was clear and he stayed afloat for a while. Then, unseen, something began pulling him under. He could feel his mouth filling with liquid. He surfaced again, but his mouth filled again…

Gordon woke up, turned his head to one side, coughing up water. He immediately felt the weight of his aching body bring him back to reality. He hurt everywhere. Gordon realized someone had been giving him water. He blinked repeatedly to clear his vision and said, "Thank you, but I don't need more water."

"Yes you do," a familiar voice said. "But I didn't mean to nearly drown you with it."

"Aline? Is it really…how did you? Where have you…?" Gordon tried to rise out of bed, and was stopped by the pain in his chest and stomach. Aline gently laid him back down.

"Be careful, my king, I know I'm not a healer like Loren, but I can tell that you need to rest," said Aline.

His uncle. He was suddenly ashamed that he had forgotten his uncle, even for a moment. He feared the two men that had murdered the king of Thure would never be found, that he would never get out of this place. But now, Aline was here and alive to give him hope.

"What happened to you?" asked Gordon.

"Well, I found out that I really don't like to travel by watership. I lost track of you when I was swept off deck, but I saved most of my gear, including my weapons. I was far away from the ship when it went down. I was able to float on a barrel from the ship for most of that next morning. A fishing ship came along and they brought me back to Aspora. I was finally able to make a connection with Mantuan."

Gordon asked excitedly, "You found him?"

Aline said, "More like he found me. The sailors had been looking for us. They were friendly with Mantuan and our people in Aspora."

Gordon asked, "I'm so glad you're okay."

Aline smiled, "I'm glad you're okay, as well, my king. Your sweetblood was not in balance. If that thing hadn't knocked you out, you would have fainted. Your body water tested at only thirty six parts sweet. That is dangerously low. Thankfully, Loren showed me how to test it a few times. You need to eat when you're supposed to."

Gordon replied, "I was a little busy. The sweetblood and fighting monsters don't go together. Wait, did you see… did you take…? I mean…" he said, looking down at his body.

Aline smiled, "Don't worry. Mantuan took your body water. They wouldn't even let me watch..."

"Mantuan? He's here?" despite the pain, Gordon rose out of bed and stood on shaky legs, "I can rest later."

Aline said, "Well, since you are the king and you did help fight that monster last night, I suppose I have no choice but to obey. Here, let me help." Aline offered her arm for Gordon to steady himself. "Let's go see Mantuan."

They came out of the large, round structure. It was almost dark. Gordon realized he must've slept for almost an entire day.

He half-walked and half-wobbled into the clearing with Aline's help.

There was a large gathering of people. He heard a loud booming voice in the language of the people here, but it did not sound like the leader. As they approached the group, the men and women were all laughing and talking back and forth in their strange musical language. He was glad to see Number Eight laughing as well, with only a few scratches.

Lantovas was also there. He had healing cloth around his chest and scratches on his face and arms, but looked otherwise alright. Lantovas came to Gordon. He went down on one knee in front of him and said, "I was wrong to doubt you. I've never seen someone your age be so brave. Thank you for saving my life, Gordon. "

Gordon was embarrassed. "Please, stand up. I was only one person last night. There were lots of us there. I couldn't just let that thing eat you."

The man rose and stretched out his hand for Lantovas. "Not too hard, my king, I'm still sore from last night."

Gordon replied, "Me too, maybe shaking hands wasn't such a good idea." They both laughed. "What was that thing anyway?"

Aline said, "It was what the people here call a Fasgonn. From what they tell us, it likes the meat cooked."

Lantovas said, "Lucky me. I guess I looked like a hearty meal."

That made Gordon laugh, which he found out was the last thing his achy body wanted. Aline and Lantovas helped Gordon to the group of men, where they could sit. As Gordon got closer, a great cheer came up among the men. At first he thought they were cheering for Mantuan or Lantovas, but he quickly realized they were cheering for him. Gordon blinked and didn't know what to say.

A large man said, "It is not a small thing to command the respect of the Copway people. You have made quite the impression, my king."

The man walked up to Gordon. He was huge. Gordon thought he must be nearly seven feet high, with huge arms and legs like tree trunks. He had a black leather patch over his eye. As he approached, Gordon tried not to stare at the patch.

"Everyone stares at the patch, my king, it's alright to look," Mantuan said as he extended his arm to Gordon, who winced as he extended his own arm in friendship. Mantuan's hand could've wrapped around Gordon's entire wrist.

"It's so good to finally meet you. I've heard…" Gordon said, stopping himself, "… actually, not very much about you at all."

Mantuan let out a large, long laugh. "Aline, you are right. I think we've found the right king."

"I think I need to sit down again," said Gordon. Aline and Mantuan helped him sit down.

"Loren taught Aline how to keep your body in balance while you slept. Are you feeling well?" asked Mantuan.

"I feel alright, just very sore. That thing last night… I guess it took a lot out of me," replied Gordon.

"I would imagine. The Copway never hunt those creatures. Too dangerous. They rarely come out in the day. It probably was agitated by the sound of the airship that passed by," Mantuan said. "You are lucky you weren't spotted, by the way."

"How do you know so much about these people? Why do you speak their language? Where are we, exactly? I'm sorry, I have a lot of questions," said Gordon.

"Of course you do. We are on the island lands of Yajan. And these are the Copway people," Mantuan said. "Since I have been 'dead' to the rest of the world, I have had to travel over many lands. The Copway do trading with Aspora and a few others. Mostly they keep to themselves, but I have been honored to be taught their language. Once you learn the melody, it never leaves you. And once you meet people that are good in their hearts like the Copway, that doesn't leave you either. It's not an easy language, but it is beautiful when you get it right. I'm glad they took you in. We feared that we had lost you forever."

Gordon asked, "Who is we? What is going on exactly? I…I have so many questions."

The sun had gone down completely. It was dark, and the men who had been laughing and joking a few moments earlier were all quiet now. Mantuan joined in their somber mood. "I know you do, my king. But that will have to wait just a little longer. Now we have to send off the dead."

Gordon said, "Dead? You mean, from last night?"

"Yes, that monster killed two men last night. You are very lucky that you weren't one of them. But the men that did survive, did so because of your bravery. Everyone is proud of you, but we will have to get you trained a little more before you take on more monsters," Mantuan said. "Come. They want you to lead them down to the water."

"Me?"

"Yes. We will walk down to the beach and let their dead float out into the waters," Mantuan said. "There is no burial here."

"But won't they be eaten by… creatures in the water?" asked Gordon.

"They believe in a circular life. They release their dead to the waters which feeds the life out there, which, in turn, helps feed them later on."

Gordon almost thought it seemed like they were cannibals after all, in a way, by eating the creatures that had eaten their dead.

Mantuan continued. "It is also a practical idea; they have limited space on these islands. And beasts might dig up their dead if there were buried."

"I see," Gordon said, but still thought it a little strange. People only ever got buried in his own kingdom. But Gordon would honor the people that protected him, fed him, and saved him.

They all followed behind Gordon, musicians playing simple drums and wind instruments. The two dead men were carried on simple wooden rafts. They looked rickety and barely put together, but Gordon realized they would float for only a short time before sinking, which must be the point.

As they all solemnly walked in silence, Gordon couldn't help but feel responsible for their deaths. They would not have gone after that monster unless Gordon had insisted. He'd help save one life, but cost two. He didn't know how to live with that.

They arrived at the water's edge, and Gordon stood aside as they quietly placed the bodies and their shallow rafts into the waters. They waited a while until the tide was right, and then it took them out to sea.

Gordon stood there watching the low, small rafts go out. He wondered how long it would be until some creature dragged them under the water, not wanting to think about it, but thinking about it anyway. Aline put a hand on Gordon's shoulder, and then the musician's song changed, getting louder. It seems almost happy.

"What's happening?" asked Gordon.

Aline replied, "Now we celebrate the lives of those men. They look on the passing of these men as a celebration of their life. They believe their spirits go to a safe, happy island far away. They don't cry at funerals here."

They all walked back to the village at a faster pace. Along the way, many of the villagers were dancing and singing. Gordon and Mantuan were now at the end of the line of people. Up ahead, Aline started dancing.

Mantuan noticed Gordon looking at Aline. "She's wonderful, isn't she?"

Gordon realized he was staring at Aline. "Aline? Oh, well, she's… alright."

"I have known Aline since she was a young girl. You would be a fool not to be in love with her at least a little. She's beautiful, she's strong and she's funny. Granted, usually at the most inappropriate times…" said Mantuan.

Gordon said, "I haven't really seen the funny yet."

Mantuan laughed his large, full chested laugh. "No, I suppose visions, poisons and ship wrecks don't bring out the funny."

"I should be thinking of those men that died," said Gordon, looking down.

"I know you're feeling guilty. These are a peaceful people, but they know how to fight when necessary. They have told me what you asked them to do, and they were proud to fight with you. Sometimes, someone gets taken by a Fasgonn. They disappear, and the Copway believe that is the price they have to pay to live in peace. All they could talk about this morning was how it was right to fight for that man. They appreciated the fact that you brought out their courage."

"But two men died to save one man. How is that a good thing?"

"Two men died last night, but because you reminded them that sometimes you have to fight, how many will be saved in the future?" offered Mantuan.

Gordon just walked for a while, not saying anything. Mantuan did the same. When they had nearly returned to the village, Gordon said, "Will you answer my questions now?"

Mantuan said solemnly, "Yes, my king. This is a night for answers. You have certainly earned them."

CHAPTER 36
ANSWERS

The celebrations were getting louder. Aline was still dancing and having a good time. Gordon liked to see her smile. He hoped he would see more of that. Mantuan was also smiling and lifted his drink. Aline motioned for Mantuan to come join her dancing, but Mantuan waved her off. She gave up and kept dancing with the others.

"Where did you meet her?" asked Gordon.

"You might say we grew up together, in a way. I literally fell into her life and she into mine. Aline was living alone with the good people of the fortress. She was the first person I saw when I arrived there. She helped heal me, and I helped raise her up all these years. She's like the daughter I never had."

Gordon asked, "Was that in Aspora?"

"Yes. Aline has grown into a very fine warrior, too. She's had to, with all we've been through together," said Mantuan.

"There are so many questions that I want to ask. I almost don't know where to begin," said Gordon.

Mantuan said, "I understand. What's the first question that comes to mind?"

"Why do you wear a patch?" Gordon blurted out.

Mantuan let out such laughter that several people stopped dancing, but his laughter was contagious, and soon they were all laughing and went right back to dancing. "Of all the questions I was prepared to answer, that is the last one I thought you'd ask. And you know… it is quite the question."

Gordon said, "Sorry. If you don't want to…"

Mantuan replied, "No, no. I said I would answer any question and I will. I have been in many battles. I have fought creatures worse than you did last night. I have fought in wars with thousands of men. I have fought with, and against, every kind of weapon you can imagine. This patch is legendary. People used to talk about it in song and poem," he said, pointing to his own patch, "and you want to hear the strangest thing? No one has ever asked me why I wear it. Care to guess?" Mantuan stared at him.

Gordon guessed. "Was it a knife? Or an arrow?"

Mantuan did not immediately answer.

Gordon kept guessing, "Some type of fire that burned your eye? Was it acid?"

Mantuan said, "Keep guessing."

Gordon couldn't think of much else. "Umm… A snake bite…?"

Mantuan laughed, "No… but I like the snake idea. It was a tree."

Gordon didn't understand. "A tree? What do you mean?"

"Well, you see, my king, when I was a young man I'd already made a name for myself as a fighter. Coming back from a battle, we were all feeling good about the victory, and we were already reenacting the battle as we were walking back to camp. Our camp was in the woods, so as we were laughing and messing about, I tripped over my own foot and ran right into a big knot right where my eye was… and that was it."

"A tree poked out your eye? You mean… you mean it was just an accident?"

Mantuan raised his patch, and Gordon was surprised to see that his eye was still there. "Everyone thinks there's no eye under here, but it's there. It knocked me so hard that I fell to the ground. When I woke up, and ever since, I can see three of everything instead of one. It's no good seeing three warriors coming at you with a longknife when there is really only one. So, I wear the patch. I've been fighting with one eye so long that it actually serves me better than both my eyes did."

As Mantuan put the patch back in place, Gordon asked, "So all the battles you were in, and all the fights and all the training, you can't use your eye because of a tree?"

Gordon didn't know how big a laugh could be until he heard Mantuan, who laughed loudly again. "Accidents do happen, my king, to everyone. When I am in battle, I am always protective of my eyes. It's when you're not paying attention that bad things happen," he tapped his eye patch. "Believe me, it's a lesson everyone needs to learn."

Gordon sat there, thinking on the idea.

Mantuan said, "Come, my king, there must be something more important than that you want to ask me."

"Well, I guess I want to know, well… who are you and what is going on exactly?" asked Gordon.

Mantuan said, "Right to the point, good. I suppose with the speed everything is happening to you, that no one's really explained it all. I used to be the firstman of the kingdom."

"You were firstman? When?"

"Before Brenddel," said Mantuan.

"But… but you don't have any firstman stripes," Gordon said.

Mantuan laughed, "Firstman stripes are there for the ceremony. Brenddel had them permanently inked on his own face. I just painted mine on before ceremonies and battles."

I served the king, but when the king died, I was no longer useful. I was suddenly an enemy of my kingdom and literally thrown out. I was taken in by a small group of good people. That's where I met Aline. She was like an orphan in a place that didn't know what to do with orphans. She latched on to me and I trained her to be the warrior that she is now."

Gordon asked, "Orphan? But I've met her mother, Sandrell."

"Yes, she has a mother, but Sandrell was away. Sometimes by choice, sometimes not. It's a complicated thing between them," Mantuan said.

"I guess that's why Aline didn't seem very happy to see her," Gordon said.

"It's a long story, but it's not mine to tell. You can ask Aline about that another time. Although, I don't think she would tell you everything," cautioned Mantuan.

"Aline said that you are the reason that I was chosen king. Is that true?" Gordon asked.

Mantuan looked directly into Gordon's eyes and said, "Yes, it's true."

Gordon asked, "But why?"

"It doesn't seem like it should be, but that's a complicated answer. There is far more going on than you know. Plans that have been in the works for many years by the firstcouncilor and others to completely change the kingdom. Trunculin has had power for a long time. He controls both councils and has controlled most of the kings," said Mantuan.

"But I don't understand. The two councils were supposed to be independent of each other, and the king is supposed to be independent of them. They make the laws together, like three sides of a triangle, each equal to each other."

"That's right, my king, the three sides of the triangle are supposed to weigh against each other, so that no one side of the triangle has more power than the other," said Mantuan. "But that is not how it has worked for a very long time. There are many of us that know Trunculin has changed the very nature of how our kingdom works, so that the power of the kingdom is his to wield in secret. I saw this myself as firstman. It took me a long time, but I slowly realized that the kingdom I thought I was living in, was not the kingdom that the first thirteen had envisioned."

Gordon said, "But how can that be? There is still a king. And there are still two councils that make laws."

"It only appears that way. Trunculin controls everything. That's why he hand picks the king. He picks boys that are easy to manipulate, easy to fool and easy to control. He would never have chosen you, because you are too strong and smart," said Mantuan.

Gordon was a little embarrassed. He certainly didn't feel special in any way. "So why did *you* choose me then? I'm nobody."

Mantuan said, "You are not nobody. But Loren would never have agreed to you being chosen king. I feel badly about not telling him first. But it had to be done. You are important in many ways. By choosing you, we sent a clear message to the firstcouncilor that his days of control are coming to an end. We had hoped to surround you with people in our cause while you were king, to teach you and to show you what was really going on. We have a large group of people in our cause, even some close to Trunculin. As king, you could have publically challenge Trunculin's lies and removed him from power. We did not count on how much the firstcouncilor was willing to go to control you. I didn't think he would actually try to kill you. We also didn't expect you to have that vision."

"What happened to me? What did that vision mean?" asked Gordon.

Mantuan shook his head. "The truth is, we don't know. We suspect that Trunculin uses mystics to help him control the minds of the other kings, and maybe some councilors as well. I believe a mystic was inside your head trying to plant some thought, or to control you when it triggered something like a dream vision."

"I don't understand. I'm not a mystic, I don't get visions."

Mantuan said, "The fact that you had this dream, this glimpse, means something. But I'm more concerned about what else you saw. Aline tells me that there were many kingdoms at war."

"Yes, it was like the world was on fire and everyone was fighting each other. Trunculin is the shadow, which makes sense now. In the last one there were two shadows. But, the part that worries me the most is that I was falling from an airship."

"Yes, my king, I recommend you don't do that. It isn't much fun," Mantuan said with a smile.

Gordon replied, "Well, I sure don't plan to. But, what does all the fighting mean?"

"I can only guess. Maybe he's making secret alliances or starting friction between kingdoms that will end very badly for us all," replied Mantuan.

When Gordon tried to think about it, the concept was just too distant. He was worried about immediate problems, "What about Uncle Loren? How are we going to get him out of prison?"

"We have to prove your innocence. We can't risk getting him out by force. That would make it appear like you're both guilty. No, we have to continue your quest to find the people that poisoned the king of Thure. We leave tomorrow morning for Artoth, the kingdom of the gods."

Aline was still dancing with some Copway people. She came over to Mantuan. She took his hand and made him get up to dance. Gordon smiled, wanting to watch the great warrior dance. To his horror, Aline took Gordon's hand too. He stopped smiling as he was led to dance. He resisted, but Aline was determined. He swallowed hard and thought that he would rather face another monster than embarrass himself in front of Aline.

CHAPTER 37
STRANGE ALLIANCE

"To what do I owe this... honor?" said the queen's Grandmother as Darion entered her chamber.

Darion said, "I've always felt that you and I started out badly. Maybe it was something that I said or maybe something you said. I've always thought that we were more alike than we care to admit."

"We are nothing alike. One of the reasons I don't like you is that you lie to get what you want, instead of just saying what you mean," said the grandmother.

"I suppose I have no talent for being blunt. But I will try. I believe you and I can help each other. I have an idea, and you could help me see it through," offered Darion.

"Why would I help you do anything? You tried to keep my granddaughter from the throne."

Darion said, "I tried to keep her away from *my* throne. You know the law and so does she. But the people have spoken and she is in, and I am out. I understand that. But what she needs now is an alliance. A true alliance with other kingdoms so that she can be insulated from anyone trying to overthrow her."

"The only person that would try to overthrow me, is you, dear brother-in-law," said the queen as she entered the chamber. "What is he doing here, grandmother?"

The grandmother replied, "Trying to convince me of something. He still hasn't gotten to the point. Spit it out boy! What do you want?"

Darion began, "We all know Gordon didn't poisoned the king. I want the true murderers discovered. And the people want justice. A public execution of the boy's uncle is a terrible way to follow up a funeral. They don't want their new ruler chopping people's heads off."

"You want me to let the prisoners go? We don't know that Gordon is innocent. He and his uncle could have planned the whole thing. The boy did run away," offered the queen.

"That makes no sense. Even if Gordon had done it, he is already dead. Loren had no reason to kill my brother. This plot may extend farther than we know. I can't have the crown, but I want real justice for my brother. I loved him, just as you did."

The queen paused, but finally said, "It's true that I never liked you, but you were a good brother and he loved you. What do you propose?"

Darion said, "I want to go look for the people that killed him and try to unravel this plot. If I left to do it on my own, it would look like I was undermining you. If you send me on this mission, it will show the kingdom that we are in alliance and not enemies. It would show that you care more about truth than vengeance."

The queen responded, "Why should we prove that Gordon is innocent? The boy fled and the god of the sea swallowed him up as punishment. And let's not forget that the fortune I now have would be returned to Denogg if his innocence is proven."

Darion continued, "I have thought of that. You have coin now and you don't want to let go. I certainly understand. But there's still a way to keep the coin. The king did die in Denny's house, probably by one of his servants. He doesn't need to be a prisoner to be ruined. We can find some legal reason to keep the coin. I'm more concerned about how our people perceive the truth."

The queen said, "Even if I agree to your logic, I can't risk upsetting this young new king. He's just a boy, but their kingdom is still the strongest, especially with their airships. We need that alliance."

Darion smiled. "There's another way I can help. I have befriended the boy. He is much smarter than people think he is, and I'm sure he would see the logic in this. It could be a venture both our kingdoms do together. It could sew this alliance together. Acts that the people could see are better than words."

The grandmother said, "The boy king might agree, but he has no real power. It's obvious that the firstcouncilor controls him and makes all the real decisions. I think it's a mistake."

Darion continued, "That may be true. I can only try to convince them. But there's a bigger issue. Who wanted my brother dead, and why? If Gordon was the target, why? No one knew he was in Thure yet. My sources believe the murderers came from the kingdom of the gods. True, there is a lot of trouble there, but it is also a gateway to another land that I fear is up to something very bad."

"Dard? You think the scum that destroyed my kingdom and renamed it could be behind this?" asked the grandmother.

Darion said, "I think it likely, or at least possible. Although I can't get any spies into that kingdom, I have heard disturbing rumors."

"Very clever, trying to gain my support by making this about the scum that threw me off my throne… and it worked, my boy. Maybe he should try to convince the king. Finding the real murderers would be better than a bloodbath in the public square," said the grandmother.

The queen was silent for a long time, looking back and forth from her grandmother to her brother-in-law. "Alright, go talk to the king. I think this is pointless, but if the king and the firstcouncilor say yes, I will agree that you can go search for these men. However, if you find there are no murderers, and there is no plot, I will expect you to swear your loyalty to me in public. Agreed?"

"Agreed," said Darion as he politely bowed and left the room. "I better go see the boy king."

"We can't trust him," said the grandmother after he left.

The queen said, "I know that. That's why I'm sending him away. The kingdom of the gods is a dangerous place, ruled by two dangerous men. Even if he's able to convince king Asa, I would be very surprised if my dear brother-in-law comes back from this mission at all."

The grandmother smiled. "My dear, now you're sounding like a true queen."

Darion wasted no time going to see the young king. The guards let him go in, and he was apparently walking in on an argument.

"… My king, it is not a good idea…," said Trunculin.

"I don't see why not. Brenddel, doesn't the firstcouncilor have to follow my orders?" asked Asa.

"It is not my place to say, my king. But it is the firstcouncilor's job to advise you... and we have a visitor," Brenddel said as he motioned to Darion.

"I'm sorry to interrupt, but may I have a moment of your time, my king?" said Darion.

"Not at all. The king always has time for someone of noble birth," said the firstcouncilor.

"He was talking to me. I can speak for myself," the king said, and then he turned to Darion and said with a smile, "How can I help you, Darion?"

Darion said, "Well, it's actually how we can help each other. I want justice for my brother and I don't believe Gordon killed him. Nor does the queen. I would like your help to go hunt down the men that poisoned him. I believe I can find them in the kingdom of the gods and bring them back for justice. That would make it much easier for you to take Gordon's uncle back to your own kingdom for whatever justice you see fit."

Trunculin replied, "The former king's uncle is guilty of many crimes. But we are content to have the queen administer the punishment. After all, we want to build an alliance, not insult the queen. Gordon is dead. It's a generous offer, but unnecessary…"

Asa interrupted, "I think that's a great idea. Brenddel will ready an airship to get you there faster. Brenddel will be a big help in finding these men."

Trunculin said, "My king, might we discussed this in private? There are a lot of implications…"

Asa replied, "I've made my decision, firstcouncilor, I don't see…"

"… Will you stop interrupting me!?" The mood in the room had changed. Trunculin was visibly angry. Brenddel looked carefully at each of the men, then back to the king.

Trunculin continued a bit calmer. "Well, what I mean to say… my king, is that this decision needs to be made very carefully. I think I could give you some strong points that…"

"My decision is made," Asa said, interrupting on purpose, "I'm the king and you have given your counsel. Brenddel, please make the arrangements," Asa said, looking right at the firstcouncilor, trying to hide how nervous he really was to be standing up to Trunculin.

Brenddel said, "My king, I will do as you ask, but my rightful place is here at your side." He looked at the firstcouncilor again. "My job is to protect you and keep you safe. I can send other men with Darion."

Asa said, "Thank you, Brenddel, but I have the rest of my personal guard here and since you trained them, they should be able to protect me from anything. Besides, you are the best soldier. I would feel better if you were leading them. Doesn't that make some sense, firstcouncilor?"

Trunculin was smiling very brightly now. His mood had abruptly changed. "As you wish, my king."

Darion said, "Thank you, my king. It's very generous of you to offer your best man for the mission. And the airship will make this a much faster journey," said Darion.

Brenddel looked from the king to the firstcouncilor and said, "I'll make the arrangements right now, my king." Trunculin was still smiling very widely. Brenddel was afraid to wonder what he was thinking.

Asa said, "Good. Please find. It would be nice to go home soon."

"Thank you again, my king," Darion said as he left the room to inform the queen.

Trunculin added, "Oh, and Brenddel, the agent I told you about earlier, he has some business in Artoth. He will go with you."

Brenddel nodded agreement and reluctantly left Trunculin and Asa alone.

CHAPTER 38
WHAT IS JUST

The Copway had prepared a sunrise feast with all kinds of exotic delicacies made just to celebrate the travelers. Gordon still felt embarrassed by the whole thing. Lantovas was healing quickly and was also enjoying the feast.

"Are you sure you want to go with us, Lantovas? You don't have to. We can send word from Artoth that you're here and I'm sure your kingdom will send a watership," asked Gordon.

Lantovas said, "Not even my beloved king would've done something as brave as you did for me. I will get back to my kingdom eventually. But since I am supposedly dead, that gives me a little time to go and try to find the real murderers of the king. Let's go find these murderers together."

Aline said, "Looks like your building quite the army, one at a time, my king."

Mantuan said, "That reminds me, one of your new friends has a gift for you."

Number Eight stood as Gordon approached, smiling. The leader adjusted his eye glasses and spoke to Mantuan, who translated, "He says Jaiwan has a gift for you."

Gordon replied, "Jaiwan? Oh, is that his name? I feel bad that I thought his name was Number Eight. I figured his body ink meant that he fought as hard as eight warriors."

Before Gordon realized it, Mantuan had translated what he had said. Everyone laughed. Jaiwan replied and Mantuan translated, "Jaiwan says the symbol on his neck is the never ending cycle of life. But he says you can call him Number Eight if you want to."

Jaiwan handed him something. Gordon asked, "Is it…is this a claw from that Fasgonn monster?"

Jaiwan smiled even before Mantuan had translated.

Gordon said, "If I knew the claws were this big, I might have let that thing eat you, Lantovas." Everyone laughed again when Mantuan translated.

All of the men and women hugged them goodbye. Before long, everything was ready and loaded on their ship. The leader said some words to Gordon which Mantuan translated as words of long life and success. Then they were on the ship headed to Artoth, waving goodbye to their Copway hosts.

After the initial flurry of activity to get the ship underway, Gordon and Aline were on the deck together, looking towards the new day. Aline said, "Great, another ship. I hope this one goes better than the last one."

Gordon smiled, "Let's hope so," then he got serious and said, "I was really worried about you Aline. I tried to hold onto you when the ship went down, but, I don't know what happened, you were just gone. When I woke up on the beach and couldn't find you, I was very… I'm just glad you're okay."

Aline punched him in the arm. Gordon winced and said, "What was that for?"

Aline smiled and said, "Thank you Gordon, I'm glad you're okay too. But don't get all soft and mushy on me. After I realized I was still alive, floating there, I was so mad at myself for failing to keep you safe. If we lost you, I don't know how we would set the kingdom right again."

Gordon replied, "I still don't see how I'm important. Everyone treats me like I'm something special. Why? Mantuan told me some of what's going on, but I still have more questions than answers…"

"You will get your answers. There should be time soon to talk. So much has happened, and so fast. There just hasn't been time. It always seems like the odds are against us. But we will win," said Aline confidently.

"Win what, exactly? My crown back? They already crowned the new king. Everyone thinks I'm dead. What exactly are we fighting for?" asked Gordon.

"Something is deeply wrong in your kingdom. Don't you feel it?" asked Aline, "That kingdom used to be a place where everyone wanted to go, because you could be free to live as you wanted. You've read stories of the first thirteen kings. You know why they went there to start a new kingdom. But now because of Trunculin, and people like him, it's rotting from the inside; being re-made into something dark. It is so far gone from what the first kings envisioned, and it is becoming as corrupt as all the other kingdoms."

Gordon asked, "But how can we fight that? Isn't it natural that a kingdom changes over time? The ideas that the first kings put down on paper were hundreds of years ago. Isn't it natural that what they thought then, doesn't… I don't know, doesn't work anymore?"

Aline said, "Of course things change over time. We have different ways to get around, like the airships. They didn't exist back then. We wear different clothes. Many things have been invented or discovered that they didn't know back then. The tools we use change, but basic truths do not. Look at the places you've been so far. The kingdom of Thure. It's a kingdom, similar to yours. What are the differences?"

Gordon said, "Well, in our kingdom, the king is chosen by fate. Or at least is supposed to be. In their kingdom, a king is born from an important family."

Aline said, "Do you think that's fair? I mean the last king of Thure was a very good king. Everyone loved him. But his grandfather started many wars, tortured people, and put people in prison without a trial ... all kinds of terrible things. But by their way of doing things, both men *deserved* to be king. There was no difference. They both had some sort of right to be king."

Gordon said, "What gave them the right?"

Aline continued "Exactly. Does it make sense a king can do terrible things to people, just because he feels like it? A poor man and a king are both humans. All men bleed red, and all men are made the same. What makes one better than the other?"

Gordon said, "I don't know. That's just the way it's always been there. The people have no power to change it, and the people in charge have no reason to change."

Aline replied, "That's right. What gives the right to any man to say to another, 'you do what I say. I rule, you follow'."

Gordon said, "But if the person doesn't do as the king says, the king could have them arrested, or killed."

Aline said, "So a king rules by fear, then? Some kings would arrest us just for having the conversation. Is that just? In your kingdom, it used to be that you could say anything you wanted to, even if it was something stupid. Nowadays, an army of people report back to Trunculin what is said. People are afraid to say what they think."

Gordon said, "But he probably thinks that it's his job to keep order..."

"To keep order, not to control what people think. He's made changes over many years and is now turning the kingdom into something it was never intended to be: a kingdom ruled by one will. One man's will, choosing for all the people, and Trunculin wasn't chosen by anyone. He proclaimed himself in charge, and he's doing it all in secret," said Aline.

"But how can that be? We still have the laws from the first kings. There on display for everyone to see," said Gordon.

"Are they? Have you seen them? Have you been to the law room? They wouldn't let you in if you tried," said Aline.

"I didn't think to ask. I'm sure they would let the king go there," said Gordon.

"Even King Stathen couldn't get in. He was king for ten trials. We believe that the original words written by the first kings have been changed, forged, hidden or destroyed. If you control the history, you control what people believe," said Aline.

Gordon thought about that. "But that doesn't make any sense. There are old people who would remember the 'real' history and how it used to be. Trunculin can't erase people's minds."

Aline agreed. "That's true, he can't. But he has been on a secret campaign for years to intimidate people into silence. It's a vast conspiracy, but Mantuan believes it all leads back to Trunculin. We can only guess at what other plans he has."

"But how do you know for sure? If you've never seen the original words, how can you know that Trunculin's documents are false?"

Mantuan joined them. "Because there's one person that has an original law book, the law keeper."

"Who is he? Where is he?" asked Gordon.

"I've been searching many years for him. We think he was a councilor who turned on Trunculin and fled with an original law book. Everywhere I've gone searching, I just seem to miss him. He has been hiding a long time," said Mantuan.

The pilot walked up to Mantuan urgently and handed him a long spy glass. Mantuan scanned the sky and finally settled on a dark speck far away.

"Is that...?" Gordon began.

"Yes." Said Mantuan.

"Where do you think they're headed?" said Aline.

"Well, if they keep the straight line, the airship must be going to Artoth, just like us. They should get there a full day ahead of us," replied Mantuan.

Mantuan handed the spyglass to Gordon and pointed to where he should look, "Why would an airship be going to Artoth?" asked Gordon.

Mantuan said, "Not sure. Maybe someone else believes you didn't poison the king. We have to be especially careful. There are few that are loyal to our cause in Artoth, and it will be harder to get around with the airship guards watching. If they let the airship in at all, that is. The two kings of Artoth both hate airships. They offend all of their gods."

CHAPTER 39
ANNOYING GUEST

The airship was over open waters. "I want two men at each arrow gun. Keep an eye out for shadow fins and yell out if you spot one," Brenddel ordered, as Darion stood nearby.

"I thought those things were only legend. You mean they're actually out there?" asked Darion.

"We all thought that they were legends," confirmed Brenddel. "But since we've created the airships, they have come back from wherever they were. Airships seem to make them angry… or crazed. They don't seem to attack waterships, just us. In the early days, nothing. One of the two brothers that created the airships reported seeing a fin once, but he went mad before he died, so no one believed him. Recently, they have made themselves known, and they're getting bolder. I'm sure it's the sound of our rotators that brought these things out of legend, some say it's the shadow the ship casts on the waters. The superstitious say it is a punishment for men daring to fly. And they are as big as the old books say they are."

Darion suddenly took a new interest in the waters below and stood scanning. Abruptly, Brenddel heard yelling coming from inside the canopy. "… Where is he, then?" said the firstcouncilor's assistant Arasta. "There you are!" the small man said as he snapped his fingers in Brenddel's direction. "You there, firstman. The sleeping arrangements are unacceptable. I cannot sleep in a primitive hanging bed made from ropes. I will be taking your bed, is that clear?"

Brenddel stood at the railing without speaking as the man approached him. Darion decided the conversation might be amusing and wandered toward the two men. Darion looked with interest from the small man to Brenddel.

Brenddel did not look at Arasta as he spoke. "I don't have another bed for you. I sleep in a rope bed just like my men. And you seem to be a little confused. I am the firstman of my kingdom, and I command this ship..."

"Excuse me firstman, but I will not be spoken to that way. Councilors always outrank soldiers. I must have a good night sleep before I tend to my business tomorrow," said the small councilor.

"Firstly, if you interrupt me again, little man, this will not be a happy trip for you," Brenddel warned, "and secondly, what exactly is this business? Our kingdom is not overly friendly with Artoth..."

The little man said, "It's a delicate matter I'm sure you couldn't possibly understand. When we land I will..."

Brenddel quickly went to the man and lifted him against the inner canopy. Brenddel's nose almost touched Arasta's. "That is the last time you interrupt me, little man. Let me be clear, you will tell me about your mission. I will know everything that goes on aboard my ship. And you have no rank on my ship. You are nobody to me. So, if you bother my men again, or don't do exactly as you're told, you will be punished. Is that clear?"

"How dare you... you insignificant..." the man began, squirming against the canopy.

Before the man could finish his thought, Brenddel quickly extended his other open palm, hitting just under the man's throat. The pressure was not hard, but the man was immediately grasping for air and Brenddel let him fall to the deck.

"We spotted one!" said an arrowman.

"Arrows at the ready. How far?" replied Brenddel.

The arrowman said, "Four hundred feet. It's breaking the surface now."

Down below them, the water was churning as they saw two great wings rising from the water. The creature breeched the surface and was headed straight for them.

The large arrow was aimed at the beast, which was coming up in a straight line. "Wait until it gets to within fifty feet and fire. Just like the drills. And please… don't miss," Brenddel said.

The small councilor was up on his feet again barely able to speak. "You… you can't touch me like that," the man croaked.

Darion was over at the railing again, watching the finned beast come towards them. It was coming up very fast, its enormous wings leaving a rain of sea water spraying behind it. The huge mouth was open, showing its rows of deadly teeth, ready to take a bite out of anything in its way. The beast was very close, certainly within fifty feet, Darion thought urgently.

"Fire!" said Brenddel and the large arrow let loose, hitting the creature where a wing connected. The beast made a strange sound, faltered and fell back to the deep waters. All the men yelled and shouted. Brenddel smacked the back of the man who had fired the arrow. "Good shot. Get another arrow ready. There's more than one out there."

Another shout came from the opposite side of the airship. "Another one! I see a fin."

Brenddel turned his attention back to the small councilor. "What is happening?" the small councilor began to say as Brenddel dragged him by his shirt.

Brenddel told his arrowman, "Tie him to the large arrow bolt there."

"What?" said the small man, beginning to realize his true rank on the airship. Two men were already lifting him onto the arrow, and a third grabbed a coiled rope from the railing. The soldiers started to tie him to the arrow as the small man was screaming, "Take your hands off me..."

A second man was watching the waters closely. "Breech! I see wings breaking the surface, shall I fire?"

"Not yet." Brenddel turned back to the soldier who was tying the small councilor to the large arrow. "Is he secure?"

"Yes. The ropes will hold."

"What is your mission?" Brenddel asked the councilor.

The small man replied, "Trunculin will have you killed. You're insane ..."

"Yes I am, and Trunculin is not here. What is your mission?"

The man did not answer.

Brenddel said, "Okay men, load him up."

The men placed the large arrow bolt on the arrow gun, pointing it straight down towards the beast. The man began to scream.

"How close?" Brenddel asked.

"Three hundred feet and coming fast," said the arrowman.

The small councilor reconsidered his position. "I'm... I'm meeting with an agent from Extatumm. I'm to meet with the contact in Artoth and then move on to their lands to negotiate. Now un-tie me.... please."

Brenddel said, "That's better. It took all of this just to get a 'please' from you. What else?"

"I can't tell you anything else. The firstcouncilor would kill me," he said, looking down at the beast flying directly at them.

Brenddel replied, "But if you don't tell me, then I'll kill you. Kind of a bad situation for you..."

The beast was coming fast. The small man was screaming again as he saw the beast and its giant teeth.

"Tell me quickly, that beast looks hungry," Brenddel said over the piercing screams of the man. The beast was getting closer.

The man looked around feverishly, realizing he had no choice. "It's about airships."

Brenddel leaned far over the railing and extended his arm. He let loose a bolt from his arm arrow gun. Before it hit anything, he had reloaded and another arrow was fired. Both found their target, one near the fin and one pierced through the beast's eye. As the momentum continued upward towards them, the beast came nearer the airship.

The beast's body slowed and started back down again. The water from its body hit the face of Brenddel and the councilor in a fine mist. Brenddel watched the beast fall back down and splash into the waters far below.

The small man was still on the arrow, screaming. The man's wild eyes darted around, his face wet with sea water. A man went to untie the small councilor, but Brenddel stopped him and said, "What about airships?"

Arasta said, "They have been building airships. An army of them."

Brenddel said, "You lie. Only our kingdom knows how to build airships. Only our kingdom has the gas. Explain."

"They have been building them for years, based on our plans. We used to sell them gas quietly. Now they have found a way to make a different type of gas. Their airships are bigger, more complex. They test them where other kingdoms can't see them."

"If they already have airships, why go? What else are you doing there?" asked Brenddel.

The man said, "The firstcouncilor is building an alliance. A treaty. He wants our kingdom to join forces with Extatumm."

Brenddel looked at the man. "The contact. Is this a man you've dealt with before?"

Arasta shook his head. "No. He's a new contact. I'm to meet him in the old part of the kingdom at the ruins of Tanlum. We are both to wear a red cloak."

Darion had been watching the events, and said, "Councilor, you should have lied and said it was someone expecting only you."

"What? Why?" said the small councilor.

"He means, because now I am free to do this," said Brenddel as he motioned for the arrowman to point the arrow gun back down at the sea again.

Panic rose in the man again. "But you said if I told you the truth, you would let me go," the man said, nearly hysterical.

"I said nothing of the kind. I made no promises. I simply said I hate secrets," replied Brenddel calmly.

"We will be taking bets on whether you'll drown, get eaten, or die from the fall," said Darion.

The small man found his arrogance again. "You wouldn't dare. Not really. This was just to scare me. How would you explain it to Trunculin?"

Brenddel replied, "People fall from airships. The slaver king fell from an airship, and the last firstman fell. It happens. When you don't make it back, I'll have a story ready."

"But...," said the small councilor, "...but, you're just a soldier. You can't possibly negotiate…"

Darion asked, "Can I say it?"

Brenddel said, "At your pleasure..."

"Fire," said Darion to the arrowman.

The arrow bolt, and the man tied to it, went straight for the waters. Because the arrow was not meant for so much uneven weight, the arrow did not go straight. It made a strange looping circle as it descended. The man's screams could be heard for a surprisingly long time, until the arrow finally hit the water with a distant splash.

CHAPTER 40
LIKE A FRIEND

"So tell us about your kingdom. We hear so very much about kings and councilors, but what are the people like? Is there many poor in your kingdom?" asked the queen as the fourth course was being served.

Asa had just taken a mouthful of food and decided to finish chewing first. "Sorry, my queen, I don't mean to be rude. Everything is really good, by the way. I'm sorry, what was the question again?"

The grandmother interrupted, "I think what my granddaughter is trying to ask is, what are the poor villages like there? Isn't that where you came from, before this… choosing ritual?"

Asa answered, "Well, my villages aren't really that poor. We live pretty close to the palace city and all my family get enough to eat. My father's a stone layer, and we have a small farm where we grow food."

"Oh, how charming. You come from a long line of builders, then? No other kings in the family?" asked the grandmother.

"No. No one in my family has ever been chosen before. I just hope I can just be a good king when I get back."

"I'm sure it will be very challenging with so little education and no royal blood. It's always been a very curious system, your kingdom," added the grandmother.

Trunculin was sitting next to the grandmother. "It must be very odd for you, who comes from such a distinguished line of kings and queens."

The grandmother said, "Very odd indeed. I don't see how you can ignore good breeding and just 'choose' kings from the crowds. Although, I suppose it's a little better than elections where you have to trust the uneducated mobs to pick a leader."

Asa said, "It is interesting to learn about all the different kings and queens. One of our first kings said something about 'when all the kings come from the same family, that eventually, the stupid cousin will be king one day'."

The queen smiled, "That is an interesting point, my young king."

Asa felt good that he remembered a lesson and continued. "Was it your kingdom that had Jorann the blood king? The one that killed all those people when he first became king?"

Trunculin had just taken a bite and started to cough.

"Yes, king Asa, I have heard of him. He ruled in the kingdom of Dard," replied the queen, smiling.

Asa continued, "They say he was actually crazy, that he talked to people that weren't there, right?"

Trunculin was still coughing and was just about to speak.

"Jorann was my grandfather," said Alonnia, the queen's grandmother.

Trunculin had finally gotten his food down, but before he could speak, king Asa said, "Oh no. I've said something wrong again. Please, my queen, I'm sorry…"

The queen smiled, "You really are a charming boy. Don't worry. You're right, my distant great grandfather was an insane, evil man who did terrible things. That's why the people rose up against him. I really can't blame them for killing him and hanging him from that bridge. There is much to be said for your way of doing things. Your kingdom has risen to be the richest and, some say, most popular kingdom there is. New ways of doing things aren't always bad. We simply believe in certain traditions in Thure." As she leaned over to Asa, she winked and said, "Maybe we still have a thing or two to learn, here in the old kingdom of paper."

Trunculin added, "It really is just a different way of doing things. No better or worse than any other way. True, we do have our different ways, but many of the ideas came from Thure, in a way. Three of our first thirteen came from Thure."

"Precisely, because there would never have been kings here," said the grandmother not smiling. "I have lost my appetite. If you excuse me, my dear, honored guests, I think I will retire."

Asa said, "I'm really sorry. I didn't mean to offend anyone. I still have so much to learn. I hope you can forgive me," said Asa.

"I can't expect the boy king of thirteen to understand the world of men and women. Good night," the grandmother said as she walked away.

"Please, let me escort you. I would love to hear some of the history of your noble family of Dard," said Trunculin getting up from the table to walk with her.

"I would be honored, firstcouncilor. I would love to talk about my truly royal family."

The two walked away, leaving the queen and Asa to finish their meal. Asa was now distracted, fearing he did more damage with every word he said.

The queen said, "Don't worry about offending her. She is an old woman with very old ways of thinking. She's still bitter about losing her throne to those that now call her land Extatumm. There are many things that I want to change in my kingdom. My husband always had great plans and had already started to change things for the better. I think our kingdom would benefit from being a little more like yours."

Asa smiled. "Thank you. Maybe I should go to bed too. It's been a long day. If you will pardon me, my queen."

"Of course, my king, sleep well," said the queen, smiling as Asa left.

Asa did not go back to his chamber. He was determined to have another conversation with Loren. Luckily, it was the same guard on duty. This time he would not be interrupted by Brenddel, either. As he made his way to the back of the prison cells, Loren was once again standing at the bars, as though he was waiting for him. "Hello again, Asa," Loren said with a smile.

Asa replied, "It's kind of nice *not* hearing the word king before my name. How are you?"

Loren just shrugged and looked at the bars.

"That's a dumb question, sorry," said Asa. "I wanted to come down and let you know that I've convinced the queen that Gordon didn't poison anyone. I sent Brenddel and an airship to find the murderers in Artoth. There's no guarantees, of course, but I think we will get you out of here."

Loren looked concerned. Once again, Denogg quietly came out of the shadows. "Was the firstcouncilor there when you made this decision?"

Asa smiled a little. "Yes. I don't think he's very happy with me. But he hasn't said anything. In fact, he really hasn't talked to me much since then. He's been smiling a lot more, though. I think he might like the queen's grandmother."

Denogg and Loren exchanged worried glances.

Loren said, "Did you openly defy him in the presence of anyone else?"

"Well, Brenddel was there, and Darion. He went with Brenddel to try and help. I think there was another guard there too. Strange, but I don't really notice the guards anymore. They are always just there. It felt good to make my own decision for once."

Loren said, "Asa, you need to understand something. You cannot trust Trunculin. He is a very bad man. I worked at the palace as the firsthealer and had to treat many people for injuries that Trunculin had ordered. I mean torture, Asa. If you openly defy him again, he will find ways to punish you. I want you to understand that, and be very, very careful. He's tried to kill me. He tried to kill Gordon. And there have been accidents in the past. Not all kings survive their trials."

He looked back and forth at the two men, "But… but I'm the king. There are guards around all the time. What could he do?"

"You may be king, but you are also a thirteen year old boy surrounded by guards that are loyal only to the firstcouncilor," said Denogg. "I don't know this Trunculin, but from what I've heard, you may be in a lot of danger."

"I hadn't thought of that. I mean, I thought the guards would protect me. But…" Asa stood there as a tear rolled down his cheek. "I never wanted to be king. Why is this happening…?"

"Being chosen is a great responsibility, no matter how you were chosen. You are stronger than you think, Asa. You need to trust in yourself. And be very careful," said Loren.

"I don't really think the firstcouncilor would try anything with the queen's guards as witnesses," added Denogg.

Asa nodded and could find no other words, so he said goodnight and went back to his chamber. Asa passed guards the entire way back. He tried to look at their faces and imagine what they were thinking. None of them would look at him.

As he opened the door to his chamber, he was surprised to see the firstcouncilor sitting in the chair, four guards behind him. He was right in the middle of the room, smiling very widely.

Almost like a friend.

CHAPTER 41
BRENDDEL'S BETRAYAL

"Good. You're getting better," said Aline as she thrust her longknife at Gordon, who blocked her with his own curved blade and retreated a few steps away from her attack.

"Thanks. I know I have a lot to learn," he said as he made a slashing movement towards Aline. She skillfully dodged, and his longknife swung down and stuck into the deck of the ship. Aline used her foot to push Gordon over. He didn't let go of the longknife, and as his body rolled, the knife came out of the wood. Gordon was quickly back on his feet.

"Not bad, my king. Improvising. You may not die in your first battle after all. But you need to keep your legs farther apart, and work on keeping yourself firmly planted," said Aline, circling him.

"I'll keep that in mind," Gordon said as he put his foot forward and thrust his longknife at Aline. She blocked his blow and spun her body so that she was behind him. She had her shortknife out and was just touching Gordon's side with the blade.

"Remember this, also," Aline said to Gordon, who quickly realized that he had lost the fight. "There is no such thing as a fair fight. Not in the real world. It is not just about clashing blades and making a lot of noise. Don't focus too much on the weapon. Use your mind." Aline tapped Gordon's head to make the point.

"Well said, Aline," said Mantuan as he approached. "It's also about what is around you. Fighting on the deck of a ship that is constantly moving is much different than fighting among trees or on flat land. Even the deck of an airship moves differently than a ship on water. My turn, Aline."

"This is going to be fun to watch. Don't kill him, Manny," said Aline as she put her knives away. Gordon held his knife and watched as Mantuan took his own longknife out of its sheath.

"Um, I don't think I'm ready to fight you," said Gordon, and felt new sweat appear on his brow.

"You're not. But you are way behind on training. And since I was firstman once, in a way it is my duty to train you for combat. Come for me, my king," said Mantuan.

Gordon looked back to Aline. She was smiling. He turned back to Mantuan, raised his longknife in both hands and walked in a circle, ready to strike. "Why aren't you the firstman anymore? You said you trained Brenddel. What really happened?"

Mantuan yelled loudly and charged Gordon, swinging his knife downward. Gordon raised his knife but the blow was too powerful and sent Gordon to his knees. Mantuan said, "Brenddel betrayed me the day King Daymer died."

Gordon got to his feet and raised his knife just in time for Mantuan to swing horizontally. Gordon jumped backwards out of Mantuan's reach. "Daymer? The slaver king, right?"

Mantuan charged again with a loud roar, longknife raised. Gordon put up his own blade to block it. Instead of swinging his knife down, Mantuan came in under Gordon's blade and slammed upwards into him with his shoulder. Gordon was pushed into the air and landed on the deck of the ship.

Before Gordon could raise his blade again, Mantuan had his knife close to Gordon's throat. "Slaver king? That was a lie invented by Trunculin. The king had nothing to do with slaves. He never would've allowed slavery in his kingdom. The king was stabbed and thrown off an airship by Brenddel." Mantuan sheathed his longknife and offered Gordon his hand. Gordon was quickly up on his feet and sheathed his own knife.

"You saw it happen?" asked Gordon, rubbing his shoulder.

Mantuan said, "Yes. Brenddel was my secondman. I trusted him completely. I rescued him as a boy and he was like my adopted son. King Daymer was facing away from me, looking down over the land. I didn't see Brenddel approach him. I looked up just as Brenddel stuck in the knife and pushed the king off the airship. The king made no sound as he fell. I will never forget that silent fall, or my failure."

Aline came back over to them and put her hand on Mantuan's arm. "That's the day we first met. Quite the surprise for a little girl."

"No more surprised than I was. I knew that I was going to die and then suddenly I landed on something solid and saw people all around me. It was a very strange day," said Mantuan.

Gordon asked, "What happened?"

"Brenddel tried to kill me just after he killed the king. He was enraged and called me slaver scum, among other things. I'm sure that Trunculin made him believe that the king and I were somehow responsible for the slave trade at the gas fields. I tried to reason with him, but he was out for blood. I was winning the fight for a while. Rage usually unbalances an opponent, but Brenddel used his to focus. I finally fell."

"Fell… from the airship? How did you survive *that*?" Gordon asked.

"The king had wanted to see the haunted forest in Aspora. We were over a large dense canopy of trees. I must've fallen twenty feet before I hit the canopy. That slowed me down, but I was still falling. I stopped when I landed on something flat. It hurt, so I knew I wasn't dead. There were people around that were just as surprised to see me. It was the fortress, as we now call it."

Aline said, "I was the first one to approach you. Everyone else was scared to come up to you. People don't usually fall through the trees over three hundred feet up."

"How high? Um, I think I'm confused," said Gordon.

Mantuan and Aline laughed. Mantuan said, "That does sound confusing if you haven't seen them. In Aspora, there are trees that grow to be hundreds of feet tall. The trees are bigger around than you can imagine. There is a large group of people who have built a city in the trees."

Gordon said, "You mean like a kid's treehouse?"

Aline said, "Like the most amazing treehouses you've never seen. The people create houses out of parts of the trees, connecting decks and platforms between the trees in an amazing system. Hundreds live in the fortress, high in the trees. We even grow food up there. There are systems for bringing water up and for getting down to the ground from the trees. It's a beautiful place. Its home."

Mantuan agreed. "And I have also called it home since that day. I've traveled through all the kingdoms building alliances and gathering information. But home has been in the trees. When we have everything we need to destroy Trunculin, I will return to my first home, our kingdom."

CHAPTER 42
OFFENDING THE GODS

The airship slowed as it approached the canal gates. Brenddel could see the great canal beyond the first gate and understood how careful he would have to be. His kingdom, and the kingdom of the gods, had a fragile understanding. He wasn't sure if he would be allowed to land peacefully, or if they would try to shoot them out of the sky. He knew that he could fly around the high mountains, avoiding the canal. But this would look suspicious, and Artoth might think it was an attack.

Darion asked, "What do you think is the best way in?"

"The best option is usually the front door. The two kings have their own guards that each control one side of the canal. I think we should ask for permission just like everyone else," replied Brenddel.

"That would be the best way not to get shot down, I reason. When we get closer they'll see that the arrow guns are empty. What do you think our odds are of getting in?" asked Darion.

"About even. There's only one way to find out." Brenddel ordered his men to steer the ship directly for the first gate of the canal. They flew in very low and slowed to a stop just close enough to shout to the guard.

"Apparently they saw us coming," said Darion as he pointed to the large amount of arrowmen lining the outer gate, pointing right at their airship.

"What is your business here?" said a large, muscular man standing next to the gate.

Brenddel shouted back, "We believe the men that killed the king of Thure may be hiding in your kingdom like cowards. May we pass over the canal and land outside your kingdom?"

Among the arrow men and guards were a few men with books in their hands. These were the councilors of the king. The main guard was nodding as the councilor spoke to him.

The guard finally said, "You may pass for double the standard fee over this gate. But the far gate is controlled by the other king. They may not let you pass. Your floating ship is an insult to all gods. Fair warning."

"Agreed, with our thanks," said Brenddel, as he told his men to fly over the gates. There were vast mountains on either side, shooting into the air, the tops hidden by clouds. The canal was wide enough for the largest ships from any kingdom. The Artoth canal was the largest in their world and made travel much shorter to Artoth, Extatumm and the lands beyond.

Darion looked at the mountains and wondered how high they were. He said, "I've always wanted to see the canal. How lucky Artoth is, to be in the middle of all the kingdoms and be able to charge a fee for any ship wanting a shortcut."

"Quite the shortcut. Going around the canal takes an extra sixteen days by watership. And they are rough seas," said Brenddel.

"Speaking of rough waters, what if the other king's gate won't let us through?" asked Darion.

Brenddel answered, "This kingdom may be founded on the love of their gods, but like most kingdoms, this one considers coin above everything else."

"You're not suggesting that there's any corruption in this kingdom, are you?"

Brenddel said simply, "No. I'm suggesting that all kingdoms are corrupt."

The airship slowed as it approached the second gate. They were twice as many arrow men at this gate as there were at the first. They were all dressed in the black and orange leather armor of their king. An arrow flew by Darion as a warning. "You will stop and state your business," came a loud booming voice.

Darion looked at Brenddel with alarm as the firstman said, "We believe the cowardly murderers of the king of Thure to be hiding in your glorious kingdom."

There were two councilors speaking to the guard of this gate. The guard nodded and said to Brenddel, "Are you mocking our glorious kingdom, air man? Your floating insult should be a meal for the beast of the canal."

Brenddel replied, "I do not mock. We want only justice for the kingdom of Thure."

The guard said, "You serve the boy kings of the thirteen. Why are you here on a mission for a dead Thurian king?"

Darion spoke, "The firstman of his kingdom was nice enough to give me a ride to your truly glorious kingdom. I am Darion, the brother of Russel, king of Thure."

The councilor spoke to the guard again. The guard said, "You may pass this glorious gate for triple the normal rate, but you must land your floating abomination far outside of the kingdom walls. May the gods be with you. I doubt they will." The man spat on the ground.

"Agreed," said Brenddel as he motioned for the airship to pass. Brenddel felt weary of this kingdom before he even entered the gates. He was also feeling a strange mix of emotions. Brenddel had not been back to Artoth since Mantuan found him as a child.

As they passed over the second gate, they were out in open waters again briefly before the airship made the turn to the left. Darion actually gasped as the kingdom of Artoth came into full view, with the great mountains rising behind it.

The sun was glistening off the ancient stone of the kingdom walls and towers beyond. Darion couldn't stop staring at the kingdom of the gods, but Brenddel looked to the right, past the mountains and deep into the great lands that led to the ancient kingdom of Dard, now called Extatumm.

Since it had become Extatumm, no outsiders were allowed in. *What is Trunculin doing?* Brenddel forced his attention back to the terraced kingdom of Artoth.

"I had no idea how beautiful it was. Paintings do not represent it properly," said Darion in awe.

"Don't let the pretty buildings fool you. Besides Aspora, the land a thousand kings, this can be a very dangerous kingdom,"

"When two kings rule one kingdom, and hate each other at the same time, believe in completely different gods, and have been at war with each other for thousands of years, I can see how things might get a little… strange," replied Darion.

"The murderers couldn't have picked a better place to hide. Because of the two kings hatred for each other, there are secret markets on both sides where people buy and sell everything you can imagine. Artoth's secret nature will hide them well," said Brenddel.

"What if we can't find them? What if your connection doesn't come through?" asked Darion.

Brenddel replied, "Then our trip will be short. I will at least find the councilor's connection and beat some answers out of him."

Darion asked, "Is that how you get all your answers?"

"Just the important ones."

Brenddel spotted a clearing to land outside the kingdom walls. The ropes descended and the crew went down them to secure the ship for landing. As they touched down, Brenddel gave instructions to his men. "Three of you come with me, the rest stay with the ship. When we've paid the ridiculous fees at the kingdom gates, you three will escort the coin chest back to the ship, and then get the ship back up in the air. If there are any surprises, I want you to see them coming. If we are not back before nightfall, send five men down on ropes to look for us."

Smiling widely towards the gates of Artoth, Darion said, "Let's go see the sights."

CHAPTER 43
SWEET GESTURES

"Are you sure you wouldn't like more to eat, my king? You barely touched anything," said the queen as they were having their meal. The guards were standing closer to the king than usual, as King Asa, The queen, Trunculin and the queen's grandmother ate. Trunculin and the grandmother were quietly talking about history across the table.

Asa responded, "No thank you… my queen. My stomach hurts a little today. But thank you anyway."

"Oh, I'm sorry," said the queen. "Would you like to go to one of my healers? Or I could have one come to your chamber..."

"Oh, I'm sure the king will be fine," Trunculin said, smiling at Asa. "Are you quite well, my king?"

Asa just looked down at his plate and said, "Yes, firstcouncilor. I'm fine."

The queen said, "I see you have more guards here today. I hope you're not expecting someone to stab you at my table?"

Asa looked at Trunculin and said to the queen, "No, of course not. It's just that… The firstcouncilor pointed out that I have fewer guards around me than other kings. He just thought I should… do it the proper way."

Trunculin added, "I thought it important to go back to our regular routine. For when we go back to our kingdom, the king will better understand how life will be for him at home."

The queen said, "Speaking of that. We will have to find some time to talk about the prisoners. If our men do actually find a plot, I assume you'll want Gordon's uncle returned to you?"

The queen had been speaking to Asa, but Trunculin answered, "Yes, assuming it goes well, our kingdom has plenty of ways to punish wrongdoers."

"I was speaking to the king, firstcouncilor," she said, turning back to Asa. "What do you say, King Asa?"

"Well… my queen, the firstcouncilor speaks… with my voice. I'm sure what he says is best," Asa said as he looked down at his plate again.

"Public trials are usually best," said the grandmother. "That way the mobs feel like they're involved somehow. My father used to have public executions almost weekly. Good for the spirits of the kingdom."

"Do you think the courts will want to kill Loren?" asked Asa. The queen wasn't sure if he was asking the question to anyone in particular. The young king's mind seemed far away.

"Being a traitor to our kingdom is punishable by death. Of course, I have no way to know what the courts will actually do, but the law is clear," said Trunculin.

The grandmother said, "I should hope that they would put him to death. He took your king. Or at the very least, he helped the boy run away like a coward…"

"I have something for you, my queen," said Asa abruptly, and slowly rose from his chair. He took a piece of paper out of his pocket. He was about to hand it to the queen, but the firstcouncilor was too fast. Trunculin snatched the piece of paper out of the king's hand before he could give it to the queen.

Trunculin said, "My king. You know that I must edit every communication we have between kingdoms. I wouldn't be doing my job if I let you give something to her that was…" Trunculin stopped as he finished reading the piece of paper, "…what is this?"

"It's a poem that I wrote for the queen. She has been so kind to us since we got here, that I thought… may I read it, firstcouncilor?" Asa said looking at Trunculin and extending his hand. The queen thought the boy was shaking.

Asa asked Trunculin, "Please?"

Trunculin smiled his famous public smile and handed the piece of paper back to Asa, "Of course, my king, I think it's a lovely gesture. The queen is quite beautiful, isn't she?"

The queen smiled, and Asa blushed as he read,

"For a queen most fair,
A smile light as air,
I beg your love,
To fly like a dove,
Read my heart, and
Please make a start,
That two birds
May soon fly together."

Asa sat down and slowly folded the paper again. The queen, her grandmother, and even Trunculin clapped along with a few tables that were close by.

The queen said, "Well, I don't know what to say. That was lovely, my king."

The grandmother remarked, "It's a good thing that you were chosen king. I'm not sure that you would ever make a poet," the grandmother said, smiling. "What exactly are your intentions towards my granddaughter, young man?" Asa wondered if that was the first time he had seen the grandmother smile. It made him nervous.

Asa said, "Nothing. I… I know it's silly. You can keep the poem if you want. I know it's…. maybe someday, someday soon, two hearts might be saved?" Asa looked into the queen's eyes and handed her the poem.

The queen smiled back, "My king, I'm flattered, truly. But with my husband so recently gone, and me being old enough to be your… well, young aunt, I think we should discuss this a few years down the road."

Asa avoided looking at the firstcouncilor, and then glanced at the queen before looking down at the table again. Asa smiled a little sadly. "Well, you can't blame a king for trying."

The queen and her grandmother laughed as did several people at the tables around them. Even the firstcouncilor laughed as he stared at the boy king.

Later, alone in her chamber, the queen was writing a stack of letters. She had the poem unfolded and propped up against her desk so she could see it. Something about the poem intrigued her. It was so surprising, and so flattering. After being married for many years, to have someone suddenly fall in love with her, even just a boyhood crush made her feel good.

As she wrote her letters, she kept looking back at the poem. Something about it seemed odd. She assumed it was just a poem written by a boy who was not used to writing poetry. But it was the way the beginning rhymed, and the end did not, that she kept coming back to. *Read my heart. Two birds fly together… Two birds.* And then he said that strange thing to her about two hearts being saved.

She decided to consult her grandmother. When the queen explained what she was thinking, the grandmother said, "That's ridiculous."

"I know it seems ridiculous, but what if that's what he was trying to say?' said the queen.

The grandmother responded, "You honestly think the boy was saying he wants you to release the prisoners? That makes no sense, my dear. Why would he want them released, and against the firstcouncilor's advice?"

The queen said, "I don't know. It's just a strange feeling I have. Why was he behaving so strangely? The extra guards, the firstcouncilor being especially overbearing. And then this poem that sounds like a code. What if the firstcouncilor is controlling him?"

The grandmother replied, "I say, good. The boy has no idea what he's doing. Honestly, choosing some boy out of the filthy mob to be your king. It's a disgusting idea. If Trunculin is controlling the boy, I say ... good! He's doing his job. At least someone with brains and cunning is getting things done in that kingdom."

"I'm going to go see the king. I have to know."

The grandmother said, "Well I hope the boy doesn't try to kiss you. He's embarrassed himself enough for one day."

The queen left the room.

As she approached Asa's door, she noticed more guards were here as well. She thought she heard raised voices, someone yelling, but she wasn't sure as the guard knocked on the door. The guard entered and returned a moment later to escort the queen inside. As she came in, Asa was sitting on a chair in the middle of the room, with the firstcouncilor standing over him.

"How may we serve you, my queen?" asked Trunculin smoothly.

"I would like to speak to the king… alone."

King Asa looked quickly to Trunculin, who smiled thinly. Asa said, "The firstcouncilor is teaching me…um, so much right now. Are you sure he couldn't stay?"

The queen replied, "There are some things that must be discussed between only a king and a queen. I'm sure the firstcouncilor will understand the delicacy."

"My apologies, my queen, but that is up to the king, and he has asked me to stay," said Trunculin.

The queen replied, "While I appreciate the loyalty to your king, I would hate to have to remind you that you are still a guest in my palace. I will speak to the king alone. Now. Is that clear?"

"Of course, my queen," Trunculin said as he left the room. "But, of course, the guards will have to stay in the room. It is only for my king's protection."

The queen looked around to the guards. They looked defiant, insolent. When Trunculin was gone and the door firmly closed, she leaned down to whisper into Asa's ear. "Was this poem for love or for something else? Don't answer. Blink your eyes once from love, twice for something else."

Asa blinked twice.

She leaned in again. "Was this about the 'birds' I have captured? One blink yes, two blinks no."

Asa blinked once.

She looked at the guards again, and at the door Trunculin was surely behind, trying to listen. "You want me to release these birds? One blink yes, or keep them where they are, two blinks."

One blink.

"Now you're going to have to talk to me, but quietly. You can whisper in my ear very softly. Why do you want the birds free?" The queen started to put her ear to Asa's mouth, but he shook his head no.

He looked in her eyes and made her follow his gaze. He winced as he raised his shirt. The queen put her hand on her mouth but didn't speak. Asa's chest and stomach were covered in dark bruises.

Asa winced again as he dropped his shirt slowly so the guards wouldn't see. The queen looked back at the door that Trunculin had gone through and looked slowly around at the guards.

She gently put her hands on either side of Asa's face and wiped away his tears. The queen gently kissed him on the mouth. Then she sternly looked him in the eyes again, nodded slightly, wiping her own tears. She left quietly.

There was something important she had to do.

CHAPTER 44
FRIEND IN ARTOTH

"The gate. Is that it?" asked Gordon.

"No, nice try," said Aline, as she punched his arm.

Mantuan had put a coin between them and told them the first one to see the gate could keep it. They were both fiercely watching for the gate when Mantuan came up to them. "You have good eyes Gordon, yes, that is the gate."

Gordon snatched up the coin and smiled. Aline punched him in the arm again.

He rubbed his arm and glanced sideways at Aline. He asked, "If the gates are controlled by two different kings, what happens when they get mad at each other?"

"Chaos," said Aline, getting up, smiling and punching Gordon on the other arm.

Mantuan said, "I remember a year when the kings were at war with each. They only let a few ships through each day. Their prices to pass the gates were unbelievable, and there was a line of ships as far as you could see waiting to get through. There was so much traffic that they woke up the beast of the canal. They lost three ships each week for nearly a year."

"I don't think it really exists. I think those boats just sank, then they blamed it on a beast," said Aline.

Mantuan said, "Oh no. The canal beast exists. I saw it take a ship down once. There are lots of strange creatures deep under the waters. They dug the canal through the land so deep because they wanted to get larger ships through. One of these things ended up in the canal between the two gates. Some say it comes and goes, some say it stays there, waiting. And some like Aline, say it doesn't exist…"

"Doesn't exist, Manny," said Aline.

"Does. And it's been the source of a lot of bad blood between the two kings. The orange king's faith believes it's a sacred animal. It is said to have taken down the ship of the blue king long ago. So, one side wants to kill it for ancient revenge, and one side believes that it proves their gods are stronger, because it killed the king from the other side. It is a very complicated kingdom."

"Is Artoth like the old books say it is?" asked Gordon.

"Very curious, I like that," Mantuan smiled. "This kingdom is truly the oldest kingdom. Thure is called the old kingdom, but Artoth was there before anyone even thought of Thure. Many great kings have ruled there, going back so far that no one remembers."

Aline said, "And the waterfalls and terraces are beautiful."

"They are," Mantuan agreed. "It's called the kingdom of the gods because the two kings who rule it believe in completely different gods. Half of the kingdom believes in the pact with man and the other half believe in so many dark gods I can't keep track."

"Don't forget the third faith," said Aline.

"I haven't. Because it's not a faith. It's just a bunch of young idiots who don't believe in anything," said Mantuan.

Aline offered, "They are very friendly…"

"…yes, and very stupid," said Mantuan, then walked away.

"The orange half of the kingdom believes in dark gods that do really bad things. Their god of healers is also the god that takes away the dead…"

"But that doesn't sound so bad…" said Gordon.

"… And eats them," finished Aline.

"Ugg. Seriously?" asked Gordon.

"And all their soldiers and guards…well, I will let you see that for yourself," said Aline.

Gordon turned around to look from the front of the ship. As they got close to the gate, Gordon saw how huge it was. He could tell that it had been there a long time because of the rust, but it didn't take away from its beauty.

There were several ships going ahead of them. One of them was stopped outside the gate. He couldn't see what was going on, but then the gates slowly started to open with a strange, deep, rusty sound. The gate split open in two halves and swung open toward the ship.

Mantuan explained that they opened out, so that a large ship couldn't just push through the gates. The ship that was moving through the gate had a very tall mast, but it was still not as tall as the gate. The gates slowly swung shut after the ship had passed through it.

Once again, the great metal doors came together to reveal what looked like a metal sun either breaking or setting over the gate. Gordon wasn't sure which.

They all watched a few other ships pass through. As they got closer, Gordon saw that the men near the gate were all very large, with huge muscular arms and legs. Gordon thought it was interesting that large powerful men were not fighting, but used as guards instead. Councilor-like men were among them, writing things down.

They had arrived at the gate. "What business do you have in the great kingdom of Artoth?" asked the guard.

"God's business. We come to see the first kingdom of men and gods," said Mantuan to the guard. Gordon noticed that he had removed his patch.

"How many on your ship? Do you bring any goods?"

"Just good people, eight of them," replied Mantuan.

Councilors were scribbling in their books and the guard said, "Normal fee applies. You may pass. The second gate is controlled by a different king. They may not let you pass. Fair warning. May the Gods be with you."

Mantuan made a slight bow and the gates opened. As they passed through, Gordon got a closer look and wondered, "How old are the gates?"

"Some say over a thousand years. Although I don't think that is true. This may be the oldest kingdom, but it's a dangerous place run on ancient grievances, deceptions and lies," replied Mantuan seriously, "but I know at least one honest man in the kingdom who may be able to help us."

Gordon's attention drifted as they made their way down the canal. He looked up at the steep, sheer mountains that rose as high as he could see. The ship suddenly rocked back and forth in the calm waters. Gordon struggled to remain standing. "What was that?"

"Something swam underneath us. Let's hope the beast of the canal is not hungry today," replied Mantuan, who said it much too calmly for Gordon's taste.

Aline was already at the railing, trying to see below the dark waters. Gordon decided he was going to stay where he was. If it had been the beast, it gave them no more trouble as they neared the second gate. Aline was still looking over the railing when Gordon gasped, startled when he saw the men guarding the second gate. Aline smiled at his shock.

They were just as large and muscled as the men of the first gate, but there was something very different about them. They were all bald and had marks on their faces. But the biggest difference was when the main guard spoke. "What is your business in the kingdom?" Gordon couldn't stop looking at his teeth, which were all sharp and pointed like an animal's fangs.

"That is our business, guard. Do you want the fee or not?" said Mantuan.

The guard looked at Mantuan for a long moment. A small councilor came up to him. He said something to the guard, but the guard continued to look at Mantuan, who stood there, staring back with his arms crossed.

The guard bowed slightly and nodded, "You may pass. Normal fee applies. May the Gods protect you."

The gate opened and they sailed into the large open waters. When they were out of earshot of the guard, Gordon asked Aline, "Why was he so rude to that guard?"

Aline replied, "The second gate is controlled by men that hate weakness. If Mantuan had been polite to the man it would've raised suspicion. To these men, strength gains respect," said Aline.

Gordon wasn't sure he understood that exactly, but he had very little time to ponder it as the ship turned. Gordon suddenly saw the kingdom of the gods for the first time. The sun glistened off the buildings of Artoth. There were great walls around the kingdom, but the buildings rose high above them. Gordon could see some of the different levels of the terraced kingdom. He had always read about the great terraced levels, connected by stairs and bridges. The buildings looked different from each other as well, like they had been built by the greatest builders, in every style imaginable.

Gordon asked, "Is it really true that the water never stops flowing in Artoth?"

Aline said, "It's true. The mountain above feed a constant flow of water around the terraces and into secret storage places underneath the kingdom. They say Artoth has enough fresh water to quench the thirst of the whole world."

"Get below Gordon. Now," said Mantuan. Aline grabbed Gordon's arm. As they both went below, Gordon saw the airship floating outside of the kingdom. Mantuan joined them below. "As I feared, they made it here before us."

"But if the ship is floating there, is it safe to enter the kingdom?" asked Gordon.

"It will be safe enough. When visiting a hostile land, only a small group go on their mission. The rest of the men stay armed and ready in the air where no one can touch them. From there, they can see anything coming. Trust me, I'm the one that invented the tactic," said Mantuan.

"What's the plan?" asked Aline.

Mantuan answered, "The plan is the same. The three of us will go to make contact. We will wear hoods so that no one is recognized. I'll have to go without my patch, so you'll be my guard Aline. Let's get ready."

Lantovas asked, "May I accompany you? I want justice for my king."

Mantuan answered, "I need you to do something else. Let me tell you in private." Mantuan gave his idea to Lantovas. The Thurian guard smiled and accepted his mission.

They docked the ship, making sure it was the farthest dock from the airship. At the entrance to the kingdom, there were fee collectors. They paid both their fees to the blue and orange guards and went through the kingdom gates.

Gordon couldn't help but smile at the enormous, tall buildings everywhere he looked. It was like walking into an old painting. Many of the buildings looked even taller than they were, since they were on terraces that were higher than the ones they came in on. Gordon didn't like the reason for his travels, but he was glad to see so many new places he'd only read about.

A group of girls a little older than Gordon approached them just as they were entering the kingdom. They were all smiling brightly and each had a flower just over the ear. They were dressed in simple, white clothes. Very clean, Gordon thought.

"Have you met the mother?" asked one of the girls coming up to Gordon.

"Sorry, what?" replied Gordon.

The girl handed Gordon a card with a drawing of a woman's face. Her eyes were closed and she was smiling. Her hair seemed to be made of flowers. "The true mother. This is your pass to meet her. Please come. Just follow the flowers."

Another girl and a boy about the same age tried to hand cards to Aline and Mantuan. "The mother loves us all…"

Mantuan said nothing and waved his hands at the young people. Aline said, "No thank you. I already have a mother… and I think she loves me." Aline tugged on Gordon's arm and they left the group of young people. As they continued down the stone streets, Gordon looked at the card and said, "What was that about?"

Aline said, "It's one of the newer faiths. They pray to a motherly goddess that they say protects us all. They dress the same, and they try to get new travelers to come to their gatherings. They seem nice enough."

"They seem nice enough. But this mother has apparently removed their brains. When you have no brains, anyone can put a bad idea in your head. My advice is to stay away," said Mantuan.

Gordon put the card in his pocket and they continued on. They came to the first set of stone stairs that led up to the next terrace. Gordon looked over the stairs and down to the rushing water below. When they got up to the next terrace, he realized how big the kingdom must be. He could see terraces up ahead, like large cities floating over streams of water, all connected to each other. He wondered how many different terraces and levels there were. He asked, but Aline just said, "No one knows."

They walked for quite a while through open air markets, down narrow passageways and through crowds large and small. This was a large kingdom with a lot of people. They had already climbed up or down eight separate terraces. Or little cities on each terrace, as Gordon came to think of them.

Gordon noticed how many different kinds of people there were. Not just different from him, but different from each other. There were people dressed in clothing of all styles and colors; wearing headdresses, bald, tall, short, skinny, muscular, tiny. People of all skin color, all going about their business on the sunny day. Most were walking, but some were on horses who didn't seem to mind the stairs between terraces. There were a few small carriages with people in them being carried by men at each end. Gordon realized it would be hard for any carriage on wheels to navigate this kingdom because of all the stairs.

Artoth reminded him of Thure, but much older. Many different languages were being spoken. He thought he could tell where some of the people were from, others he couldn't even imagine. What struck him most were the smells, old and deep, and totally different somehow. And there was also something about the light that was unique from anywhere else he'd been. Being in this kingdom was like he was in a completely different world.

Gordon noticed a man begging. The man looked old until Gordon got closer. As they walked by, Gordon realized that the man was only a boy a few years older than him, maybe seventeen or eighteen. He looked like a living skeleton. Gordon stopped when he read his sign, his blood turning to ice. It read, *sweetblood sickness please help.*

Gordon fished into his pocket. He realized he had the same coin he had been holding the day he put his name in the tower. Aline put her hand on Gordon's shoulder as the coin fell into the man's metal cup. They walked on, not talking about the fact that the boy had no legs.

They finally arrived at a large tall building that resembled a tower and entered the courtyard. They got to the great door with a large metal knocker. It made a deep musical sound and the door opened with two large eyes staring at them, "Yes?"

"I'm here for Santovan," said Mantuan.

"Your business?" asked the young woman.

"Personal," Mantuan said as he lowered his hood and put his patch on.

The young woman looked surprised and closed the door briefly. The young woman smiled and motioned for them to come in. She led them up winding stairs until they reached the upper part of the building. The girl excitedly asked them to wait for a moment as she ran off. From the other room they heard, "It can't be," as a large man came out to meet them. "They said you were dead!"

"They say a lot of things. How are you, my friend?" Mantuan and the stranger embraced. Gordon got the feeling that he had met this man before, even though he knew he couldn't have. *Something about his face,* he thought.

"And who are these two fine young people?" asked the man.

"Santovan, meet Aline. And Gordon…" Mantuan said cautiously "… the rightful king from far away."

Santovan looked them over, smiled and said, "My house is suddenly full of dead people. You were king for a day and you are already famous all over our world. Nice to meet you, my king. And always nice to meet a lovely young lady. Come, let me feed you."

CHAPTER 45
RED CLOAK

"Any other ideas?" asked Darion, eating an apple.

Brenddel stood in the open market with a dark expression and said, "No. I was counting on those two contacts to lead me in the right direction. Now I have no one else to ask... wait, maybe one more. He's a merchant that lives here in the kingdom, but he's hardly a friend. Anyway, we are close to the meeting place, let's go find this contact of the little councilor first."

"Lead on," replied Darion.

Brenddel was wearing the red cloak the councilor was supposed to have worn. It was much too short, but he hoped that would not matter. "We have to find out if what the councilor said was true. If Extatumm has an army of airships, then all of our kingdoms are in danger."

Darion noted, "You seem to know your way around this kingdom fairly well," he glanced down at the rushing water below, as they went over a wooden bridge.

"You have an annoying habit of asking a question without asking a question. I respect those that say what they mean," said Brenddel.

Darion laughed, "Fair enough. In my kingdom, you never say what you actually think. There are many games played in my kingdom and they can be exhausting. So, how do you know your way around Artoth so well?

"I was born here. I lived here when I was a boy," Brenddel responded.

"I didn't expect that. How long.... Rather, many kings have you served in your adopted kingdom of the thirteen?" asked Darion.

Brenddel didn't immediately answer, but finally said, "Five, if you count Gordon."

"Five. That would mean you first served under... the slaver king Daymer?" asked Darion. Before Darion knew what was happening, he found himself a foot off the ground, up against a stone wall.

Brenddel said very slowly, "I don't discuss that king. Ever. Nod your head to show me that you understand."

Darion looked into Brenddel's eyes and slowly nodded his head. Brenddel let him down and they continued on their journey. They didn't speak again until they reached their destination.

Darion asked, "Where are we exactly?"

Brenddel responded, "This part of the kingdom is one of the oldest sites known to man. It is mostly ruins from an even more ancient kingdom that no one talks about. Both ancient faiths had gods that were supposedly born here. It is for visitors now, with street vendors around the old remains of the water fountains."

"How are we going to find him in all these people?" said Darion. "I see people wearing red everywhere."

It was true. There were people wearing red hats, red scarves, red shirts, red capes, and even red pants. There were also people yelling, with signs in their hands. One read, *the gods are angry*. Another man was shouting, *death form the skies, turn back to the gods.*

Brenddel ignored them. "If this meeting was so important, he should be looking for us," replied Brenddel, slowly moving around the old ruins.

They had been walking for half of an hour among the different water fountains. Many people had their eyes closed, saying silent promises to their gods at the fountains.

Darion and Brenddel scanned casually for anyone to make eye contact with them. They finally saw a man standing in a shallow archway, staring. Brenddel looked away for a moment and then looked back, and the man was still looking at him.

The man walked to them, "Pardon me, but I couldn't help notice the fine fabric of your red cloak. May I ask where you got it?"

"It was a gift from the firstcouncilor Trunculin. Perhaps you've heard of him?" Brenddel replied.

The man nodded, "I have. Perhaps we could go somewhere more private and discussed it."

"That is what I had in mind," said Brenddel

They went to an old ruin far away from the crowds. The man said, "I wasn't expecting two contacts."

"The firstcouncilor has a new ally. This is Darion of Thure, the brother of the murdered king. The firstcouncilor asked me to bring him along," said Brenddel.

"What The Father has in mind did not include other kingdoms. It was not agreed," replied the man.

"I know it seems strange," said Darion, "but the queen has stolen my birthright. I'm a man without a kingdom and I'm looking to make new alliances. So are my men, who are loyal only to only me. My army is in Aspora now, ready for my instructions. Surely your inner council is looking for allies that have a private army."

The agent responded, "It won't be hard to find out if you speak the truth. I think there might be a place for you in our plans. I am Coltun. Before I look foolish, how much do you know?"

Darion jumped in. "We know you're building an army of airships. This would change the power structure of all of our kingdoms. Whether it is to attack, or merely to threaten, I want to be on the right side of history. The winning side."

Brenddel was surprised at how blunt Darion was being. Either he meant every word he said, or he was a very good actor.

The man nodded. "The firstcouncilor shared much with you. He would not have told you this, unless you were indeed an ally. Yes, we have built many airships. We have modified and expanded the original plans. Our newest ships look very different than the other airships. We are not quite ready to let the world know what we are doing."

Brenddel said, "The firstcouncilor shared much with us. But there are a few unanswered questions. How are you getting all the gas you need?"

The man said, "Well, I am here for a specific set of reasons. I can't discuss all of our plans. I can only say that we make our own gas. If the firstcouncilor is worried about how much coin your kingdom is losing by us not buying your gas, it is more than made up for by the price we paid for the airship plans and our coming alliance. All we are required to talk about today is how soon we can arrange the meeting."

Brenddel knew nothing about any meeting. It was difficult for him to control his anger at hearing that the firstcouncilor had sold their kingdom's biggest secret. But he had to know more. "The meeting can be very soon."

The man looked at him suspiciously. "So, we're still on schedule? The inner council had feared that this Gordon business would put things on hold."

Brenddel lied. "Nothing has changed. Gordon was discredited, and now he's dead. A new king has been chosen.

The meeting is still on schedule," said Brenddel hoping that partial truths would get more information from the man.

"That is the good news the council was hoping for. TrTorrin, our great father, will be escorted to meet with your king and firstcouncilor. We will need an airship escort for our delegation, as planned. If we are agreed on the basics, I am to escort you back to Extatumm, where we can meet with the father. In secret, of course."

Brenddel replied, "Of course. Unfortunately there is another matter that I must attend to before we leave. Trunculin wants me to follow up a lead on the men who poisoned the king of Thure."

The man looked confused for a moment and then said, "How… how can I help?"

"I need to go see a man. He's a merchant named Santovan of the family Xoss," said Brenddel.

Darion looked confused for a moment, but Brenddel clarified, "Denogg's brother." Darion understood and nodded.

Brenddel continued, "He lives not far from here. I don't know if he'll help me or not."

Darion offered, "He also won't like the fact that his brother is in prison. Surely he's heard by now,"

"We still have to try. Shouldn't take long," said Brenddel.

"I will accompany you. I am at your service," said Coltun, their new ally.

CHAPTER 46
OLD WOUNDS

"That's why you look familiar!" said Gordon.

"Yes, Denogg is my brother. I'm very sorry to hear that the first meal you had with him went so badly. At least, badly for the king of Thure," said Santovan.

They were finishing their lavish meal and Gordon was still picking at his raisin cakes, careful to stay balanced with his sweetblood. Not being able to test his blood, Gordon had to trust how he felt. That just made him think of his uncle again.

Mantuan finished his tea and brought up the subject that he had come here for. "So you're positive that the murderers are agents from Extatumm?"

"Oh yes. When I heard about what happened in my brother's house, I started finding out whatever I could. They were definitely Extatumm agents. I just confirmed it yesterday with a contact that does some trading near their lands. But they will be deep back into their protected circle by now," said Santovan.

"But why? Why would they want to kill me, or the king of Thure? Why would they want to interfere with any other kingdom at all?" asked Gordon.

"Here in Artoth, we are Extatumm's closest neighbor. We hear whispers of what goes on in their secretive lands. What they say and how they behave are two very different things. I can only guess why they wanted one of you dead. But as far as interfering with other kingdoms, they had been doing that ever since their 'great and glorious transformation' as they call it. They have agents in nearly all the kingdoms, and they have a nasty habit of taking people in the middle of the night. The two kings of Artoth have mostly let it happen, since most taken are from the lower classes. The kings almost feel as though they're doing my kingdom a favor, taking people no one would notice."

"Why would they want to take anyone?" asked Gordon.

"When they overthrew the king and queen of Dard, they declared their ideas. Some of them sounded fine. The people ruling themselves with no king to tell them what to do. The workers being taken care of like never before, freedom for all, everyone equal. They all sounded very nice. But from what we hear, the reality is much different. We know there are large mining operations and gas fields. They still have leaders, they just don't call themselves kings. And they are a very suspicious people. The leaders keep Extatumm very closed to outsiders," said Santovan.

Aline seemed bothered by something and she excused herself to go into the next room.

Gordon asked, "I thought you said everyone was equal. How can they have leaders?"

Santovan continued, "From what we have heard, it is a very strange system. Some leaders get elected, some get appointed. They have some sort of ruling body that makes all the decisions. Apparently, some are more equal than others."

Gordon said, "A few people saying that everyone is equal, but then saying 'but we will be in charge,' seems confusing."

"They don't see any contradiction," said Santovan.

Mantuan said, "There's always a leader. And when there's great power involved, they rarely give up that power. So, finding the murderers is out of the question. We will find another way to get your brother and Loren out of prison. There is another way you can help, old friend."

Santovan seemed intrigued. "I'll help anyway I can..."

"We need to find the law keeper," said Mantuan.

"...Anyway but that," said Santovan. "The law keeper does not want to be found."

Mantuan smiled, "So you do know where he is?"

"Yes," Santovan said with a puzzled look. "You do know who the law keeper is, don't you?"

"He is the one that's going to help us take down Trunculin and all his evil plots, once and for all," said Mantuan.

"I seriously doubt that. It would be difficult for you to even reach the law keeper, who has stopped travelling and settled in one place. And you will never convince the law keeper to get involved with your kingdom again."

"If what I've heard is true, he found many documents that will prove what Trunculin has been doing, many of his secrets. We need this proof to convince our people," said Mantuan.

"I believe the law keeper does have these documents. Every kingdom was searched quietly for years by the law keeper. But to do what you propose, would open up more wounds than you know."

"Opening up old wounds is always dangerous. But if we don't, they won't heal correctly. Right now my kingdom is rotting from the inside out. We have to destroy the illness and restore the kingdom," said Mantuan.

Santovan looked weary. "The problem is not finding the law keeper. The hard part is getting there. The law keeper is high in the snowy mountains. Agents of mine climb the mountains with supplies once a year. It takes a full week to climb the mountain. And I lose men every year in the attempt. It is an impossible idea."

"Too bad we don't have an airship," Gordon jested.

Mantuan laughed, "Too bad indeed. I don't think Trunculin will loan us one. We will have to make the climb. We will find the law keeper with or without your help Santovan."

"How can I say no to a man back from the dead? The law keeper will be very angry." Santovan let out a heavy sigh. "Please say you beat the information out of me. I will give you maps that show exactly where the law keeper is. But I will warn you that the path you're on, there's no turning back. It will be sad for you to come back from the dead only to die again," said Santovan, indicating Gordon and pointing to the next room where Aline had gone, "...and then taking these nice young people with you."

"Not very much faith for someone who lives in the kingdom of the gods," said Mantuan.

Santovan said, "I believe in a great many things. I also live in the real world. I'm convinced that we can never go backwards. I will help you on one condition. Find a way to get my brother out of prison."

"You have my word. I will get him out if I have to fight all of Thure myself," Mantuan promised.

"I would say I'm going to regret this, but I already do. Come with me," said Santovan leading them into another room for the maps and a list of things they would need to make the climb.

Mantuan sent Aline ahead to ready the men at the docks, giving her specific instructions on how to prepare them for the next step. Santovan warned them to dress warmly and sent Gordon and Mantuan on their way. They said their goodbyes and came out of the door. As Gordon and Mantuan were walking into the street, Mantuan suddenly stopped. Without saying a word, he drew his longknife.

Three men were walking towards them and they also stopped. Gordon didn't recognize two of the men. But there was no mistaking the man in the center. It was Brenddel. The firstman had drawn his own longknife and was already running straight at them.

CHAPTER 47
IMPRISONED

Loren and Denogg stood by the bars in their cells.

"... No, it was just me and my brother Santovan," said Denogg. "Our parents were merchants. We both followed in their footsteps. Although my brother was much more defiant, he dared to go far away from home. I never had the urge. Of course I've traveled and have business dealings in many kingdoms, but I like the comfort of home."

Loren said, "I'm sorry that home is gone. Sorry that we involved you at all, Denny. Although I certainly couldn't have seen any of this coming."

"Oh stop. I will be fine, providing that they don't cut my head off. That would ruin my day. How about your family?" asked Denogg.

Loren said, "Just one sister. I..." they both heard noises coming down the hall toward them.

Denogg said, "I hope that's not the executioner already..."

The queen walked down the corridor quickly, giving orders to several soldiers. Denogg and Loren stood there. The queen said, "You're getting out of here. Now. I'm giving you a full pardon."

"To what do we owe this… honor, my queen?" asked Denogg cautiously.

One of the guards opened the cell doors, and the queen said, "I'm convinced you were not involved in my husband's death Denny, or you Loren, nor Gordon. I am sorry about Gordon, by the way. And I'm getting you out of here so that your insane firstcouncilor does not kill you."

Loren asked, "Did Trunculin do something? What has happened?"

"Many things happened," said the queen. "Some of them too disturbing to talk about now. Besides, there's no time. Denny, you both need to leave the kingdom now. How fast can you make arrangements?"

"Just release my ships back to me when I arrive at the docks. We can leave right away. Why the urgency, my queen?"

"Because as soon as my grandmother finds out what I've done, she will tell Trunculin and his men will be after you," said the queen.

"What's the best way out?" asked Loren.

"Like all palaces, we have secret ways out," the queen said, handing something to one of her guards. "These guards will get you to the docks. I have given him a sealed letter releasing any goods you need. Go quickly… ".

The queen stopped as she heard metal clanging and voices coming towards them. "She was faster than I thought. Go, it's that way."

Denogg, Loren and the two guards made for the secret exit the opposite way from the fast approaching commotion. The queen turned to see several of Trunculin's guards running towards them. The guards had their longknives out and started to surround the queen. Her own guards drew their longknives.

The queen said, "How dare you draw your knives in my kingdom?"

"Put your knives away," said Trunculin as he strode in with the grandmother. He asked, "Where are they, my queen?"

"How dare you…" the queen started.

The grandmother rushed in and slapped the queen across the face. The guards froze, not used to protecting the queen from her own grandmother. "You stupid girl. I should have realized from your mother that brains could skip a few generations. We need this alliance. You have royal blood, act like it!"

The queen recovered and rubbed her face. She stared at her grandmother. "I will act like a queen who was just struck by one of her subjects. Guards, put my beloved grandmother in that cell," said the queen wiping the blood from her lip.

"You wouldn't. I…" began the grandmother.

The guards hesitated for a moment but complied. "And gag her," added the queen. "I can't speak to the brains, grandmother, but I thank the gods that cruelty skips generations as well."

The firstcouncilor stood there watching. The queen could tell from his expression that he didn't know what to expect next.

The queen turned on Trunculin. "You vile filth. If I could find a way to save that poor boy, I would. I should kill you where you stand, but I'm not stupid. I know your airships would come over and rain fire on my kingdom. I know that I cannot win in a war with you." She took a step toward Trunculin. "But I can throw you the hell out of my kingdom."

Trunculin stepped towards her. "You have far more enemies than you think, my queen," he said, nearly spitting the words. "We will leave. And we will catch the prisoners. Don't worry, I'll return Denogg to you after I catch them, from my airship. The fat pig should make quite the stain in front of your palace. And if I ever choose to come back here, it will not be for a friendly chat."

Before the queen had time to respond, Trunculin and his guards had walked back down the corridor. The queen fully understood that the ally she'd hoped to gain was now her enemy.

She looked over to the cell where the grandmother was gagged. Her hands were tied, but she was furiously trying to shout through the gag. The queen slowly went up to the bars. The two women made eye contact.

The queen said only one word to her grandmother before she walked away. "Rot."

CHAPTER 48
MANTUAN AND BRENDDEL

Mantuan was in the middle of the street as Brenddel charged him. Brenddel only faltered for a moment when he saw the boy and realized Gordon was alive. Mantuan used that moment of hesitation to attack. He swung at Brenddel, but Brenddel twisted his body backwards and leapt to avoid the knife. He didn't land on his feet, but he was up on them quickly enough to block Mantuan's second blow.

The other two men in Brenddel's party didn't move to help, but instead the man from Extatumm asked Darion, "Who is that boy?"

Darion said, "Believe it or not, that is the boy king Gordon. And that is the legendary warrior Mantuan. Looks like it's a day of the dead in the kingdom of the gods."

Gordon has drawn his longknife as well, and wanted to help Mantuan, but he had no idea how to engage without being in the way.

"Did you bring it with you?" Mantuan asked Brenddel as they battled in the middle of the street.

Brenddel took a step back and aimed his wrist arrows. Mantuan pushed over a small wooden table, spilling fruit everywhere. With one hand, he turned it into a shield and the small, thick arrow made a "thktt" sound as the head of the arrow came through the wood. Mantuan launched the table at Brenddel and it hit his arm, shattering his wrist mounted arrow gun. "I told you that thing is useless in a real fight."

The blow sent Brenddel tumbling down the stone steps to the next terrace. People scrambled to get out of his way. Mantuan charged down the steps, not wasting a moment. "*Is it here?*" Mantuan shouted again.

Brenddel stood up and took a few paces backwards. He knew that Mantuan had the advantage on the higher ground, looming over him on the steps. Both men's hearts raced as they shouted over the rushing water below the steps. "What are you saying, dead man?"

Mantuan made a shout and charged Brenddel again, blocking his knife and pushing him back. Brenddel went flying backward into a cart full of pottery. He rolled over the ruined cart, getting up quickly. Mantuan said, "My battle axe. I want it back before I kill you."

Gordon raced down the steps after them, still hesitating to enter the fight. Brenddel had just gotten up, when Mantuan's shortknife went flying at Brenddel. He shielded his face instinctively and it sunk into the back of his arm.

Brenddel yelled and pulled the knife out. Gordon's hesitation didn't matter, and apparently Mantuan needed no help. Gordon knew how strong Brenddel was, but it was clear he would lose this fight. Brenddel knew it too.

Mantuan advanced on Brenddel slowly, step by step. "I can throw you down into the waters of Artoth, or you can run. Your choice."

"*You* should run, dead man," said Brenddel, holding his arm. Blood was pouring from the open wound. "I have a full airship. We will be coming for you."

Mantuan replied, "I'm counting on it. Next time we meet, I want my axe back."

Brenddel broke off the attack and started running back to the gates of the kingdom and his airship. Memories of his childhood rushed into his mind as he ran. Brenddel realized this part of the kingdom was not far from where Mantuan had found him. And from where his parents had been taken.

He used the fury of these memories to rush to his men on the airship.

*

Darion and the Extatumm agent watched the action from the distance. They saw the fight move down the steps to the terrace below.

Darion said, "Well, it looks like we will be headed to Extatumm alone."

Coltun said, "Yes, it appears that way. I have transportation out of the kingdom at the far gate. I need to make an urgent stop first."

At the next block, Darion waited as the man went into a small building with a woman's face painted above the door. A few young women and young men all wearing white were milling around outside. Coltun was only inside a moment. After he came out, he saw a group of girls with flowers in their hair leave the building. They all seem to be running back the direction they had just come.

They stood at the edge of the fight again and saw Brenddel leave to retrieve his men.

"Should we wait until he gets back?" asked Coltun.

Darion saw the first of the Artoth guards coming. "No. We should go now." Coltun and Darion left for Extatumm.

*

Mantuan did not pursue Brenddel, but gathered Gordon and took an alternative route. They tried to walk quickly, without drawing attention. He removed his patch again. He knew the skirmish in the street had been witnessed by a lot of people. Both kings had guards everywhere. He just hoped to get out of the kingdom in time.

It was slow going, winding through the ancient terraces, streets and alleyways. Mantuan was sure that they would get away, when he saw a group of guards shouted for them to stop.

"Blast, I would've preferred to have dealt with the blue king's men. Those pointy toothed guards are very skilled." They stopped and ducked into a nearby alleyway. "Gordon, I need to take care of these guards. Stay here in the alley..."

"I want to fight," Gordon said.

"You are not ready, my king. This is no place to test your skills. Wait here. I insist," Mantuan said as he drew his longknife. He was back in the street quickly, the guards nearly on him. There were four guards dressed in orange leather armor, and Gordon could see they were all bearing their sharpened teeth. They all had their knives drawn and Mantuan leapt into them as though he was a beast attacking prey.

"Hello."

Gordon was startled by the greeting from behind him. He turned around to see a young woman in a white dress standing in the alleyway. He turned back to the fight. Another girl said, "Hello."

Gordon saw that Mantuan had already defeated one man and was just besting another. The man fell and would not get up again.

"Do you know the mother?" asked one girl to Gordon.

"Would you like to meet the father?" asked another.

"What? I'm sorry I'm a little busy right now…" Gordon said as three more of the girls came smiling at him. Gordon looked confused as one of them came close to him and opened her palm.

Gordon said, "I really can't…"

The girl blew a fine powder into Gordon's face.

Mantuan had defeated the third guard, when movement caught his attention from the alleyway. He looked for Gordon. To his shock, Gordon was being carried off by girls all dressed in white.

Mantuan shouted, "Gordon!"

One of the pointy toothed guards took advantage of the distraction and slashed at Mantuan, slicing him on the left arm. Mantuan growled and used the pain to fuel him. He ran the man through with his longknife and the man dropped to the ground. Turning, Mantuan shouted, "Gordon!"

Mantuan put pressure on his wound and starting towards the alleyway. He could no longer see the girls or Gordon. What he saw coming instead were dozens of guards. They were coming at him fast.

From either side of the alleyway, there were guards wearing the colors of both kings. They successfully cut Mantuan off from Gordon.

Mantuan knew he had no choice and fled. He had temporarily lost Gordon, the best hope for the kingdom. He sheathed his longknife, running back to his men and Aline.

CHAPTER 49
CATCHING THE PRISONERS

King Asa just watched as his men packed up all of their things. The firstcouncilor had said nothing since he had returned, except that they were going back to their kingdom. Everything was done quickly, and in what seemed like only moments, they were aboard the airship.

Asa thought about asking to say goodbye to the queen, but he knew that would only make Trunculin angrier, if that was possible. They boarded the airship and took to the skies. Trunculin knew that leaving at night was dangerous with the fin creatures, but he had no choice.

He had only a small contingent of soldiers after all, and one airship was nothing against the entire kingdom of Thure. Trunculin had many plans, but starting a war now was not one of them.

It wasn't until they were up in the air that Trunculin turned to Asa and said, "You did it all for nothing, you know. Loren and Denogg are fleeing Thure by ship, you stupid boy. This airship is twice as fast. We will find them. And I will make sure you remember their screams as you watch them fall."

Asa sat looking down at the deck of the ship. Then he slowly rose out of his chair to look right in the firstcouncilor's eyes. He tried very hard not to wince at the pain from the bruises. Asa's eyes were wet, but he tried not to blink, saying nothing. He just stood there looking at Trunculin.

Trunculin smiled a thin, arrogant smile. Asa thought that this was his true smile, not the one he showed to the public.

"You want to be defiant, do you?" said Trunculin. "Do you enjoy the punishment? Because I have many more ways to punish you, little king."

Asa stood there, staring at Trunculin.

"Guards. You two there. The king would like some fresh air," said Trunculin. The guards seemed to understand as they came towards Asa.

Asa tried not to look frightened, remembering the 'punishment,' as the firstcouncilor called it. Asa didn't know any way to fight Trunculin, but he still stood there.

Trunculin smiled. "The king would like a closer look. I think by the ankles would be the best view."

The two guards grabbed and lifted the small, defenseless king and held him by the ankles over the railing backwards, so he was staring straight down at the kingdom of Thure. The wind was cold and Asa told himself that he would not yell out.

Trunculin taunted, "Do you see them yet, my king?"

Asa said nothing.

Trunculin asked the pilot, "Are we close to the docks?"

"Yes, firstcouncilor, we're almost there," replied the pilot.

The guards held Asa, suspended by his feet over the railing. Asa's shirt slid down his body to reveal his bruises. The guards that had made them laughed as they held his ankles. It was freezing cold on his bare skin, but Asa refused to cry out.

"How's the view, boy?" asked one guard.

Another guard said, "Did you spot them yet? Even from here you should see the fat one."

Asa raised his head the best he could and shouted over the wind to Trunculin, "Why don't you just kill me?"

Trunculin replied, "Oh no, my king, that would be far too easy. For your insolence, and the crimes you have committed against me, staying king is a much worse punishment for you. I can't wait to meet your family when we get back. I have some punishments for them as well."

Asa closed his eyes. He wished he'd never seen the palace, never put his name in that tower.

He opened his eyes again and was starting to feel a little dizzy. He saw the lights at the docks, all the ships. The night was windy, but clear. There were so many lights. It was almost like staring down at the sky full of stars. Even at this height, Asa could smell sea water.

Then, something strange happened. The lights started flickering off, one by one. It was as though every light of the dock was being snuffed out like a candle. Asa watched, as what must have been a thousand little lights blinking out. It made the area very dark.

"Firstcouncilor, you need to see this," said one of the guards that had punished Asa.

Trunculin said, "What is it?"

"The lights at the docks," said the guard, "...they are all… going out."

Trunculin rushed to the front of the airship and the guard was right. Every light at, or near the docks was nearly gone. Even lights that should be lit for the boats were out. They were looking down into pitch black. It was though they were floating over nothingness.

Asa smiled as he heard the firstcouncilor yell of anger. It was a deep, enraged sound.

The guard said, "There's no way to find them, not in that darkness."

Asa's dizziness stopped, as he felt the firstcouncilor grab him and yank him back onto the deck of the airship. Asa slowly rose to stand. He thought he'd seen the firstcouncilor angry, but his face had never looked like this. Asa was glad for the dim light on the deck from the lanterns. More frightening than Trunculin's rage, was what slowly turned into the most terrifying smile Asa had ever seen.

CHAPTER 50
AT THE DOCKS

Brenddel and his men were running for the docks in Artoth. He had left only two men on the airship just outside the kingdom gates. He would take no chances this time, with his men behind him. He reached the docks to find soldiers from both kings waiting for them.

"What is the meaning of this attack?" asked one of the blue king's men.

A guard from the orange king's army said, "You dare attack our kingdom? Do not mistake the fact that we have two kings for weakness."

Brenddel motioned for all his men to put their knives away. "We are not attacking your kingdom. I was attacked in the street by a man. He and his men are hiding on these docks. I am Brenddel, firstman of the kingdom of the thirteen. I know our kingdoms have not always been friendly, but I swear to you this is not an attack. I am here on behalf of my king to look for the men that poisoned the king of Thure."

"These murderers from Thure attacked you?" asked the blue guard.

Brenddel tried not to be frustrated. "I was looking for the murderers when this *other* man attacked me. The man is very large and has a black leather patch over one eye."

"That sounds like a man that died a long time ago," said the orange guard.

Brenddel said, "I thought so too. But I saw him in the streets and I know he's on these docks somewhere. Will you help us search?"

The blue guard said, "We will have to ask the king's councilors first. We have only your word…"

The orange guard interrupted, "Why did you kill our men?"

Brenddel said, "We killed no one. It must have been Mantuan, trying to get here to the docks. Will you help us search for those that killed your men?"

The orange guard said, "We will have to ask our councilors."

"Can you at least stop ships from leaving the docks? They could be escaping as we argue!"

The blue guard said, "You are a guest here. You will watch your tongue."

The orange guard asked, "Is that your airship?"

Brenddel tried not to snap at the man, but replied calmly, "Yes. We paid both proper king's fees and agreed to keep it outside of the kingdom. We will put it back in the air as soon as we return with Mantuan."

"Brenddel?" said one of his own men behind him.

Brenddel turned around, "What!?" he shouted, losing his temper at the interruption. The man looked terrified and said nothing. He simply lifted his finger and pointed. Brenddel whipped around in fury and followed the man's finger.

His airship was floating away.

Brenddel watched one of his men fall over the railing of the airship. Although he could not see the faces of the people on board, he could see arms waving at him and knew that Mantuan had stolen his airship.

"Why would your men leave without you?" asked the guard of the blue king.

"I don't think those are his men," one of the orange guards said, laughing through his sharpened teeth. The guards of both kings all began laughing.

Brenddel did not cry out. His rage could find no voice.

When the guards stopped laughing, a blue guard said, "I think it's time you talked to our kings. All of you, come with us."

Brenddel turned back one more time to see his airship flying off. It looked very small now. He turned away from it and went with his men to go meet the two kings of Artoth.

END OF BOOK 1

AUTHOR NOTE

I just want to write a note to explain why this book leaves everyone hanging off the proverbial cliff. It was a hard decision, but the book I originally wrote was just too long. To tell the story properly, it needed more than one book. This was not a marketing gimmick. I just didn't want to scare off my first readers with a 900 page book.

I hope you continue Gordon and Asa's story.

You'll like what happens next.

M J Sewall,

June 2015

THANKS AND ACKNOWLEDGEMENTS

To everyone that helped me with my story at every stage, thank you.

But especially:

Anthony Pico
Brian Hall
Danielle O'Brien
Irene Getchel
Janet Wallace
Jenna Elizabeth Johnson
Lizann Flatt
Marshall Jones
Michele Casteel
Nellie Sewall
Rose Torres
Ryne Torres
Sarah Harris
Terri Jones
The McAlister family (John, Susan, Aidan and Colin)
A special thanks to you Aidan, for being the first boy to read my book.

INDEX OF NAMES AND TERMS

Adinn (Pronounced: AYE-DINN) – King before Stathen. Almost died on third trial, saved by Loren, and was later killed in a riding "accident."

Aline (AYE-LEEN) – Girl that helped Gordon.

Alonnia (UH-LONE-EE-UH) – Former queen of Dard, grandmother of the queen of Thure.

Anthsia (ANTH-SEE-UH) – Mountain in Dralinn, dormant volcano.

Arasta (A-RASS-TA) – Councilor and Trunculin's agent.

Arm arrows – Small wrist mounted arrow gun, like a small crossbow.

Arrow guns – Similar to crossbows or large arrow weapon like a ballista.

Artoth – Also known as the kingdom of the gods, rules by two kings.

Asa (AYE-SUH) – King after Gordon.

Asgonan (AZ-GO-NAN) – Island between Extatumm and Artoth, in dispute for centuries.

Aspora – Also known as the land of a thousand kings.

Banner of The kingdom of the thirteen – Banner with a triangle in the middle, surrounded by thirteen longknives pointed outward.
Borenn – First king, ruled the kingdom of the thirteen.
Brenddel – Firstman for five kings (Asa, Gordon, Stathen, Adinn and Daymer).
Coltun – Assistant to Extatumm leader.
Copway people – The friendly people of Yajan.
Corinn – The firsthealer of the kingdom of the thirteen.
Dard – Kingdom that was overthrown and renamed Extatumm.
Darion – Younger brother of Russel the third, king of Thure.
Daymer (DAY-MER) – aka Slaver king. Ruled the kingdom of the thirteen.
Denogg of the family Xoss – wealthy merchant of Thure.
Dinmar - Asporan leader saved by Stathen at the marshes.
Dralinn (DRAY-LINN) – Port, dangerous, aka Murderer's Bay, on same landmass as the kingdom of the thirteen.
Enricca – A girl Gordon and Asa know.
Extatumm – Formerly the kingdom of Dard.
Eyonna – Queen of Thure, married to King Russel the third.
Family Xoss (Pronounced ZOSS) – Wealthy merchants, Denogg and Santovan are brothers from this family.
Fasgonn – Creature that can use two front legs like hands. Prefers cooked meat.
Fire bugs - They are explosive when agitated. Their natural defense is like a bee – to sacrifice themselves to damage an enemy. Left alone, they are like lightning bugs. They are naturally attracted to sugar cane. By themselves, one exploding bug is like a spark. When enough are together, they can start a small fire.
Fire gun – Aka rainmaker – Fire weapon mounted on airships.
Fortress – Group of people in the haunted forest of Aspora.
Giber (GUY-BURR) – King of old, kingdom of the thirteen.
Gordon – A thirteen year old boy.

Haunted Forest – Forest of large trees in Aspora.
Jaiwan (JA–EYE-WAN) – Referred to as Number Eight, warrior from Yajan.
Jannfarr – Thurian king of old.
Jenae (JA-NAY) – Serving girl, works for Denogg.
Jhalgon Fish (JALL-GONE) – Giant flying fish, also known as shadow fins. Can reach up to sixty feet in length. Their flight capability is limited, they rarely venture over land. The wings can get them to great vertical heights, but their weight appears to limit mobility over long distances. Like any fish, they cannot survive out of water indefinitely.
Jorann the blood king - Grandfather of the former queen of Dard (Alonnia).
Joreh (JORE-UHH) – King that was chosen, but was scared and refused the crown.
Kingdom of the thirteen – aka the new kingdom – Gordon's kingdom.
Lantovas (LAN–TOE-VAH-SS) – Firstman of Thure.
Lawkeeper – 1) Workers that attend to the great law rooms. 2) Name of elusive councilor being hunted for knowledge.
Longknife and shortknife or great knife and Smallknife – Similar to long swords and short swords.
Loren (LORE-ENN) – Gordon's uncle.
Mantuan (MAN-TOO-UNN) – Has a patch on his right eye.
Mural of the 100 kings – In Thurian throne room, painted by Ninian.
Ninian (NIN-EE-ANN) – Famous artist, painted the mural of the one hundred kings in Thure.
Ninnith – Blue king of Thure.
Outlands – Many of these lands are unknown.
Pact with man – Faith of the Blue king of Artoth.
Queen Ellice (ELL-EE-SS) – a.k.a. Slaver queen, grew up in a village with Daymer.
Rainmaker - Fire gun weapons on airships.

Rolem (ROLL-EM) – Trunculin's assistant at the palace.
Rolenn – King of old, Kingdom of the thirteen.
Russel the Great – Thurian king of old. Ancestor to the current king Russel.
Russel the third – Current king of Thure.
Salenn the peacemaker – Queen of old, kingdom of the thirteen.
Sandrell – Aline's mother.
Sanjee – Eight year old girl that chose Gordon.
Santovan – Denogg's brother.
Skyler – Friend of Gordon and Asa.
Sochatt & Norum – Boys that see Brenddel come out of water at Murderer's Bay (Dralinn).
Sour cake – Cakes that Loren makes Gordon for the sweetblood, helped lower blood sugar. Purple medicine cakes that contain insulin from animals.
Stathen (STAY-TH-ENN) – King before Gordon.
Swamp rot – Tranquilizer on the dart that Aline uses.
Talinna – Eight year old girl that picked King Stathen.
Tanlum – Famous old ruins in the kingdom of Artoth.
Tethon, son of Torr – Orange king of Artoth.
Thorny root – Poison.
Thure – aka Old kingdom.
Tobee – Guard of prisoners in Thure.
TrTorrin (TRUH-TORE-INN) – Ruler of Extatumm, also called the father.
Trunculin (TRUNK-YOU-LINN) – Firstcouncilor of the kingdom of the thirteen.
Valren (VAL-RENN) – Mystic from the mystic guild.
Yajan – (YA-ZSAH-NN) Island lands.
Zoress Bread or dough – Used to extract poison.

AUTHOR BIOGRAPHY

M J Sewall is a native Californian and a lover of all things strange, magical, mysterious and awesome. Loves writing about the fact that he hates talking about himself. He is the father of four, and glad that he did not pass on any of his bad habits. Well, maybe some. He is sometimes subliminal, often nebulous, only occasionally trepidatious and other fancy words. Writing since the age of twelve, Mr. Sewall has a backlog of stories that may have already filled the Sargasso Sea. He had a strange fascination with lemurs, until they became cool. Now he's on to ocelots.

This is his first novel.

For more information please visit,
MJSewall.com

PREVIEW FROM BOOK 2 IN THE CHOSEN KING SERIES

The monsters were getting out of hand.

The large watership bobbed in the gray day, the waters mesmerizing the man standing on deck. The cold wind swirled around his muscular frame, the wind playing with his beard. Bare chested, he refused to let the cold touch him. He willed it away.

"A fin, two hundred feet off shore, father," said one of the crew rushing up to him.

The man knew this was the first time the boy had been on a ship, the son of a young man from the inner council. He patted the young man's face that held only a wisp of a beard, "Let's go kill it."

The young man smiled, and yelled to the crew, "Long boats at the ready!"

The man smiled as he saw the crew begin to lower the long boats, *just like the legends,* he thought. He jumped into one of the three boats as the winches lowered the narrow wooden vessels.

The man shouted, "Are you ready to reclaim your place in history?" the six men on each boat cheered as the man spoke, "Our ancestors hunted these monsters back in the mists of time. Now they have returned. Let's send them back into legend!"

The crew of young men cheered louder. The men treated him like a god. That worried the man. *The old superstitions must die for us to finish our work,* thought the man. Best to show them that I am a man, and that man is more than any god ever was. He couldn't tell his crew that he had other reasons for killing these beasts. Three of his airships had gone missing. That was not a coincidence. All of them had been lost over the waters, no survivors. *I will not let these things take my ships one by one. Time to fight. If it raises the moral of my men by leading them like a hero... well, some lies were necessary, if they served a greater purpose.*

The man cranked the device. His thinkers said the creatures must be attracted to the sound of the airship's rotators. Trunculin has written of similar problems, *but of course we are both liars,* he thought.

To the man, the sound the device made was different than the noise of the rotators, but before he had a chance to decide if this would bring out the beasts, a Jhalgon fish erupted out of the water to the right of their boat. Its leathery wet wings pushed it straight up into the air. The longboat rocked both their boats, and the third boat just twenty feet away.

It was massive. He had read the reports, interrogated those that spotted them. But to see sixty feet of monster go straight into the air was a marvel. The men were all frozen with shock. *They look more like boys than ever,* thought the man.

The monster arced, and the man realized it was coming down. It opened its massive jaws to reveal three rows of teeth. *Each tooth must be bigger than my hand...* but his thought turned to the other boat. The sea water rained from the giant fish, but they realized what was happening too late for them to get away. His own men were frantically rowing to escape wherever the beast might land. The monster landed on the second boat, the beast forcing the longboat under the waves before it snapped in two under the pressure.

The shock of new waves hit the boats. It felt like a tidal wave as the two remaining longboats fought to stay upright. A circle of red emanated out from the where the beast had gone under, fragments of the broken longboat no bigger than the size of a plate floated there, riding the waves.

Luckily, the red was the only part of his men they saw, the rest must have gone under, or been swallowed by the beast. The two remaining boats continued to bail the water out that had lapped over the sides. The man stood up, grasping the giant metal spear. It was longer than the man was tall, but he stood straight, feeling the cold metal slick with sea water. He stood on sure legs, riding the rocking motion, scanning for a sign of the beast.

"Fin!" A man shouted from the other boat. The man smiled. It was headed for the other boat. *No, monster, come for me,* he thought. He realized he was smiling as he looked at the young man with the wispy beard, his face horrified and desperate. When he saw the bare chested man looking at him, the young man's face changed to a hardy resolve. He bailed water faster.

The fin came up from the water, parting it, standing five feet above the waves. The man cranked the machine again, imitating the sound of the rotators form the airships. The top of the beast crested the water, a gray hint of the massive monster under the waves. It didn't change direction, still headed for the second boat.

"Damn you!" the man shouted, "men, row!" he commanded, as the young men heeded the command and rowed directly into the path of the fin. The man ignored the terror that gripped his crew, and raised the long metal spear. The three hooks came to a steely point, a rope tied to the end. Water sprayed as the boat rocked. The fin rose with the beast, the wings throwing sea water at them as the beast rose even higher. The second boat still its target, the man realized it was only jumping their boat to get to the other.

The beast was out of the water, using its wings to help arc the body. Just before it was directly over their boat, the man thought, *you're mine now,* as he flung the spear at the belly of the Jhalgon fish. It struck the beast, the hooks at the end of the great spear doing their job. The man held fast to the rope, wrapping it around his arm, ignoring the burn of the rope as it slid through his hands. He grabbed it firmly and was lifted off the boat.

Hurt, the beast changed its angle and missed the second boat. The beast and the man hit the icy waters. His bare chest exploded with a thousand needles as the beast dragged him down. The man strained his muscles and forced himself to climb along the rope toward the beast. It was dragging him deeper, but he ignored the pressure building in his head. Hand over hand he pulled himself along the rope until he finally reached the beast. He groped for his shortknife, fearing he had lost it. One hand held the rope tight as he fumbled to find the knife, ignoring the pains in his chest. He finally found it and he jammed it into the beast. Over and over again he stabbed, warm blood flowing past him from the beast as he was dragged deeper.

The man had done all he could. He let go of the rope, and used the last of his strength to push up to the light. He had no air. *No, this is not how I die,* but it was getting harder to think. The cold felt like knives going deeper and deeper, aiming for his heart. Still he moved his legs, pushing toward the light, the air. Just when he thought his muscles would fail him, he felt the precious air fill his lungs.

His hearing was filled with the sound of water, like the sea had invaded his mind. As he took his second and third gulps of air, he heard the cheering. The two boats were far away from him, but the shouting was fierce. It stopped abruptly when the fin appeared again. It shot straight up out of the water not far from the man. The man groped for his knife, but realized he had dropped it while searching for air and light. The fin bobbed up again, then slowly rolled to one side. The leathery wings splayed out on either side of the beast, the beast bobbed with the waves, surrounded by blood draining from its wounds. The blood reached the man and warmed him.

The great cheers got louder and became a chant, "Father! Father! Father! Father..."

The man smiled, *yes, my children, let's begin this new day with blood.*

CHOSEN KING
BOOK TWO: TRIALS OF BOY KINGS

AVAILABLE SOON

11729492R00176

Printed in Great Britain
by Amazon.co.uk, Ltd.,
Marston Gate.